D0655165

THE TAVERN KNIGHT

THE
TAVERN KNIGHT

RAFAEL SABATINI

THOMAS NELSON AND SONS LTD
LONDON EDINBURGH PARIS MELBOURNE
TORONTO AND NEW YORK

THOMAS NELSON & SONS LTD

3 HENRIETTA STREET, LONDON, W.C.2
PARKSIDE WORKS, EDINBURGH
25 RUE DENFERT-ROCHEREAU, PARIS
312 FLINDERS STREET, MELBOURNE
91–93 WELLINGTON STREET WEST, TORONTO
385 MADISON AVENUE, NEW YORK

First published in this edition September 1947

CONTENTS

THE TAVERN KNIGHT

CHAPTER I

ON THE MARCH

HE whom they called the Tavern Knight laughed an evil laugh—such a laugh as the pious might conceive on the lips of Satan.

He sat within the halo of yellow light shed by two tallow candles, whose sconces were two empty bottles, and contemptuously he eyed the youth in black, standing with white face and quivering lip in a corner of the mean chamber. Then he laughed again, and in a bottle-hoarse voice broke into song. He lay back in his chair, his long, spare legs outstretched, spurs jingling to the lilt of his ditty.

> " On the lip so red of the wench that's sped
> His passionate kiss burns, still-O !
> For 'tis April time, and of love and wine
> Youth's way is to take its fill-O !
> Down, down, derry-do !

> " So his cup he drains and he shakes his reins,
> And rides his rake-helly way-O !
> She was sweet to woo and most comely, too,
> But that was all yesterday-O !
> Down, down, derry-do ! "

The lad started forward with a scowl and a shudder.

" Have done," he cried, in a voice of loathing, " or, if croak you must, choose a ditty less foul ! "

" Eh ? " The ruffler shook back the matted hair from his lean, harsh face, and a pair of eyes that of a sudden seemed ablaze glared at his companion ; then the lids drooped until those eyes became two narrow slits—cat-like and cunning—and again he laughed.

" Gad's life, Master Stewart, your temerity should save you from grey hairs ! What is't to you what ditty takes my fancy ? 'Swounds, man, for three weary months have I curbed my moods, and worn my throat dry in praising the Lord ; for three months have I been a living monument of Covenanting zeal and godliness ; and now that at last we've shaken the dust of your beggarly Scotland from our heels, you—you milksop—chide me because, the bottle being done, I sing to keep me from contemplation of its emptiness ! "

There was a scorn unutterable on the lad's face as he turned away.

" When I joined Middleton's Horse and took service under you, I held you to be at least a gentleman."

For an instant that dangerous light gleamed again from his companion's eyes. Then, as before, the lids drooped, and, as before, he laughed.

" Gentleman ! " he mocked. " Gentleman ! And what may you know of gentlemen, Sir Scot ? D'ye think a gentleman is a Jack Presbyter, or a droning member of your kirk committee, strutting like a crow in the gutter. Gadswounds, boy, when I was your age, and George Villiers lived——"

"Oh, have done," broke in the youth impetuously. "I'll leave you, Sir Crispin, to your bottle, your croaking, and your memories."

"Ay, go your ways, sir; you'd be sorry company for a dead man—the sorriest ever my evil star brought me into. There's the door, and should you happen to break your saintly neck on the stairs, it is like to be well for both of us."

And with that Sir Crispin Galliard lay back in his chair once more, and took up the thread of his interrupted song—

"But, heigh-o! she cried, at the Christmas-tide,
That dead she would rather be-O!
Pale and wan she crept out of sight, and wept
'Tis a sorry——"

A loud knock, that echoed through the mean chamber, fell in that instant upon the door. And with it came a breathless cry of—

"Cris! Open, Cris! Open, for the love of God!"

Sir Crispin's ballad broke off short, whilst the lad paused in the act of quitting the room, and turned to look to him for direction.

"Well, my master," quoth Galliard, "for what do you wait?"

"To learn your wishes, sir," was the sullen answer.

"*My* wishes! Rat me, there's one out there whose wishes brook less waiting! Open, fool!"

Thus rudely enjoined, the lad lifted the latch and set wide the door, which opened immediately upon the street. Into the apartment stumbled a large man in the accoutrements of a soldier. He was breathing hard, and his rugged face was grey, be it from exhaustion or from fear. An instant he paused to close the door after him, then turning to Galliard, who had risen and who stood eyeing him in astonishment—

" It's sanctuary I'm needing, Cris. Hide me somewhere," he panted—his accent proclaiming his Irish origin. " My God, hide me, or it's a dead man I am this night ! "

" 'Slife, Hogan ! What's amiss ? Has Cromwell overtaken us ? "

" Cromwell, quotha ? Would to Heaven 'twere no worse ! I've killed a man ! "

" If he's dead why run ? "

The Irishman made an impatient gesture.

" There's a party of Montgomery's Foot on my heels. They've raised the whole of Penrith, so they have, and if I'm taken, soul of my body, 'twill be a short shrift they'll give me. The King will have me served like poor Wrycraft two days ago at Kendal." He broke off, as his ear caught a sound of feet and voices from the lane. " Mother of Mercy ! Have you never a hole I can be creeping into ? "

" Up those stairs and into my room with you ! " said Crispin shortly. " Leave me to head them off. Away with you ! "

Then, as with nimble alacrity Hogan obeyed him, and slipped from the room, he turned to the lad, who had been a silent spectator of what had passed. From the pocket of his threadbare doublet he drew a pack of greasy playing cards.

" To table," he said laconically.

But the boy, comprehending what was required of him, drew back at sight of those cards as one might shrink from a thing unclean.

" Never ! " he began.   " I'll not defile——"

" To table ! " thundered Crispin.   " Is this a time for Presbyterian scruples ?   To table, and help me play this game, or, by the living God, you'll never play another."

His vehemence promised a violent answer to disobedience.   He leaned forward until Kenneth felt his hot, wine-laden breath upon his cheek.   Cowed by the words, the gesture, and above all the glance, the lad drew up a chair, mumbling in explanation—intended as an excuse to himself for his weakness—that he submitted only because a man's life was at stake.

Opposite him Galliard resumed his seat with a smile that made the boy wince.   Taking up the cards, he flung a portion of them across the table, whilst those he retained he spread fanwise in his hand as if about to play.   Silently the subdued Kenneth imitated him.

Nearer and louder came the sounds of the approach, lights flashed before the window, and the two men, feigning to play, sat on and waited.

" Have a care, Master Stewart," growled Crispin sourly, then in a louder voice—for his quick eye had caught a glimpse of a face that watched them from the window—" I play the King of Spades ! "

A blow was struck upon the door, and after it followed the command :   " Open in the King's name ! "

Softly Sir Crispin rapped out an oath.   Then he rose, and with a last look of warning to Kenneth, he went to open.   And as he had greeted Hogan he now

greeted the troopers and the townsfolk that surged
in their wake about the threshold.

"Sirs, why this ado? Has the Sultan Oliver
descended upon us?"

In one hand he still held his cards, the other he
rested upon the edge of the open door. It was a
young ensign who stood forward to answer him.

"You are merry, Sir Crispin. One of Lord Middleton's officers has done a man to death not half an
hour since. He is an Irishman—Captain Hogan by
name."

Crispin's countenance became grave. "Hogan—
Hogan?" His tone was that of one who fumbles in
his memory. "Ah, yes—an Irishman with a grey
head and a hot temper. And he is dead, you say?"

"Nay, it was he who did the killing."

"That I can better understand. It'll not be the
first time, I dare swear."

"And I dare swear it will be the last, Sir Crispin."

"Like enough. His Majesty's grown strict since
we crossed the Border." Then in a brisker tone:
"I can't think why you should trouble to bring me
this news," he said, "and I regret that in my poor
house there is nothing in which to drink His Majesty's
health before you continue your search. I'll give
you good night, sir, and go back to the cards." He
drew back a pace, and signified his wish to close the
door and be quit of them.

The officer hesitated a moment; then, "We
thought," he said, "that—that perhaps you would
assist us——"

"Assist you!" Crispin broke in, with a fine assumption of anger. "Assist you take a man? Sink me, sir, I am a soldier, not a tipstaff!"

The ensign's cheeks grew crimson under the sting of that veiled insult.

"There are some, Sir Crispin, that have yet another name for you."

"Like enough—when I am not by," sneered Crispin. "The world is full of foul tongues in craven heads. But, sirs, the night air is chill and you are come inopportunely, for, as you'll perceive, I was at play. I'll thank you to suffer me to close the door."

"By your leave, Sir Crispin. We know that our man came this way."

"What then?"

"We'll search the house, by your leave."

Crispin yawned.

"I will spare you the trouble. It's impossible that he should be here without my knowledge. I have not stirred from this room for these two hours past."

But the officer was dogged. "'Twill not suffice. We must satisfy ourselves."

"Satisfy yourselves? What better satisfaction can I afford you? 'Swounds, sir jackanapes," he added, in a roar that sent the other back a pace as if he had been struck. "First you invite me to turn tipstaff, then you add your cursed innuendoes of what people say of me, and now you end by doubting me! You must satisfy yourself!" His anger flamed more fiercely at every word. "Linger another moment on the threshold, and damn me, sir, I'll give you all the satisfaction you'll be needing, and maybe something over. Good night to you."

Before that hurricane of passion the ensign recoiled.

"I will report to General Montgomery," he threatened.

"Report to the devil! Had you done your errand in seemly fashion you had found my door thrown wide in welcome. As it is, sir, the cause for complaint is on my side, and complain I will. We shall see whether the King permits an old soldier who has followed the fortunes of his family these eighteen years to be flouted by a malapert cockerel of yesterday's brood."

The subaltern paused in dismay. Some demur there was in the gathered crowd. Then the officer fell back and consulted an elderly sergeant at his elbow. The sergeant was of opinion that the fugitive must have gone farther. Moreover, he could not think, from what Sir Crispin had said, that it would have been possible for Hogan to have entered the house. With this, and realizing that much trouble and possible loss of time must result from Sir Crispin's obstinacy, did they attempt to force a way into the house, and bethinking himself, also, maybe, how well this rascally ruffler stood with Lord Middleton, the ensign determined to withdraw, and to seek elsewhere.

And so he took an ill-tempered leave with a parting threat to bring the matter to the King's ears, upon which Galliard slammed the door before he had finished.

There was a tight-lipped smile on his face as he walked slowly to the table, and resumed his seat.

"Master Stewart," he muttered, as he spread his cards anew, "the comedy is not yet played out. There is a face glued to the window at this moment, and I made little doubt that for the next hour or so we shall be spied upon. That pretty fellow was born to be a thief-taker."

The boy turned a glance of sour reproof upon his companion. He had not stirred from his chair while Crispin had been at the door.

" You lied to them," he said at last.

" Sh ! Not so loud, sweet youth," was the answer that lost nothing of menace by being subdued. " And let us be accurate. Let me discriminate. A mere *suppressio veri* ; at most a *suggestio falsi*. But a lie ! Sweet, sir, I hope I am incapable of that. Still, if you insist, to-morrow I will account to you for offending your delicate soul by so much as suggesting a falsehood in your presence. To-night we have a man's life to save, and that, I think, is work enough. Come, Master Stewart, we are being watched. Let us resume our game."

His eye, fixed in cold command upon the boy, compelled obedience. And the lad, out of awe of that glance, out of no desire to contribute to the saving of Hogan, mutely consented to keep up this pretence. But in his soul he rebelled. He had been reared in an atmosphere of honourable and religious bigotry. Hogan was to him a coarse ruffler ; an evil man of the sword ; such a man as he abhorred and accounted a disgrace to any army—particularly to an army launched upon England under the auspices of the Solemn League and Covenant. Hogan had been guilty of an act of brutality ; he had killed a man ; Crispin had made himself an accessory ; and Kenneth deemed himself little better, since he assisted in harbouring instead of discovering this murderer, as he held to be his duty. But under the suasion of Galliard's inexorable eye he sat limp and docile, vowing to himself that on the morrow he would lay the matter before Lord Middleton, and thus not only endeavour to make amends for his present guilty silence, but rid himself also of the companionship of this ruffianly Sir Crispin, to whom no doubt a hempen justice would be meted.

Meanwhile, he sat on and left his companion's occasional sallies unanswered. In the street men stirred and lanthorns gleamed fitfully, while ever and anon a face surmounted by a morion would be pressed against the leaded panes of the window.

Thus an hour wore itself out during which Captain Hogan sat above, alone with his anxiety and unsavoury thoughts.

CHAPTER II

ARCADES AMBO

Towards midnight at last Sir Crispin threw down his cards and rose. It was close upon an hour and a half since Hogan's advent. In the streets the sounds had gradually died down, and peace seemed to reign again in Penrith. Yet was Sir Crispin cautious—for to be cautious and mistrustful of appearances was a lesson life had taught him.

"Master Stewart," said he, "it grows late, and there's no need to keep you longer from your bed. Give you good night!"

The lad rose. A moment he paused, hesitating, then in a minatory tone, "To-morrow, Sir Crispin ——" he began.

But Crispin cut him short. "Leave to-morrow till it dawn, my friend. Give you good night. Take one of those noisome tapers with you and go."

A moment yet the boy hesitated, then in sullen silence he took up one of the candle-bearing bottles, and passed out through the door leading to the stairs.

For a moment Crispin remained standing by the table, and as the door closed the expression of his face was softened. A momentary regret of his treatment of the boy stirred in him. Master Stewart might be a milksop, but Crispin accounted him leastways honest, and had a lurking kindness for him in spite of all. He crossed to the window, threw it wide and leaned out, as if to breathe the cool night air, what time he hummed the refrain of " Rub-a-dub-dub " for the edification of any chance listeners.

For a half-hour he lingered there, watchful, alert for the least movement among the shadows of the street. Reassured at last that the house was no longer under any observation, he drew back, and closed the lattice.

Upstairs he found the Irishman stretched upon his bed, awaiting him.

" Soul of my body ! " cried Hogan, sitting up, " I was never nearer being afraid in my life."

" You were fully as near as ever I should care to be," was the dry answer, followed by a request for the tale of what had passed.

" It's a simple tale enough, faith," said Hogan. " The landlord of ' The Angel ' is the father of an angel —maybe 'twas after her he named his inn—with a pair of the sauciest eyes that ever a man saw perdition in. We were becoming the sweetest friends, when, like an incarnate fiend, a loutish clown, whom I take to have been her lover, sweeps down upon us, and —bad cess to him—with more jealousy than wit, struck me across the face ! Soul of my body, think of it, Cris ! " And he empurpled at the recollection. " I took him by the collar of his mean smock and flung him into the kennel—the fittest bed he ever lay in. That made us quits, and had he chosen to bide there all had been well ; but the fool, in his vanity, with the girl's eyes upon him, must be coming back, to demand satisfaction. I gave it him since he insisted, and—plague on it—he's dead ! "

Crispin looked at him and his eyes were stern. "An ugly tale."

"Och now! Don't I know it?" returned Hogan, spreading out his palms, "but what choice had I? The fool came at me, bilbo in hand. He forced me to draw."

"But not to slay, Hogan!"

"'Twas an accident. Sink me, it was! I sought his sword-arm; but the light was bad, and my point went through his middle instead."

For a moment Crispin stood frowning, then his brow cleared, as though he had put the matter from him.

"Well, well—since he's dead, there's an end to it."

"Heaven rest his soul!" muttered the Irishman. He crossed himself piously, and with that dismissed the subject of the great wrong that through folly he had wrought—the wanton destruction of a man's life, and the poisoning of a woman's with a remorse that might be everlasting.

"It will tax our wits to get you out of Penrith," said Crispin. Then, turning and looking into the Irishman's great, good-humoured face—"I am sorry you should be leaving us, Hogan," he added.

"Sure now, there's no call for tears at all. It's glad to begone I am. Such a march as this is little to my taste. Bah! Charles Stuart or Oliver Cromwell, 'tis all one to me. What care I whether King or Commonwealth prevail? Shall Harry Hogan be the better or the richer under one than under the other? Oddslife, Cris, I have trailed a pike or handled a sword in well-nigh every army in Europe. I know more of the great art of war than all the King's generals rolled into one. D'ye think I can rest content with a miserable company of horse when plunder is forbidden, and even our beggarly pay doubtful? And if things go ill—as well they may, faith, with an army ruled by parsons—the wage will be a swift death on field or gallows, or a lingering one in the plantations, as fell to the lot of those poor wretches Noll drove into England after Dunbar. Soul of my body, it is not so that I had looked to fare when I took service at Perth, with never a chance of loot, according to the usages of warfare, as a fitting reward for a toilsome march and the perils gone through. Thus I know war, and for this have I followed the trade these twenty years. Instead, we have thirty thousand men, marching to battle as prim and orderly as a pack of shavelings in a Corpus-Christi procession. 'Twas not so bad in Scotland— haply because the country holds naught a man may profitably plunder—but since we have crossed the Border, 'slife, they'll hang you if you steal so much as a kiss from a wench in passing."

Crispin shook his head. " The King has a tender stomach, as I should have in his place. He will not allow that we are marching through an enemy's country ; he insists that England is his kingdom, forgetting that he has yet to conquer it, and——"

" Was it not also his father's kingdom ? " broke in the impetuous Hogan. " Yet times are sorely changed since we followed the fortunes of the Martyr. When I rode with Rupert you might help yourself to a capon, a horse, a wench, or any other trifle of Round-head gear, without ever a question asked. Why, man, it is but two days since His Majesty had a poor devil hanged at Kendal for laying violent hands upon a pullet. Pox on it, Cris, that was enough for me, so it was. When I saw that wretch strung up, I swore to fall behind at the earliest opportunity, and to-night's affair merely makes it necessary."

" And what may your plans be ? " asked Crispin.

" War is my trade, not a diversion, as it is with Wilmot and Buckingham and the other pretty gentlemen of our train. And since the King's army is like to yield me no profit, faith, I'll turn me to the Parliament's. If I get out of Penrith with my life, I'll shave my beard and cut my hair to a comely and godly length ; don a cuckoldy steeple hat and a black coat, and carry my sword to Cromwell with a line of text."

Sir Crispin fell to pondering. Observing him, and imagining that he guessed the reason of his thoughtfulness, Hogan's glance quickened.

" I take it, Cris, that you are much of the same mind ? "

" Maybe I am," replied Crispin carelessly.

" Why, then," cried Hogan, " there'll be no need to part company ? "

There was a sudden eagerness in his tone, born of the affection in which this rough soldier of fortune held one whom he accounted his better in that same harsh trade. But Galliard answered coldly—

" You forget, Harry."

" Not so ! Surely on Cromwell's side your object ——"

" T'sh ! I have well considered. My fortunes are

bound up with the King's. In his victory alone lies my profit ; not the mere profit of pillage, Hogan, but the profit of those broad lands that for nigh upon twenty years have been in usurping hands. The profit I look for, Hogan, is my restoration to Castle Marleigh, and for this my only hope lies in the restoration of King Charles. If the King should not prevail—which God forfend !—why, then, I can but die. I shall have naught left to hope for from life. No, no, Harry, I remain."

Still the Irishman urged him, until realizing at last the futility of his endeavours, he sighed and moved uneasily in his chair, whilst the broad, tanned face was clouded with regret. Crispin came to lay a hand upon his shoulder.

"I had counted upon your help in what's to do when the time is ripe. But if you go——"

"Faith, I may help you yet. Who shall say ? " Then of a sudden there crept into the voice of this hardened campaigner a note of soft concern. "What if there be danger to yourself in remaining ? "

"Danger ?   To me ? " echoed Crispin.

"Ay—for having harboured me. That whelp of Montgomery's Foot suspects you."

"Suspects ?   Am I so light as to be blown over by a breath of suspicion ? "

"There is your lieutenant, Kenneth Stewart."

"Since he has been a party to your escape, his only course is silence, lest he set a noose about his own neck. Come, Harry," he added briskly, changing his manner, "the night wears on. It's time you were stirring."

Hogan rose with a sigh.

"Find me a horse," said he, "and by God's grace next week shall see me a Roundhead. Heaven prosper and reward you, Cris."

"You'll need clothes more fitting than those—a coat more staid and better suited to the Puritan part you are to play."

"And where will you be having such a coat?"

"My lieutenant affects the godly black, from a habit taken in that Presbyterian Scotland of his."

"But I am twice his bulk."

"Better a tight coat to your back than a tight rope to your neck, Harry. Wait."

Taking a taper, he left the room, to return presently with the coat which the now sleeping Kenneth had worn that day.

"Off with your doublet," he commanded, and as he spoke he set himself to empty the pocket of Kenneth's garment; a handkerchief and a few papers were all he found in them, and these he tossed carelessly on the bed. Next he assisted the Irishman to struggle into the stolen coat.

"May the Lord forgive my sins," groaned Hogan, as he felt the cloth straining upon his back and cramping his limbs. "May He forgive me, and see me safely out of Penrith and into Cromwell's camp, and never again will I resent the resentment of a clown with whose sweetheart I may make too free."

"Pluck that feather from your hat," said Crispin.

Hogan obeyed him with a sigh.

"Truly it is written in Scripture that man in his

time plays many parts. Who would have thought to see Harry Hogan playing the Puritan ? "

" Unless you improve your acquaintance with Scripture you are not like to play it long." Crispin surveyed him. " There, man, you'll do well enough. Your coat may be tight in the back and short in the skirt ; but neither so tight nor so short but that it's better than a winding-sheet, and that is the alternative, Harry."

Hogan replied by roundly cursing the coat and his own lucklessness. That done—and in no measured terms—he pronounced himself ready to set out, whereupon Crispin led the way below once more, and out into a hut that did service as a stable.

By the light of a lanthorn he saddled one of the two nags that stood there, and led it into the yard. Opening a door that abutted on to a field beyond, he bade Hogan mount. He held his stirrup for him, and cutting short the Irishman's voluble expressions of gratitude, he gave him " God speed," and urged him to use all dispatch in setting as great a distance as possible betwixt himself and Penrith before the dawn.

CHAPTER III

THE LETTER

It was with a dejected countenance that Crispin returned to his chamber and sate himself wearily upon the bed. With elbows on his knees and chin in his palms he stared straight before him, the usual steely brightness of his grey eyes dulled by the despondency that sat upon his face and drew deep furrows adown his fine brow.

With a sigh he rose at last and idly fingered the papers he had taken from the pocket of Kenneth's coat. As he did so his glance was arrested by the signature at the foot of one : " Gregory Ashburn."

The hand, to which no peril had ever brought a tremor, shook now as he stared at that name. Feverishly he spread the letter on his knee, and with a glance, from dull that it had been, grown of a sudden fierce and cruel, he set himself to read.

" Dear Kenneth,—These in the hope that I may yet prevail upon you to quit Scotland and your attachment to a king whose fortunes prosper not, nor can prosper. Cynthia is pining, and if you tarry longer from Castle Marleigh she can but think you a laggard lover. Than this I know no better argument to draw you from Perth to Sheringham, but this I think should prevail where others have failed me. We await you then, and whilst we wait we daily drink your health. Cynthia commends herself to your memory, as doth my brother, and soon we hope to welcome you. Believe, my dear Kenneth, that whilst I am, I am yours in affection.

"GREGORY ASHBURN."

Twice Crispin read the letter through. Then with set jaw and straining eyes he sat lost in thought.

Here indeed was a strange chance! This boy whom he had met at Perth, and enrolled in his company, was a friend of Ashburn's—the lover of Cynthia, whoever this Cynthia might be.

Long and deep were his ponderings upon the inscrutable ways of Fate—for Fate he now believed was here at work to help him, revealing herself by means of this sign, even at the very moment when he decried his luck.

In memory he reviewed his meeting with the lad in the courtyard of Perth Castle a month ago. Something in the boy's bearing, in his air, had caught Crispin's eye. He had looked him over, then approached, and bluntly asked his name and on what business he was come there. The youth had answered him civilly enough that he was Kenneth Stewart of Bailienochy, and that he was come to offer his sword to the King. Thereupon, yielding to the mysterious sympathy the lad aroused in him, he had so far interested himself in Kenneth's behalf as to gain him a cornetcy in his own company. Why he should have been drawn to a youth on whom never before had he set eyes was a matter that had at once perplexed and amused him. Now he held, he thought, the explanation. It was a thing pre-ordained.

This boy had been sent into his life by a Heaven that at last showed compassion for the deep wrongs he had suffered; sent him as a key wherewith, should the need occur, to open him the gates of Castle Marleigh.

In long strides he paced the chamber, turning the matter over in his mind. He need not scruple, he assured himself, to use the lad should the need arise. For he had never received aught but disdain and scorn at the hands of this sniveller whom he had befriended.

Day was breaking ere he sought his bed, and already the sun was up when at length he fell into a troubled sleep, vowing to mend his wild ways in order to gain the boy's favour against the time when he might have need of him.

When later he restored the papers to Kenneth, explaining to what use he had put the coat, he refrained from questioning him concerning Gregory Ashburn. The docility of his mood on that occasion came as a surprise to Kenneth, who set it down to Sir Crispin's desire to conciliate him into silence touching the harbouring of Hogan. In that matter, however, Crispin showed him calmly and clearly that he could not now inform without involving himself to an equally dangerous extent. And partly from fear of this, partly won over by Crispin's persuasions, the lad determined to hold his peace.

Nor had he cause to regret it thereafter, for throughout that tedious march he found his roystering companion oddly changed, singularly meek and kindly. As if to make amends, he seemed a different man.

His old swagger and roaring bluster had disappeared;
he drank less, diced less, blasphemed less, and stormed
less than in the old days before the halt at Penrith;
instead he rode, a silent, thoughtful figure, as self-
contained and as godly of mien as would have rejoiced
the heart of the sourest Puritan. The wild tantivy
boy had vanished, and the title of Tavern Knight was
fast becoming a misnomer.

Kenneth began to find him tolerable, deeming him
a penitent that had seen at last the error of his ways.
And thus things prevailed until the almost triumphal
entry into the city of Worcester on the twenty-third
of August.

CHAPTER IV

AT THE SIGN OF "THE MITRE"

FOR a week after the coming of the King to Worcester, Crispin's relations with Kenneth steadily improved. By an evil chance, however, there befell on the eve of the battle that which renewed with heightened intensity the hostility which the lad had fostered for him, but which lately he had almost overcome.

The scene of this event—leastways of that which led to it—was "The Mitre Inn," in the High Street of Worcester.

In the common room one day sat as merry a company of carousers as ever gladdened the soul of an old tantivy boy. Youthful cornets of Lesley's Scottish Horse—caring never a fig for the Solemn League and Covenant—rubbed shoulders with beribboned Cavaliers of Lord Talbot's company; gay young lairds of Pittscottie's Highlanders, unmindful of the kirk's harsh commandments of sobriety, sat cheek by jowl with rake-helly officers of Dalzell's Brigade, and drank long life to the King and damnation to the crop-ears in many a stoup of canary and many a can of stout March ale.

Spirits ran high and laughter filled the chamber, the mirth of some having its source in a neighbour's quip, that of others having no source at all save in the wine consumed.

At one table sat a gentleman of the name of Faversham, who had ridden on the previous night in that ill-fated camisado that should have resulted in the capture of Cromwell at Spetchley, but which, owing to a betrayal—when was a Stuart not betrayed and sold?—miscarried. He was relating to the group about him the details of that disaster.

"Oddslife, my masters, I vow that but for that roaring dog Sir Crispin Gaillard, the whole of Middleton's regiment had been cut to pieces. There we stood on Red Hill, taken like fish in a net, with the whole of Lilburne's men rising out of the ground to enclose and destroy us. A living wall of steel it was, and on every hand the call to surrender. There was dismay in my heart, as I'll swear there was dismay in the heart of every man of us, and I make little doubt that with but scant pressing we had thrown down our arms, so disheartened were we by that ambush. Then of a sudden there arose above the clatter of steel and Puritan cries, a loud, clear, defiant shout of ' Hey for Cavaliers ! '

"I turned, and there in his stirrups stood that madman Galliard, waving his sword and holding his company together with the power of his will, his courage, and his voice. The sight of him was like wine to our blood. ' Into them, gentlemen ; follow me,' he roared. And then, with a hurricane of oaths, he hurled his company against the pikemen. The blow was irresistible, and above the din of it came that voice of his again : ' Up, Cavaliers ! Slash the cuckolds to ribbons, gentlemen ! ' The crop-ears gave way, and like a river that has burst its dam, we poured through the gap in their ranks and headed back for Worcester.''

His tale was greeted by the roar of men eager to toast the Tavern Knight.

Meanwhile half a dozen merry-makers at a table hard by were baiting a pale-faced lad, sombrely attired, who seemed sadly out of place in that wild company—indeed, he had been better advised to have avoided it.

The matter had been set afoot by a pleasantry of Ensign Tyler's, of Massy's Dragoons, with a playful allusion to a letter in a feminine hand which Kenneth had let fall, and which Tyler had restored to him. Quip had followed quip until in their jests they transcended the bounds of decency. Livid with passion and unable to endure more, Kenneth had sprung up.

" Damnation ! " he blazed, bringing his clenched hand down upon the table. " One more of your foul jests and he that utters it shall answer to me ! "

The suddenness of his action and the fierceness of his tone and gesture—a fierceness so grotesquely ill-attuned to his slender frame and clerkly attire—smote the company for a moment into speechless amazement. Then a mighty burst of laughter greeted him, above which sounded the shrill voice of Tyler, who held his sides, and down whose crimson cheeks two tears of mirth were trickling.

" Oh, fie, fie, good Master Stewart ! " he gasped. " What think you would the reverend elders say to such bellicosity and such profanity ? "

" I know what gentlemen would say to this drunken poltroonery of yours ? " was the hot unguarded answer. " Poltroonery, I say," he repeated, embracing the whole company in his glance.

The laughter spluttered out as Kenneth's insult penetrated those befuddled minds. An instant's lull there was, then, as with one accord, a dozen of them bore down upon him.

It was a vile thing they did, perhaps ; but then they had drunk deep, and Kenneth Stewart counted no friend amongst them. In an instant they had him, kicking and biting, on the floor ; his doublet was torn rudely open, and from his breast Tyler plucked the letter whose existence had led to this shameless scene.

But before he could so much as unfold it, a voice rang harsh and arresting—

" You are merry, my masters. What is it you do ? "

They were confronted by a tall, gaunt man in a leather jerkin and a broad hat decked by a goose-quill, who came slowly forward.

" The Tavern Knight," cried Tyler, and his call for " A rouse for the hero of Red Hill ! " provoked a thunderous response. For despite his sour visage and ungracious ways there was not a roysterer in the Royal army to whom Galliard was not dear.

But as he now advanced, the forbidding set of his face froze them into silence.

" Give me that letter."

For a moment Tyler hesitated, frowning, whilst Crispin waited with hand outstretched. Vainly did the ensign look round for sign or word of help or counsel. None came. His fellow-revellers hung back in silence.

Thus lacking support, and far from wishing to try

conclusions with Galliard, Tyler with an ill grace surrendered the paper. Sir Crispin glanced at it, and then, with a pleasant bow and word of thanks, delivered with never so slight a saturnine smile, he turned on his heel and left the tavern as abruptly as he had entered it.

The din it was that had attracted him as he passed by on his way to the Episcopal Palace where a part of his company was on guard-duty. Thither he now pursued his way, bearing with him the letter which so fortuitously had passed into his possession, and to which he looked for further light upon Kenneth's relations with the Ashburns.

He was almost on the threshold of the palace when there was a quick step behind him. A hand fell upon his arm. He turned.

"Ah! And it's yourself, Kenneth." The boy's hand clung to his sleeve.

"Sir Crispin," said he, "I came to thank you."

"There is not the occasion." And he made shift to mount the steps. "Give you good evening."

But still Kenneth detained him.

"You are forgetting my letter, Sir Crispin," he ventured, and he held out his hand to receive it.

Galliard saw the gesture, and for a moment it was in his mind in self-reproach that the part he played was that of a bully. A second he hesitated, tempted to surrender the letter unread, and deny himself the aid of the information it might bring him. But in the end he overcame and stifled the generous impulse. His manner hardened as he made answer—

"Here's an ado about a letter, faith! Too much

to warrant my so lightly parting with it. First I will
satisfy myself that I have been no unconscious abettor
of treason. Come to me for your letter to-morrow,
Master Stewart."

"Treason!" echoed Kenneth. And before that
cold rebuff of Crispin's his mood changed from con-
ciliatory to resentful—resentful towards the fates that
made him this man's debtor.

"I assure you, on my honour," said he, mastering
his feelings, "that this is but a letter from the lady
I hope to make my wife. Assuredly, sir, you will not
now insist upon reading it."

"Assuredly I shall."

"But, sir——"

"Master Stewart, it's a matter of duty. Of duty
to myself, and were you to talk from now till dooms-
day, you would not turn me from it. So good night
to you."

"Sir Crispin," cried the boy, his voice quavering
with passion, "while I live you shall not read that
letter!"

"Hoity-toity, sir! All these heroics for a letter
you would have me believe innocent?"

"As innocent as the hand that penned it. You
shall not read it. It is not for such eyes as yours.
Believe me, sir," he added, reverting to a tone of
pleading, "I swear that it is no more than such a
letter any maid may write her lover. I thought that
you had understood all this when you rescued me
from those bullies at 'The Mitre.' I thought that
what you did was a noble and generous deed. Instead——" The lad paused.

"Oh, but continue," Galliard requested coldly. "Instead——?"

"There can be no instead, Sir Crispin. You will not mar so good an action now. You will give me my letter, will you not?"

Crispin winced. The breeding of earlier days—so sadly warped—cried out within him against the lie that he was acting by pretending to suspect treason in those feminine pothooks. Instincts of gentility and generosity long dead took life again at that call of conscience. He was conquered.

"There, take your letter, boy, and plague me no more," he growled, and abruptly thrust it upon Kenneth. Without waiting for reply or acknowledgment, he turned on his heel, and entered the palace. But he had yielded overlate for gratitude, and as Kenneth turned away, it was with a curse upon Galliard, for whom his detestation seemed to be afforded fresh cause at every step.

CHAPTER V

AFTER WORCESTER FIELD

THE morning of the third of September—that date so propitious to Cromwell, so disastrous to Charles—found Crispin in a company of gentlemen in battle-harness, assembled at " The Mitre Inn." For a toast he gave them " Damnation to all crop-ears."

" Sirs," quoth he, " a fair beginning to a fair day. God send the evening find us as merry."

It was not his good fortune, however, to be in the earlier work. Until afternoon he was kept within the walls of Worcester, chafing to be where hard knocks were being dealt—with Montgomery at Powick Bridge, or with Pittscottie on Bunn's Hill. But he was forced to hold his mood in curb, and wait until Charles and his advisers should elect to make the general attack.

It came at last, but not until they had the disastrous news that Montgomery was routed, and Pittscottie in full retreat, whilst Dalziel had surrendered, and Keith was taken. Then was it that the main body of the Royal army formed up at the Sidbury Gate, and Crispin found himself in the centre, which was commanded by the King in person. It is written that in the brilliant charge that followed there was no more conspicuous figure, no voice rang louder in encouragement to the men. For the first time on that fateful day Cromwell's Ironsides gave back before the Royalists, who in their fierce, irresistible charge, swept

all before them until they reached the battery on
Perry Wood, and drove the Roundheads from it hell-
to-leather.

It was a glorious moment, a moment in which the
fortunes of the day hung in the balance ; the turn of
the tide it seemed to them at last.

Crispin was among the first to reach the guns, and
with a great shout of " Hurrah for Cavaliers ! " he
had cut down two gunners that yet lingered. His cry
lacked not an echo, and a deafening cheer broke upon
the clamorous air as the Royalists found themselves
masters of the position. Up the hill pressed the Duke
of Hamilton on one side and the Earl of Derby on
the other, to support the King. It but remained for
Lesley's Scottish Horse to follow and complete the
rout of the Parliamentarian forces. Had they moved
at that supreme moment there are those who hold
that the issue of Worcester Field had been vastly
different. But they never stirred a foot, and the
Royalists waiting on Perry Wood cursed Lesley for
a foul traitor who had sold his King.

In overwhelming bitterness they realized then that
their great effort was to be barren, their gallant charge
in vain. Unsupported, their position grew fast un-
tenable.

And presently, when Cromwell had gathered his
scattered Ironsides, that gallant host was driven fight-
ing, down the hill and back to the shelter of Worcester.
With the Roundheads pressing hotly upon them they
gained at last the Sidbury Gate, but only to find that
an overset ammunition wagon blocked the entrance.
In this plight, and without attempting to remove the

obstacle, they faced about to make a last stand against the Puritan onslaught.

Charles had flung himself from his charger and climbed the obstruction, and in this he was presently followed by others concerned for his person, amongst whom was Crispin.

In the High Street Galliard came upon the young King, mounted on a fresh horse, addressing a Scottish regiment of foot. The soldiers had thrown down their arms, and stood sullenly before him, refusing to obey his command to help him attempt, even at that late hour, to retrieve the fortunes of the day. Crispin looked on in scorn and anger. His passion aroused at the sight of Lesley's inaction needed but this last breath to fan it into a very blaze of wrath. And what he said to them touching themselves, their country, and the Kirk Committee that had made sheep of them, was so bitter and contemptuous that none but men in the most parlous and pitiable of conditions would have stood to listen.

He was still hurling vituperations at them when Colonel Pride with a troop of Parliamentarian horse —having completely overcome the resistance at the Sidbury Gate—rode into the town. At the news of this Crispin made a last appeal to the infantry.

" Afoot, you Scottish hinds ! " he roared at them. " Will you rather be cut to pieces as you stand ? Up, you dogs, and since you know not how to live, die at least without shame ! "

But in vain did he rail. They stood sullen, unheeding, their weapons on the ground before them. And then, as Crispin was turning away to see to his own safety, the King rode up again, and again in passionate terms sought to revive the courage that was dead in those Scottish hearts. If they would not stand by him, he cried at last, let them slay him there, sooner than that he should be taken captive to perish like his father on the scaffold.

He was still urging them, when Crispin unceremoniously seized his bridle.

" Will you stand here until you are taken, sire ? " he cried. " It's time to look to your safety."

Charles turned upon the resolute, battle-grimed face of the man that thus addressed him a glance that blended wonder with indignation. Then it softened. A faint, sad smile parted his lips.

" Faith ! you are right, sir," he made answer. " Attend me." And turning about he rode down a side street with Galliard following closely in his wake.

With the intention of doffing his armour and changing his apparel, the King made for the house in New Street where he had been quartered. As they drew up before the door, Crispin looked over his shoulder and rapped out an oath.

" Hasten, sire," he exclaimed. " The damned cropears are upon us."

The King looked round to behold Colonel Pride's Parliamentarians. " It is ended," he muttered. But already Crispin had sprung from his horse.

" Dismount, sire," he commanded, and in his frenzy to assist him he almost appeared to drag him from the saddle.

" Which way ? " Charles asked, looking helplessly from left to right. " Which way ? "

Crispin had already determined. Seizing the royal arm with the same lack of ceremony, he thrust the King across the threshold, and, following, closed the door and shot its only bolt. But the shout set up by the Puritans warned them that they had been detected.

The King turned upon Sir Crispin, and in the half-light of the passage wherein they stood Galliard made out the frown that bent the royal brows.

" Oddslife, sir ! you have me in a trap."

" Not yet, sire," returned the knight. " Begone whilst there's time."

" Begone ? " echoed Charles, in annoyance. " But whither, sir ? Whither and how ? "

His last word was almost drowned in the din without, as the Roundheads pulled up before the house.

" By the back, sire," was the impatient answer. " Through door or window—as best you can. The back must overlook the Corn-market ; that is your way. But hasten—in God's name hasten !—before they think of it and cut off your retreat."

As he spoke a heavy blow shook the door.

" Hasten, your Majesty," he implored in a frenzy.

Charles moved to depart, then paused.

" But you, sir ? Must I go alone ? "

Crispin stamped his foot, and turned a face livid with impatience upon his King.

" Either that or not at all. That crazy door will not hold for a second once a stout man sets his shoulder to it. After the door they will find me, and for your Majesty's sake I trust my timbers may prove stouter. Fare you well, sire," he ended in a softer tone. "God guard your Majesty and send you happier days."

And, bending his knee, Crispin brushed the royal hand with his hot lips.

A shower of blows was clattering upon the timbers of the door, and one of its panels was splintered by a musket-stock. Charles saw it, and with a muttered word that was not caught by Crispin, he obeyed the knight, and fled.

Scarcely had he disappeared down that narrow passage, when the door gave way completely and with a mighty crash fell inwards. Over the ruins of it sprang a young Puritan—scarce more than a boy—shouting : " The Lord of Hosts ! "

But he had not taken three strides when the point of Crispin's tuck-sword gave him pause.

" Halt ! You cannot pass this way."

" Back, son of Moab ! " was the Roundhead's retort. " You stay me at your peril."

Behind the lad, in the doorway, pressed others, crying out to him not to parley, but to cut down the Amalekite that stood between them and the young man Charles Stuart. Crispin answered this by a laugh, and kept the officer in check with his point.

" Back, or I cut you down," blustered the Roundhead. " We seek the malignant Stuart."

" If by that blasphemy you mean his sacred Majesty, faith, he's where you will never be—in God's keeping."

" Presumptuous hound," stormed the lad, " give way ! "

Their swords met, and for a moment they ground

one against the other; then Crispin's blade darted out, swift as the tongue of a snake, and took his opponent in the throat.

"You would have it so, rash fool," he deprecated.

The boy hurtled back into the arms of those behind, and as he fell he dropped his rapier, which rolled almost to Crispin's feet. The knight stooped, and when again he stood erect, confronting the troopers in that narrow passage, he held a sword in either hand.

There was a momentary pause in the onslaught, then to his dismay Crispin saw the barrel of a musket pointed at him over the shoulder of one of his foremost assailants. He set his teeth for what was to come, and braced himself with the hope that the King might already have made good his escape.

The end was at hand, he thought, and a fitting end, since his last hope of redress was gone—destroyed by that fatal day's defeat.

But of a sudden a cry rang out in a voice wherein rage and anguish were blended fearfully, and simultaneously the musket barrel was dashed aside.

"I want him alive!" was the cry of that voice. "Take him alive!" It was Colonel Pride himself, who having pushed his way forward, now beheld the bleeding body of the youth Crispin had slain. "Take him alive!" roared the old man. Then his voice changing to one of exquisite agony—"My son, my boy," he was sobbing.

At a glance Crispin caught the situation; but the old Puritan's grief left him unmoved.

"You must have me alive?" he mocked. "Gadswounds, but you'll find my life will cost you dear.

Well, sirs? Who will be next to court the honour of dying by the sword of a gentleman? At your pleasure. my crop-ears.''

A roar of fury answered him, and straightway two men sprang forward. More than two could not engage him at once by virtue of the narrowness of the passage. Again steel clashed on steel. Crispin—lithe as a panther—crouched low, and took one of their swords on each of his.

A disengage and a double he foiled with ease, then by a turn of the wrist he held for a second one opponent's blade ; and before the fellow could disengage again, he had brought his right-hand sword across, and stabbed him in the neck. Simultaneously his other opponent had rushed in and thrust. It was a risk Crispin was forced to take, trusting to his armour to protect him. It did him the service he hoped from it ; the trooper's sword glanced harmlessly aside, whilst the fellow himself, over-balanced by the fury of his onslaught, staggered helplessly forward. Before he could recover, Crispin had spitted him from side to side betwixt the straps that held his back and breast together.

As the two men went down, one after the other, the watching troopers set up fresh cries of rage, and pressed forward in a body. But the Tavern Knight stood his ground, and his points danced dangerously before the eyes of the two foremost. Alarmed, they called to those behind to give them room to handle their swords ; but too late. Crispin had seen the advantage, and taken it. Twice he had thrust, and another two sank bleeding to the ground.

At that there came a pause, and somewhere out in the street a knot of them expostulated with Colonel Pride, and begged to be allowed to pick off that murderous malignant with their pistols. But the grief-stricken father was obdurate. He would have the Amalekite alive that he might cause him to die a hundred deaths in one.

And so two more were sent in to try conclusions with the indomitable Galliard. They went to work more warily. He on the left parried Crispin's stroke, then, knocking up the knight's blade, he rushed in and seized his wrist, shouting to those behind to follow up. But even as he did so, Crispin sent back his other antagonist, howling and writhing with the pain of a transfixed sword-arm, and turned his full attention upon the foe that clung to him. Not a second did he take for thought. Instinctively he knew that whilst he shortened his blade, others would rush in ; so, turning his wrist, he caught the man a crushing blow full in the face with the pommel of his disengaged sword.

Fulminated, the man reeled back into the arms of yet another who advanced.

Again there fell a pause. Then silently a Round-head charged Sir Crispin with a pike. He leapt nimbly aside, and the murderous lunge shot past him ; as he did so he dropped his left-hand sword and caught at the halberd. Exerting his whole strength, he jerked the fellow that wielded it forward, and received him on his outstretched blade.

Covered with blood—the blood of others—Crispin stood before them now. He was breathing hard and sweating at every pore, but still grim and defiant. His strength, he realized, was ebbing. Yet he shook himself, and asked them with a gibing laugh did they not think that they had better shoot him.

The Roundheads stood at gaze, hesitating. The fight had lasted but a few moments, and already five of them were stretched upon the ground, and a sixth disabled. There was something in the Tavern Knight's attitude and terrific, blood-bespattered appearance that deterred them. From out of his powder-blackened face his eyes flashed fiercely, and a mocking, diabolical smile played round the corners of his mouth. What manner of man, they asked themselves, was this who could laugh in such an extremity? Superstition quickened their alarm as they gazed upon his undaunted front, and muttered that this was no man they fought, but the foul fiend himself.

" Well, sirs," he mocked them presently. " How long must I await your pleasure ? "

Snarls answered him, yet they hung back until Colonel Pride's voice shook them into action. In a body they charged him now, so suddenly and violently that he was forced to give way. Cunningly did he ply his sword before them, but ineffectually. They had adopted fresh tactics, and engaging his blade, they acted cautiously and defensively, advancing steadily, and compelling him to fall back.

Sir Crispin guessed their scheme at last, and vainly strove to hold his ground ; his retreat slackened perhaps, but it was still a retreat, and their defensive action gave him no opening. Vainly, yet by every trick of fence he knew, did that master of the art seek to lure the two foremost into attacking him; stolidly they pursued the adopted plan, and steadily they impelled him backward.

At last he reached the staircase, and he realized that did he allow himself to go farther he was lost irretrievably. Yet farther was he driven, despite the strenuous efforts he put forth, until on his right there was room for a man to slip on to the stairs and take him in the flank. Twice one of his opponents essayed it, and twice did Galliard's deadly point repel him.. But at the third attempt the man got through, another stepped into his place in front, and thus from two, Crispin's immediate assailants became increased to three.

He realized that the end was at hand, yet craftily did he lay about him, but to no purpose. Presently he who had gained the stairs flung himself suddenly upon him sideways, and clung to his sword-arm. Before he could make a move to shake himself free, the two that faced him caught at his other arm.

Like one possessed he struggled then, for the sheer lust of striving; but they that held him gripped effectively.

Thrice they bore him struggling to the ground, and thrice he rose again and sought to shake them from him as a bull shakes off a pack of dogs. But they held fast, and again they forced him down; others sprang to their aid, and the Tavern Knight could rise no more.

" Disarm the dog ! " cried Pride. " Disarm and truss him hand and foot."

"Sirs, you need not," he answered, gasping. "I yield me. Take my sword. I'll do your bidding."

The fight was fought and lost, but he rejoiced almost that upon so worthy a scene of his life was the curtain to fall, and again to believe that, thanks to the stand he had made, the King should have succeeded in effecting his escape.

CHAPTER VI

COMPANIONS IN MISFORTUNE

THROUGH the streets of Worcester the Roundheads
dragged Sir Crispin, and for all that he was as hard
and callous a man as any that ever buckled on a
cuirass, the horrors that in going he beheld drew more
than a shudder from him.

The place was become a shambles, and the very
kennels ran with blood. The Royalist defeat was by
now complete, and Cromwell's fanatical butchers over-
ran the town, vying to outdo one another in savage
cruelty and murder. Houses were being broken into
and plundered, and their inmates—resisting or un-
resisting; armed or unarmed; men, women, and
children alike—were pitilessly being put to the sword.
Charged was the air of Worcester with the din of that
fierce massacre. The crashing of shivered timbers,
as doors were beaten in, mingled with the clatter and
grind of sword on sword, the crack of musket and
pistol, the clank of armour, and the stamping of men
and horses in that troubled hour.

And through all rang the fierce, raucous blasphemy
of the slayers, and the shrieks of agony, the groans,
the prayers, and curses of their victims.

All this Sir Crispin saw and heard, and in the
misery of it all, he for the while forgot his own sorry
condition, and scarcely heeded the pike-butt wherewith the Puritan at his heels was urging him along.

They paused at length in a quarter unknown to him,

before a tolerably large house. Its doors hung wide, and across the threshold, in and out, moved two continuous streams of officers and men.

A while Crispin and his captors stood in the spacious hall before they ushered him roughly into one of the abutting rooms. Here he was brought face to face with a man of middle height, red and coarse of countenance and large of nose, who stood fully armed in the centre of the chamber. His head was uncovered, and on the table at his side stood the morion he had doffed. He looked up as they entered, and for some few seconds rested his glance sourly upon the lank, bold-eyed prisoner who coldly returned his stare.

" Whom have we here ? " he inquired at length, his scrutiny having told him nothing.

" One whose offence is too heinous to have earned him a soldier's death, my lord," answered Pride.

" You lie, you damned rebel ! " said Crispin. " Tell Master Cromwell "—for he had guessed the man's identity—" that single-handed I held my own against you and a score of your curs, and that not until I had cut down seven of them was I taken. Tell him that, master psalm-singer, and let him judge whether you lied or not. Tell him, too, that you, who——"

A voice cold of authority interrupted him. " Peace, man. Peace to your ribaldry. Now, Colonel, let us hear you."

At great length, and with much interlarding of proverbs, did Pride relate how this impious malignant had been the means of the young man, Charles Stuart, making good his escape when otherwise he must have fallen into their hands. He accused him also of the murder of his son and of four other stout, God-fearing troopers, and urged Cromwell to let him deal with the malignant as he deserved.

The Lord-General's answer took expression in a form that was little puritanical. Then, checking himself—

"He is the second they have brought me within ten minutes charged with the same offence," said he. "The other one is a young fool who gave Charles Stuart his horse at St. Martin's Gate. But for him again the young man had been taken."

"So he has escaped!" cried Crispin. "Now God be praised!"

Cromwell stared at him blankly for a moment, then—

"You will do well, sir," he muttered sourly, "to address the Lord on your own behalf. As for that young man of Baal, your master, rejoice not yet in his escape. By the same crowning mercy, in which the Lord hath vouchsafed us victory to-day, shall He also deliver the malignant youth into my hands. For your share in retarding his capture your life, sir, shall pay forfeit. You shall hang at daybreak together with that other malignant who assisted Charles Stuart at the St. Martin's Gate."

"I shall at least hang in good company, whoever he may be," said Crispin pleasantly, "and for that, sir, I give you thanks."

"You will pass the night with that other rogue," Cromwell continued, without heeding the interruption, "and I pray that you may spend it in such meditation as shall fit you for your end. That is all. Take him away."

"But, my lord," exclaimed Pride, advancing.

"What now?"

Crispin heard half-whispered words, earnest and pleading. Cromwell shook his big head.

"It were not seemly. I cannot sanction it. Let it satisfy you that he dies. I grieve for you in your bereavement, but it is the fortune of war. Let the thought that your son died in a godly cause be of comfort to you. Bear in mind, Colonel Pride, that Abraham hesitated not to offer up his child to the Lord. And so, fare you well."

Colonel Pride's face worked oddly, and his eyes rested for a second upon the stern, unmoved figure of the Tavern Knight in malice and vindictiveness. Then, with every show of unwilling resignation, he withdrew, whilst Crispin was led out.

In the hall again they kept him waiting for some moments, until at length an officer came to bid him follow and led the way to the guard-room. Here they stripped him of his back-and-breast, and when this was done the officer again led the way, Crispin following between two troopers. They conducted him up three flights of stairs, and hurried him along a passage to a door by which a trooper was mounting guard. At a word from the officer the sentry turned, and unfastening the heavy bolts, opened the door. Crispin crossed the threshold to find himself within a mean, gloomy chamber, and to hear the heavy door closed and made fast again behind him. His stout heart sank a little as he realized that that closed door shut out to him the world for ever; but once again would he cross that threshold, and that would be the preface to the crossing of the greater threshold of eternity.

Then something stirred in one of that room's dark corners, and he started, to see that he was not alone, remembering that Cromwell had said he was to have a companion in his last hours.

"Who is there?" came a dull voice—a voice that was eloquent of misery.

"Master Stewart!" he exclaimed, recognizing his companion. "Oddslife, was it then you who gave the King your horse at the St. Martin's Gate? May Heaven reward you. Gadswounds," he added, "I had little thought to meet you again this side of Hell."

"There's little satisfaction for me in the meeting," was the doleful answer. "What make you here?"

"By your good leave and with your help I'll make as merry as a man may whose sands are all but run. The Lord-General—whom the devil burn in his good time—will make a pendulum of me at daybreak, and gives me the night in which to prepare."

The lad came forward into the light, and eyed Sir Crispin sorrowfully.

"We are companions in misfortune, then."

"At least we are consistent. For we were never companions in aught else? Come, sir, be of better cheer. Since it is to be our last night in this poor world, let us spend it as pleasantly as may be."

"Pleasantly?"

"'Twill clearly be difficult," answered Crispin, with a laugh. "Were we in Christian hands they'd not deny us a black jack over which to relish our last jest, and to warm us against the night air, which must be chill in this garret. But these crop-ears——" He paused to peer into the pitcher on the table. "Water! Pah! A scurvy lot, these psalm-mongers!"

"Merciful Heaven! Is that all you can think of? Have you no thought for your end?"

"Every thought, my lad, every thought, and I would fain prepare me for the morning's dance in a less dismal fashion than old Noll will afford me. Damn him!"

Kenneth drew back in horror. His old dislike for Crispin was all aroused by this indecent flippancy at such a time. The horror of spending the night in his company almost eclipsed the horror of the gallows whereof he had been a prey before Sir Crispin's coming.

Noting the movement, Crispin laughed carelessly, and walked towards the window. It was a small opening by which two iron bars, set crosswise, defied escape. Moreover, as Crispin looked out, he realized that a more effective barrier lay in the height of the window itself. The house overlooked the river on that side; it was built upon an embankment some thirty feet high; around this, at the base of the edifice, and some forty feet below the window, ran a narrow pathway protected by an iron railing. But so narrow was it, that had a man sprung from the casement of that prison, it was odds he would have fallen clear of it into the river some seventy feet below. He turned away with a sigh. He had approached the window almost in hope; he quitted it in despair.

"Ah, well," said he, "we will hang, and there's the end of it."

Kenneth had gone back to his seat in the corner, and, wrapped in his cloak, sat huddled, his comely young face seared with lines of pain. As Crispin looked upon him then, his heart softened and went out to the lad—went out as it had gone out to him on the night when first he had beheld him in the courtyard of Perth Castle.

He recalled the details of that meeting; he remembered the attraction that had drawn him to the boy and how Kenneth had at first appeared to reciprocate the feeling, until he came to know him for the godless ruffler that he was. He thought of the gulf that gradually had opened between them. The lad was righteous and God-fearing, truthful and sober, filled with stern ideals by which he sought to shape his life. He had taxed Crispin with his dissoluteness, and Crispin, despising him for a milksop, had returned the lad's disgust with mockery, and had found an evil pleasure in feeding that disgust at every turn.

To-night, as Crispin looked at him and remembered that at dawn they were to die in company, conscience told him that he had used him ill, that his behaviour towards him had been that of the dissolute ruffler he was become, rather than of the gentleman he had once accounted himself.

In that mood he now spoke.

"Kenneth," he said at length, and his voice bore so unusually mild a ring that the lad looked up in surprise. "You'll have heard tell that it is a common thing for men upon the threshold of eternity to seek to repair some of the evil they may have done in life."

Kenneth shuddered at this reminder of his approaching end. The ruffler paused a moment, as if awaiting a reply or a word of encouragement. Then, as none came, he continued—

"I am not one of your repentent sinners, Kenneth. I have lived my life, and as I have lived I shall die, unflinching and unchanged. Dare we to presume that a few hours spent in whining prayers shall atone for years of reckless living? A doctrine of cravens, who, having lacked in life the strength to live as conscience bade them, lack in death the courage to stand by life's deeds. I'll be no such traitor to myself. If my life has been evil, my temptations have been sore, and the rest is in God's hands. But in my course I have sinned against many men. They are not by, nor, were they, could I now make amends. But you at least are here, and what little reparation may lie in asking pardon I can make. When I first saw you at Perth it was my wish to make you my friend—a feeling I have not had these twenty years towards any man. I failed. How else could it have been? The dove may not nest with the carrion bird."

"Sir Crispin," cried Kenneth, genuinely moved, and still more amazed by this odd humility in one whom he had never known other than arrogant and mocking. "I beseech you say no more. For what trifling wrongs you may have done me I forgive you as freely as I would be forgiven. Is it not written that it shall be so?" And he held out his hand.

"A little more I must say, Kenneth," answered the

other, leaving the outstretched hand unheeded. "The feeling that was born in me towards you at Perth Castle is on me again. I do not account for it. Perhaps it springs from my recognition of the difference betwixt us ; perhaps I see in you a reflection of what once I was myself—honourable and true. But let that be. The sun is setting over yonder, and you and I will behold it no more. That to me is a small thing. I am weary. Hope is dead ; and when that is dead what does it signify that the body die also ? Yet in these last hours that we shall spend together I would at least have your esteem. I would have you forget my harshness and the wrongs that I may have done you down to that miserable affair of your sweetheart's letter, yesterday. I would have you realize that if I am vile, I am but such as a vile world hath made me. And to-morrow when we go forth together, I would have you see in me at least a man in whose company you are not ashamed to die."

Again the lad shivered.

"Shall I tell you my story, Kenneth ? I am oddly moved to go over this life of mine again in memory, and by giving my thoughts utterance it may be that they will take more vivid shape. For the rest my tale may while away a little of the time that's left, and when you have heard me you shall judge me, Kenneth. Can you bear with me ? "

Despite the parlous condition whereunto the fear of the morrow had reduced him, this new tone of Galliard's so wrought upon the lad then that he was almost eager in his request that Sir Crispin should unfold his tale. And this the Tavern Knight then set himself to do.

CHAPTER VII

THE TAVERN KNIGHT'S STORY

SIR CRISPIN walked from the window by which he had been standing, to the rough bed, and flung himself full length upon it. The only chair that dismal room contained was occupied by Kenneth. Galliard heaved a sigh of physical satisfaction.

" 'Fore George, I knew not I was so tired," he murmured. And with that he lapsed for some moments into silence, his brows contracted in the frown of one who collects his thoughts. At length he began, speaking in calm, unemotional tones that held perhaps a deeper pathos than a more passionate utterance could have lent them—

" Long ago—twenty years ago—I was as I have said, a lad to whom the world was a fair garden, a place fragrant with hope. Those, Kenneth, were my illusions. They are the illusions of youth ; they are youth itself, for when our illusions are gone we are no longer young no matter what years we count. Keep your illusions, Kenneth ; treasure them, hoard them jealously for as long as you may——"

" I dare swear, sir," answered the lad, with bitter humour, " that such illusions as I have I shall treasure all my life. You forget, Sir Crispin."

" Faith, yes. For the moment I had gone back twenty years, and to-morrow was none so near." He laughed softly, as though his lapse of memory amused him. Then he resumed—

" I was the only son, Kenneth, of as noble and upright a gentleman as ever lived—heir to an ancient, honoured name, and to lands as fair and broad as any in England.

" They lie who say that from the dawn we may foretell the day. Never was there a brighter dawn than that of my life ; never a day so wasted ; never an evening so dark as this. But let that be.

" Our lands were touched upon the northern side by those of a house with which we had been at feud for a hundred years and more. Puritans they were, stern and haughty in their self-righteousness. They held us dissolute because we enjoyed the life that God had given us, and there I am told the hatred first began. When I was a lad of your years, Kenneth, the hall—ours was the castle, theirs the hall—was occupied by two young sparks who made little shift to keep up the pious reputation of their house. They dwelt there with their mother—a woman too weak to check their ways, and holding, mayhap, herself, views not altogether puritanical. They discarded the sober black their forebears had worn for generations, and donned gay Cavalier garments. They let their love-locks grow ; set plumes in their castors and jewels in their ears ; they drank deep, ruffled it with the boldest, and decked their utterance with great oaths—for to none does blasphemy come more readily than to lips that in youth have been overmuch shaped in unwilling prayer. Me they avoided in accordance with tradition, and when at times we met, our salutations were grave as those of men on the point of crossing swords. I despised them for their coarse, ruffling

apostasy more than ever my father had despised
their father for a bigot, and they guessing or knowing
what was in my mind held me in deeper rancour
even than their ancestors had done mine. And more
galling still and yet a sharper spur to their hatred did
those whelps find in the realization that all the countryside held, as it had held for ages, us to be their betters.
A hard blow to their pride was that, but their revenge
was not long in coming.

"It chanced they had a cousin—a maid as sweet
and fair and pure as they were foul. We met in the
meads—she and I. Spring was the time—it seems
but yesterday!—and each in our bearing towards the
other forgot the traditions of the names we bore.
And as at first we met by chance, so did we
meet later by contrivance, not once or twice, but
many times. She made the world sweet for me. It
was sweet to live and to be young. We loved. How
else could it have been? What to us were traditions,
what to us the hatred that for centuries had held our
families asunder? In us it lay to set aside all that.

"And so I sought my father. He cursed me at
first for an unnatural son who left unheeded the
dictates of our blood. But later, when I had urged
my cause with all the fervour that is but of youth
—youth that loves—he relented. His thoughts went
back perhaps to the days of his own youth. He bade
me do as I listed. Nay, more than that. The first
of our name was he out of four generations to set
foot across the threshold of the hall; he went on
my behalf to sue for their cousin's hand.

"Then was their hour. To them that had been

taught the humiliating lesson that we were their betters, one of us came suing. They from whom the countryside looked for silence when one of us spoke, had it in their hands at length to say us nay. And they said it. What answer my father made them, Kenneth, I do not know; but very white was his face when I met him on the castle steps on his return. He was a cripple, who had lost the use of his right arm. In burning words he told me of the insult they had put upon him, then silently he pointed to the Toledo that two years before he had brought me out of Spain, and left me. But I had understood. I unsheathed that virgin blade and read the Spanish inscription, blurred by my tears of anger and shame; a proud inscription was it, instinct with the punctilio of proud Spain—' *Draw me not without motive, sheathe me not without honour.*' Motive there was and to spare; honour I swore there should be; and with that oath, and that brave sword girt to me, I set out to answer the insult "

Sir Crispin paused, and a sigh escaped him, followed by a laugh of bitterness. He fell to musing.

" I lost that sword years ago. The sword and I have been close friends in life, but my companion has been a blade of coarser make, carrying no inscriptions to prick at a man's conscience."

He laughed again, and again turned thoughtful, until Kenneth's voice aroused him.

" Your story, sir."

Twilight shadows were gathering in the garret, and as Crispin turned his face towards the youth, he no longer could discern his features; but his tone had been eager, and Crispin noted that he sat with head bent forward and that his eyes were intent.

"It interests you, eh? Ah, well. Hot foot I went to the hall, and with burning words I called upon those dogs to render satisfaction for the dishonour they had put upon my house. It proved a fool's errand. They sheltered their craven lives behind a shield of mock valour. They would not fight a boy, they said, and bade me get my beard grown, when perhaps they would give ear to my grievance.

"And so, a shame and rage a hundredfold more bitter than that which I had borne thither did I carry thence. My father bade me treasure up the memory of it against the time when my riper years should compel them to attend me, and this, by my every hope of Heaven, I swore to do. He bade me further efface for ever from my mind all thought or hope of union with their cousin, and though I made him no answer at the time, yet in my heart I promised to obey him in that, too. But I was young—scarce twenty. A week without sight of my mistress and I grew sick with despair. Then at length I came upon her, pale and tearful, one evening, and in an agony of passion and hopelessness I flung myself at her feet, and implored her to keep true to me and wait, and she, poor maid, to her undoing, swore that she would. You are yourself a lover, Kenneth, and you may guess something of the impatience that anon beset me. How could I wait? I asked her this.

"Some fifty miles from the castle there was a little farm, in the very heart of the country, which had been left me by a sister of my mother's. Thither I now implored her to go with me. I would find a priest to marry us, and there we should live a while in happiness, in solitude, and in love. I drew an alluring picture with all a lover's cunning, and to the charm of it she fell a victim. We fled three days later.

" We were wed in the village that pays allegiance to the castle, and thereafter we travelled swiftly and unhindered to that little homestead. There in solitude, with but two servants—a man and a maid whom I could trust—we lived, and for a season, brief as all happiness is doomed to be, we were happy. Her cousins had no knowledge of that farm of mine, and though they searched the country for many a mile around, they searched in vain. My father knew —as I learned afterwards—but deeming that what was done might not be undone, he held his peace. In the following spring a babe was born to us, and our bliss made heaven of that cottage.

" It was little more than a month after the birth of our child that the blow fell. My father had sent me word that he was ill, and I had gone to visit him. Two days I was absent, and on the second of these my man had been constrained to make a journey to the nearest town, whence he would not return until the morrow. Oft have I cursed the folly that led me to make no better provision.

" I returned earlier than I had thought to do. But I came too late. At my gate I found two freshly ridden horses tethered, and it was with a dull foreboding in my heart that I sprang through the open door. Within—O God, the anguish of it !—stretched on the floor I beheld my love, a gaping sword-wound in her side, and the ground all bloody about her. For a moment I stood dumb, in the spell of that horror, then a movement beyond, against the wall, aroused me, and I beheld her murderers, one with a naked sword in his hand.

"I think it was in that fell hour, Kenneth, that my whole nature changed. Until then it had been gentle, even weakly. But it was never so thereafter. It was, I think, in that very hour that I became the violent, reckless man that you have known. As I beheld then her cousins, my blood seemed to curdle in my veins; my teeth were set hard; my nerves and sinews knotted. I snatched up my fowling-piece from the chimney corner, and clutched it by the barrel with the fierceness that was in me—the fierceness of the beast about to spring upon those that have brought it to bay. For a moment I stood swaying there, my eyes upon them, and holding their craven glances fascinated. Then I leapt forward, the stock of my fowling-piece swung high above my head. And, as God lives, Kenneth, I had sent them straight to hell before they could have raised a hand or made a cry to stay me. But as I sprang my foot slipped in the blood of my beloved, and in my fall I came close to her where she lay. The fowling-piece had escaped my grasp and crashed against the wall. I scarce knew what I did, but as I lay beside her it came to me that I did not wish to rise again—that already I had lived overlong. It came to me that, seeing me fallen, haply those cowards would seize the chance to make an end of me as I lay. I wished it so in that moment's frenzy, for I made no attempt to rise or to defend myself; instead I set my arms about my poor murdered love, and against her cold cheek I set my face that was well-nigh as cold. And thus I lay, nor did they keep me long. A sword was passed through me from back to breast, whilst he who did it cursed me with a foul oath. The room grew dim; methought it swayed and that the walls were tottering; there was a roar as of an ocean in my ears, and then a piercing cry in a baby voice. At the sound of this I vaguely wished for the strength to rise. As in the distance, I heard one of those butchers cry, ' Haste, man; slit me that squalling bastard's throat ! ' And then I must have swooned.''

Kenneth shuddered.

" My God, how horrible ! '' he cried.

" When I regained consciousness,'' Crispin continued, as if he had not heard Kenneth's exclamation, " the cottage was in flames, set alight by them to burn the evidence of their foul deed. What I did I know not. I have tried to urge my memory along from the point of my awakening, but in vain. By what miracle I crawled forth, I cannot tell ; but in the morning I was found by my man lying prone in the garden, a dozen paces from the blackened ruins of the cottage, as near death as man may go and live.

" God willed that I should not die, but it was close upon a year before I was restored to any semblance of my former self, and then I was so changed that I was hardly to be recognized as that same joyous, vigorous lad, who had ridden eagerly home, one fine morning a year agone. There was grey in my hair, as much as there is now, though I was but twenty-one; my face was seared and marked as that of a man who had lived twice my years. It was to my faithful servant that I owed my life, though I ask myself to-night whether I have ever had real cause to thank him for it.

"As soon as I had regained sufficient strength, I went secretly home, wishing that men might continue to believe me dead. My father I found much aged by grief, but he was kind and tender with me. From him I had it that our enemies were gone to France. There were suspicions against them, and it would seem they had thought it better to remain absent for a while. He had learnt that they were in Paris, and thither I determined forthwith to follow them. Vainly did my father remonstrate with me; vainly did he urge me rather to bear my story to the King at Whitehall and seek for justice. I had been well advised had I obeyed this counsel, but I burned to take vengeance with my own hands, and with this purpose I set out. Two nights after my arrival in Paris it was my ill fortune to be embroiled in a rough-and-tumble in the streets, and by an ill chance I killed a man—the first was he of several that I have sent whither I am going to-morrow. The affair was like to have cost me my life, but by another of those miracles which have prolonged it, I was sent instead to the galleys on the Mediterranean. It was only wanting that, after all that already I had endured, I should become a galley-slave!

"For twelve long years I toiled at an oar, and waited. If I lived I would return to England; and if I returned, woe unto those that had wrecked my life—my body and my soul. I did live, and I did return. The Civil War had broken out, and I came to throw my sword into the balance on the King's side. I came, too, to be avenged, but that would wait. Meanwhile, the score had grown heavier. I went home to find the castle in usurping hands—in the hands of my enemies. My father was dead ; he had died a few months after I had gone to France ; and those murderers had advanced a claim that through my marriage with their cousin, since dead, and through my own death, there being no next of kin, they were the heirs-at-law. The Parliament allowed their claim, and they were installed. But when I came they were away, following the fortunes of the Parliament that had served them so well. And so I determined to let matters wait until the war was ended and the Parliament destroyed. The Parliament, however, survived."

The tale was told. Sir Crispin sat bowed in thought, and silence reigned between them for a spell. When, at last, he spoke again, it was on a pleading note.

" Ah, Kenneth, you have been hard upon me for my ways, for my abuses of the cup, and all the rest. But can you judge me harshly still, knowing what I had suffered, and what a weight of misery I bore with me ? I, whose life was wrecked beyond salvation ; who only lived that I might square the account with those that had so irreparably wronged me. Think you still that it was so vicious a thing, so unpardonable an offence to seek the blessed nepenthe of the wine-cup, the heavenly forgetfulness that its abuses brought me ? Is it strange that I became known as the wildest tantivy boy that rode with the King ? What else had I ? "

" In all truth your trials were sore," said the lad in a voice that contained a note of sympathy. And yet there was a certain restraint that caught the Tavern Knight's ear. He turned his head and bent his eyes in the lad's direction, but it was quite dark by now, and he failed to make out his companion's face.

" My tale is told, Kenneth. The rest you can guess. The King did not prevail and I was forced to fly from England with those others who escaped from the butchers that had made a martyr of Charles. I took service in France under the great Condé, and I saw some mighty battles. At length came the Council of Breda, and the invitation to Charles the Second to receive the crown of Scotland. I set out again to follow his fortunes as I had followed his father's, realizing that by so doing I followed my own, and that did he prevail I should have the redress so long awaited. This evil day has wrecked my last hope ; to-morrow at this hour it will not signify. And yet much would I give to have my fingers on the throats of those two scoundrels before the hangman's close around my own."

Again there was a spell of silence as the two men sat, both breathing heavily in the gloom that enveloped them. At length—

" You have heard my story, Kenneth," said Crispin.

" I have heard, Sir Crispin, and God knows I pity you."

That was all, and Galliard felt that it was not

enough. He had lacerated his soul with those grim
memories to earn a yet kinder word. He had looked
even to hear the lad suing for pardon for the harsh
opinions wherein he had held him. Strange was this
yearning of his for the boy's sympathy. He who
for twenty years had gone unloving and unloved,
sought now in his extremity affection from a fellow-
man.

And so in the gloom he waited for a kinder word
that came not ; then—so urgent was his need—he set
himself to beg it.

"Can you not understand now, Kenneth, how I
came to fall so low ? Can you not understand those
things in me which led them to dub me the Tavern
Knight after the King conferred upon me the honour
of knighthood for that stand of mine in Fifeshire ?
You must understand, Kenneth," he insisted almost
piteously, " and knowing all, you must judge me more
mercifully than hitherto."

"It is not mine to judge, Sir Crispin. I pity you
with all my heart," the lad replied, not ungently.

Still the knight was dissatisfied.

"Yours it is to judge as every man may judge his
fellow-man. You mean it is not yours to sentence.
But if yours it were, Kenneth, what then ? "

The lad paused a moment ere he answered. His
bigoted Presbyterian training was strong within him,
and although, as he said, he pitied Galliard, yet to
him—whose mind was stuffed with life's precepts, and
who knew naught of the trials it brings to some and
the temptations to which they were not human did
they not succumb—it seemed that vice was not to be

excused by misfortune. Out of mercy then he paused, and for a moment he had it even in his mind to cheer his fellow-captive with a lie. Then, remembering that he was to die upon the morrow, and that at such a time it was not well to risk the perdition of his soul by an untruth, however merciful, he answered slowly—

"Were I to judge you, since you ask me, sir, I should be merciful because of your misfortunes. And yet, Sir Crispin, your profligacy and the evil you have wrought in life must weigh heavily against you." Had this immaculate bigot, this churlish milksop been as candid with himself as he was with Crispin, he must have recognized that it was mainly Crispin's offences towards himself that his mind now dwelt on in deeper rancour than became one so well acquainted with the Lord's Prayer.

"You had not cause enough," he added impressively, "to defile your soul and risk its eternal damnation because the evil of others had wrecked your life."

Crispin drew breath with the sharp hiss of one in pain, and for a moment after was still. Then a bitter laugh broke from him.

"Bravely answered, reverend sir," he cried with biting scorn. "I marvel only that you left your pulpit to gird on a sword ; that you doffed your cassock to don a cuirass. Here is a text for you who deal in texts, my brave Jack Presbyter—' Judge you your neighbour as you would yourself be judged ; be merciful as you would hope for mercy.' Chew you the cud of that until the hangman's coming in the morning. Good night to you."

And throwing himself back upon the bed, Crispin composed himself to sleep. His limbs were heavy and his heart was sick.

" You misapprehend me, Sir Crispin," cried the lad, stung almost to shame by Galliard's reproach, and also maybe into some fear that hereafter he should find little mercy for his own lack of it towards a poor fellow-sinner. " I spoke not as I would judge, but as the Church teaches."

" If the Church teaches no better I rejoice that I was no churchman," grunted Crispin.

" For myself," the lad pursued, heeding not the irreverent interruption, " as I have said, I pity you with all my heart. More than that, so deeply do I feel, so great a loathing and indignation has your story sown in my heart, that were our liberty now restored us I would willingly join hands with you in seeking to punish those evildoers."

Sir Crispin laughed. He judged the tone rather than the words, and it rang hollow.

" Where are your wits, O casuist ? " he cried mockingly. " Where are your doctrines ? ' Vengeance is mine,' saith the Lord ! Pah ! "

And with that final ejaculation, pregnant with contempt and bitterness, he fell into silence.

He was accursed, he told himself. He must die alone, as he had lived.

CHAPTER VIII

THE TWISTED BAR

NATURE asserted herself, and, despite his condition, Crispin slept. Kenneth, huddled on his chair, listened in awe and amazement to his companion's regular breathing. He had not Galliard's nerves nor Galliard's indifference to death, so that neither could he follow his example, nor yet so much as realize how one should slumber upon the very brink of eternity.

For a moment his wonder stood perilously near to admiration ; then his pious training swayed him, and righteousness almost drew from him a contempt of this man's apathy. There was much of the Pharisee's attitude towards the publican in his mood.

Anon that regular breathing became an irritation to him ; it drew so marked a contrast 'twixt Crispin's frame of mind and his own. Whilst Crispin had related his story, the interest it awakened had served to banish the spectre of fear which the thought of the morrow conjured up. Now that Crispin was silent and asleep, that spectre returned, and the lad grew numb and sick with the horror of his position. Thought followed thought as he sat huddled there with sunken head and hands tightly clasped between his knees, and they were mostly of his dull uneventful days in Scotland, and ever and anon of Cynthia, his beloved. Would she hear of his end ? Would she weep for him ?—as though it mattered ! And every train of thought that he embarked upon brought him to the same issue—

to-morrow ! Shuddering, he would clench his hands still tighter, and the perspiration would stand out in beads upon his brow.

At length he flung himself upon his knees to address not so much a prayer as a maudlin grievance to his Creator. He felt himself a craven—doubly so by virtue of the peaceful breathing of that sinner he despised—and he told himself that it was not in fear a gentleman should meet his end.

" But I shall be brave to-morrow. I shall be brave," he muttered, and knew not that it was vanity begat the thought, and vanity that might uphold him on the morrow when there were others by, however broken might be his spirit now.

Meanwhile Crispin slept. When he awakened the light of a lanthorn was on his face, and holding it stood beside him a tall black figure in a cloak and a slouched hat whose broad brim left the features unrevealed.

Still half asleep, and blinking like an owl, he sat up.

" I have always held burnt sack to be well enough, but——"

He stopped short, fully awake and suddenly remembering his condition. Thinking they were come for him, he drew a sharp breath and in a voice as indifferent as he could make it—

" What's o'clock ? " he asked.

" Past midnight, unhappy man," he was answered by a deep, droning voice. " Hast entered upon thy last day of life—a day whose sun thou'lt never see. But five hours more are left thee in this vale of tears."

"And is it to tell me this that you have awakened me?" demanded Galliard in such a voice that he of the cloak recoiled a step, as if he thought a blow must follow. "Out on you for an unmanerly lout to break upon a gentleman's repose."

"I come," returned the other in his droning voice, "in Christian charity, to call upon thee to repent."

"Plague me not," answered Crispin, with a yawn. "Let me sleep."

"Soundly enough shalt thou sleep in a few hours' time. Bethink thee, miserable sinner, of thy soul."

"Sir," cried the Tavern Knight, "I am a man of marvellous short endurance. But mark you this—your ways to heaven are not my ways. Indeed, if heaven be peopled by such croaking things as you, I shall be thankful to avoid it. So go, my friend. Leave me before I become discourteous."

The minister stood in silence for a moment; then, setting his lanthorn upon the table, he raised his hands and eyes towards the low ceiling of the chamber.

"Vouchsafe, O Lord," he prayed, "to touch yet the callous heart of this obdurate, incorrigible sinner, this wicked, perjured, and blasphemous malignant, whose——"

He got no further. Crispin was upon his feet, his harsh countenance thrust into the very face of the minister; his eyes ablaze.

"Out!" he thundered, pointing to the door. "Out! Begone! I would not be guilty at the end of my life of striking a swordless man. But go whilst I can bethink me of it! Go—take your prayers to hell."

The minister fell back before that blaze of passion.

For a second he appeared to hesitate, then he turned towards Kenneth, who stood behind in silence. But the lad's Presbyterian rearing had taught him to hate a sectarian as he would a papist or as he would the devil, and he did no more than echo Galliard's words —though in a gentler key.

"I pray you go," he said. "But if you would perform an act of charity, leave your lanthorn. It will be dark enough hereafter."

The minister looked keenly at the boy, and won over by the humility of his tone, he set the lanthorn on the table. Then, moving towards the door, he stopped and addressed himself to Crispin.

"I go since you oppose with violence my ministrations. But I shall pray for you, and I will return anon, when perchance your heart shall be softened by the nearer imminence of your end."

"Sir," quoth Crispin wearily, "you would out-talk a fishwife."

"I've done, I've done," cried the minister in trepidation, making shift to depart. On the threshold he paused again.

"I leave you the lanthorn," he said. "May it light you to a godlier frame of mind. I shall return at daybreak." And with that he went.

Crispin yawned noisily, and stretched himself. Then, pointing to the pallet—

"Come, lad, 'tis your turn," said he.

Kenneth shivered.

"I could not sleep," he cried. "I could not."

"As you will." And shrugging his shoulders, Crispin sat down on the edge of the bed.

"For cold comforters commend me to these crop-
eared cuckolds," he grumbled. "They are all thought
for a man's soul, but for his body they care nothing.
Here am I who for the last ten hours have had neither
meat nor drink. Not that I mind the meat so much,
but, 'slife, my throat is dry as one of their sermons,
and I would cheerfully give four of my five hours of
life for a posset of sack. A paltry lot they are, Kenneth, holding that because a man must die at dawn
he need not sup to-night. Heigho! It has been said
that he who sleeps dines, but I never heard that he
who sleeps drinks. Still, if I sleep perchance I shall
forget my thirst."

He stretched himself upon the bed, and presently
he slept again.

It was Kenneth who next awakened him. He
opened his eyes to find the lad shivering as with an
ague. His face was ashen.

"Now, what's amiss? Oddslife, what ails you?"
Crispin demanded.

"Is there no way, Sir Crispin? Is there nothing
you can do?" wailed the youth.

Instantly Galliard sat up.

"Poor lad, poor lad! The thought of the rope
affrights you, eh?"

Kenneth bowed his head in silence.

"'Tis a scurvy death, to be sure. Look you,
Kenneth, there is a dagger in my boot. If you would
rather have cold steel, 'tis done. It is the last service
I may render you, and I'll be as gentle as a mother.
Just there, over the heart, and you'll know no more
until you are in Paradise."

Turning down the leather of his right boot, he thrust his hand down the side of his leg. But Kenneth sprang back with a cry.

"No, no," he cried, covering his face with his hands. "Not that! You don't understand. What odds to exchange one form of death for another? Is there no way out of this? Is there no way, Sir Crispin?" he demanded with clenched hands.

"You're maudlin," quoth the other. "Is there no way, say you? There is the window, but it's seventy feet above the river; and there is the door, but it's locked, and there is a sentry on the other side."

"I might have known it. I might have known that you would mock me. What is death to you, to whom life offers nothing? For you the prospect of it has no terrors. But for me—bethink you, sir, I am scarce eighteen years of age, and life was full of promise for me. O God, pity me!"

"True, lad, true," the knight returned in softened tones. "I had forgotten that death is not to you the blessed release that it is to me. And yet, and yet," he mused, "do I not die leaving a task unfulfilled—a task of vengeance? And by my soul, I know no greater spur to make a man cling to life. Ah," he sighed wistfully, "if indeed I could find a way."

"Think, Sir Crispin, think," cried the boy feverishly.

"To what purpose? There is the window. But even if the bars were moved, which I see no manner of accomplishing, the drop to the river is seventy feet at least, as I've said. I measured it with my eyes

when first we entered here. We have no rope. Your
cloak rent in two and the pieces tied together would
scarce yield us ten feet. Would you care to jump the
remaining sixty ? "

At the very thought of it the lad shuddered.

" There. And yet, boy, it would be taking a risk
which if successful would mean life—if otherwise, a
speedier end than even the rope will afford. Oddslife," he cried, suddenly springing to his feet, and
seizing the lanthorn. " Let us look at these bars."

He stepped across to the window, and held the
light so that its rays fell full upon the base of the
vertical iron that barred the square.

" It is much worn by rust, Kenneth," he muttered.
" The removal of this single piece of iron," and he
touched the lower arm of the cross, " should give us
passage. Who knows ? Hum ! "

He walked back to the table and set the lanthorn
down.

" He who throws a main must set a stake upon
the board. I set my life—a stake that is already
forfeit—and I throw for liberty. If I win, I win all ;
if I lose, I lose nought. 'Slife, I have thrown many
a main with Fate, but never one wherein the odds
were more generous. Come, Kenneth, it is the only
way, and we will attempt it if we can but move the
bar."

" You mean to leap ? " gasped the lad.

" Into the river. It is at least a chance."

" O God, I dare not. It is a fearsome drop."

" Longer, I confess, than they'll give you in an
hour's time ; but it may lead elsewhere."

The boy's mouth was parched. His eyes burned in their sockets, and yet his limbs shook with cold—but not the cold of that September night.

" I'll take the risk of it," he muttered with a gulp. Then suddenly clutching Galliard's arm, he pointed to the window.

" What ails you now ? " quoth Crispin testily.

" The dawn, Sir Crispin.   The dawn."

Crispin looked, and there, like a gash in the black-ness of the heavens, he beheld a streak of grey.

" Quick, Sir Crispin ; there is no time to lose. The minister said he would return at daybreak."

" Let him come," answered Galliard grimly, as he moved towards the casement.

He gripped the lower bar with his lean, sinewy hands, and setting his knee against the masonry beneath it, he exerted the whole of his huge strength —that awful strength acquired during those years of toil as a galley-slave, which even his debaucheries had not undermined. He felt his sinews straining until it seemed that they must crack ; the sweat stood out upon his brow ; his breathing grew ster-torous.

" It gives," he panted at last.   " It gives."

He paused in his efforts, and withdrew his hands.

" Let me breathe a while. One other effort such as that, and it is done. 'Fore George," he laughed, " it is the first time water has stood my friend, for the rains have sadly rusted that iron."

Outside their sentry was pacing before the door ; his steps came nearer, passed, and receded ; turned, came nigh again, and again passed on. As once more they grew faint, Crispin seized the bar and renewed his attempt. This time it was easier. Gradually it yielded to the strain.

Nearer came the sentry's footsteps, but they went unheeded by him who toiled, and by him who watched with bated breath and beating heart. He felt it giving—giving—giving. Crack!

With a report that rang through the room like a pistol shot, it broke in its socket. Both men caught their breath, and stood for a second crouching, with straining ears. The sentry had stopped at their door.

Galliard was swift to think, and as swift to act upon the thought. To thrust Kenneth into a corner, to extinguish the light, and to fling himself upon the bed was all the work of an instant.

The key grated in the lock, and Crispin answered it with a resounding snore. The door opened, and on the threshold stood the Roundhead trooper, holding aloft a lanthorn whose rays gleamed on his polished cuirass. He beheld Crispin on the bed with closed eyes and open mouth, and he heard his reassuring and melodious snore. He saw Kenneth seated peacefully upon the floor, with his back against the wall, and for a moment he was puzzled.

" Heard you aught ? " he asked.

" Ay," answered Kenneth, in a strangled voice, " I heard something like a shot out there."

The gesture with which he accompanied the words were fatal. Instinctively he had jerked his thumb towards the window, thereby drawing the soldier's eyes in that direction. The fellow's glance fell upon the twisted bar, and a sharp exclamation of surprise escaped him.

Had he been aught but a fool he must have guessed at once how it came so, and having guessed it, he must have thought twice before venturing within reach of a man who could so handle iron. But he was a slow-reasoning clod, and so far, thought had not yet taken the place of surprise. He stepped into the chamber and across to the window, that he might more closely view that broken bar.

With eyes that were full of terror and despair, Kenneth watched him; their last hope had failed them. Then, as he looked, it seemed to him that in one great leap from his recumbent position on the bed, Crispin had fallen upon the soldier.

The lanthorn was dashed from the fellow's hand, and rolled to Kenneth's feet. The fellow had begun a cry, which broke off suddenly into a gurgle as Galliard's fingers closed about his windpipe. He was a big man, and in his mad struggles he carried Crispin hither and thither about the room. Together they hurtled against the table, which would have gone crashing over had not Kenneth caught it and drawn it softly to the wall.

Both men were now upon the bed. Crispin had guessed the soldier's intent to fling himself upon the ground so that the ring of his armour might be heard, and perchance bring others to his aid. To avoid this, Galliard had swung him towards the bed, and hurled him on to it. There he pinned him with his knee, whilst his fingers gripped the Roundhead's throat, pressing the apple inwards with his thumb.

"The door, Kenneth!" he commanded, in a whisper. "Close the door!"

Vain were the trooper's struggles to free himself from that throttling grip. Already his efforts grew weaker; his face was purple; his veins stood out in ropes upon his brow till they seemed upon the point of bursting; his eyes protruded like a lobster's and there was a horrible grin upon his mouth; still his heels beat the bed, and still he struggled. With his fingers he plucked madly at the throttling hands on his neck, and tore at them with his nails until the blood streamed from them. Still Galliard held him firmly, and with a smile—a diabolical smile it seemed to the poor, half-strangled wretch—he gazed upon his choking victim.

"Someone comes!" gasped Kenneth suddenly. "Someone comes, Sir Crispin!" he repeated, shaking his hands in a frenzy.

Galliard listened. Steps were approaching. The soldier heard them also, and renewed his efforts. Then Crispin spoke.

"Why stand you there like a fool?" he growled. "Quench the light—stay, we may want it! Cast your cloak over it! Quick, man, quick!"

The steps came nearer. The lad had obeyed him, and they were in darkness.

"Stand by the door," whispered Crispin. "Fall upon him as he enters, and see that no cry escapes him. Take him by the throat, and as you love your life, do not let him get away."

The footsteps halted. Kenneth crawled softly to his post. The soldier's struggles grew of a sudden still, and Crispin loosed his hold at last. Then, calmly drawing the fellow's dagger, he felt for the straps of his cuirass, and these he proceeded to cut. As he did so the door was opened.

By the light of the lamp burning in the passage they beheld silhouetted upon the threshold a black figure crowned by a steeple hat. Then the droning voice of the Puritan minister greeted them.

" Your hour is at hand ! " he announced.

" Is it time ? " asked Galliard from the bed. And as he put the question he softly thrust aside the trooper's breastplate, and set his hand to the fellow's heart. It still beat faintly.

" In another hour they will come for you," answered the minister. And Crispin marvelled anxiously what Kenneth was about. " Repent then, miserable sinners, whilst yet——"

He broke off abruptly, awakening out of his religious zeal to a sense of strangeness at the darkness and the absence of the sentry, which hitherto he had not remarked.

" What hath——" he began. Then Galliard heard a gasp, followed by the noise of a fall, and two struggling men came rolling across the chamber floor.

" Bravely done, boy ! " he growled almost mirthfully. " Cling to him, Kenneth ; cling to him a second yet ! "

He leapt from the bed, and guided by the faint light coming through the door, sprang across the intervening space and softly closed it. Then he groped his way along the wall to the spot where he had seen the lanthorn stand when Kenneth had flung his cloak over it. As he went, the two striving men came up against him.

"Hold fast, lad," he cried, encouraging Kenneth, "hold him yet a moment, and I will relieve you!"

He reached the lanthorn at last, and pulling aside the cloak, he lifted the light and set it upon the table.

CHAPTER IX

THE BARGAIN

By the lanthorn's yellow glare Crispin beheld the two men—a mass of writhing bodies and a bunch of waving legs—upon the ground. Kenneth, who was uppermost, clung purposefully to the parson's throat. The faces of both were alike distorted, but whilst the lad's breath came in gasping hisses, the other's came not at all.

Going over to the bed, Crispin drew the unconscious trooper's tuck-sword. He paused for a moment to bend over the man's face; his breath came faintly, and Crispin knew that ere many moments were sped he would regain consciousness. He smiled grimly to see how well he had performed his work of suffocation without yet destroying life.

Sword in hand, he returned to Kenneth and the parson. The Puritan's struggles were already becoming mere spasmodic twitchings; his face was as ghastly as the trooper's had been a while ago.

" Release him, Kenneth."

" He struggles still."

" Release him, I say," Galliard repeated, and stooping he caught the lad's wrist and compelled him to abandon his hold.

" He will cry out," protested Kenneth in apprehension.

" Not he. Leastways, not yet awhile. Observe the wretch."

With mouth wide agape, the minister lay gasping like a fish newly taken from the water. Even now that his throat was free he appeared to struggle for a moment before he could draw breath. Then he took it in panting gulps until it seemed that he must choke in his gluttony of air.

" 'Fore George," quoth Crispin, " I was no more than in time. Another second, and we should have had him, too, unconscious. There ! He is recovering.

The blood was receding from the swollen veins of the parson's head, and his cheeks were paling to their normal hue. Anon they went yet paler than their wont, as Galliard rested the point of his sword against the fellow's neck.

" Make sound or movement," said Crispin coldly, " and I'll pin you to the floor like a beetle. Obey me, and no harm shall come to you."

" I will obey," the fellow answered, in a wheezing whisper. " I swear I will. But of your charity, good sir, I beseech you remove your sword. Your hand might slip, sir," he whined, a wild terror in his eyes.

Where now was the deep bass of his whilom accents ? Where now the grotesque majesty of his bearing, and the impressive gestures that erstwhile had accompanied his words of denunciation ?

" Your hand might slip, sir," he whined again.

" It might—and, by Gad, it shall if I hear more from you. So that you are discreet and obedient, have no fear of my hand." Then, still keeping his eye upon the fellow : " Kenneth," he said, " attend to the crop-ear yonder, he will be recovering. Truss him with the bedclothes, and gag him with his scarf. See to it, but leave his nostrils free that he may breathe."

Kenneth carried out Galliard's orders, what time Crispin remained standing over the recumbent minister. At length, when Kenneth announced that it was done, he bade the Puritan arise.

"But have a care," he added, "or you shall taste the joys of the Paradise you preach of. Come, sir parson; afoot!"

A prey to a fear that compelled unquestioning obedience, the fellow came clumsily to his feet.

"Stand there, sir. So." Crispin's point was within an inch of the man's Geneva bands. "Take his kerchief, Kenneth, and pinion his wrists behind him."

That done, Crispin bade the lad unbuckle and remove the parson's belt. Next he ordered that man of texts to be seated upon their only chair, and with that same belt he commanded Kenneth to strap him to it. Not until the Puritan was safely bound did Crispin lower his rapier, and seat himself upon the table-edge beside him.

"Now, sir parson, let us talk a while. At your first outcry I shall speed you into that future world whither it is your mission to guide the souls of others. Maybe you'll find it a better world to preach of than to inhabit, and so, for your own sake, I make no doubt you will obey me. To your honour, to your good sense and a parson's natural horror of a lie, I look for truth in answer to what questions I may set you. Should I find you deceiving me, sir, I shall see that your falsehood overtakes you." And eloquently raising his blade, he intimated the exact course he would adopt. " Now, sir, attend to me. How soon are our friends likely to discover this tipsy-turvydom ? "

" When they come for you," answered the parson meekly.

" And how soon, O prophet, will they come ? "

" In an hour's time, or thereabout," replied the Puritan, glancing towards the window as he spoke. Galliard followed his glance, and observed that the light was growing perceptibly stronger.

" Ay," he commented, " in an hour's time there should be light enough to hang us. Is there no chance of anyone coming sooner ? "

" None that I can imagine. The only others in the house are a party of half a dozen troopers in the guard-room below."

" Where is the Lord-General ? "

" Away—I know not where. But he will be here at sunrise."

" And the sentry that was at our door—is he not to be changed 'twixt this and hanging-time ? "

" I cannot say for sure, but I think not. The guard was relieved just before I came."

" And the men in the guard-room—answer me truthfully, O Elijah—what manner of watch do they keep ? "

" Alas, sir, they have drunk enough this night to put a debauched Cavalier to shame. I was but exhorting them."

When Kenneth had removed the Puritan's girdle a small Bible—such as men of his calling were wont to carry—had dropped out. This Kenneth had placed upon the table. Galliard now took it up, and, holding it before the Puritan's eyes, he watched him narrowly the while.

"Will you swear by this book that you have answered nothing but the truth?"

Without a moment's hesitation the parson pledged his oath, that to the best of his belief he had answered accurately.

"That is well, sir. And now, though it grieve me to cause you some discomfort, I must make sure of your silence."

He placed his sword upon the table, and passed behind the Puritan, to take the man's own scarf and gag him with it.

"Now, Kenneth," said he, turning to the lad. Then he stopped abruptly as if smitten by a sudden thought. Presently—"Kenneth," he continued in a different tone, "a while ago I mind me you said that were your liberty restored you, you would join hands with me in punishing the evildoers who wrecked my life."

"I did, Sir Crispin."

For a moment the knight paused. It was a vile thing that he was about to do, he told himself, and as he realized how vile, his impulse was to say no more; to abandon the suddenly-formed project and to trust to his own unaided wits and hands. But as again he thought of the vast use this lad would be to him—this lad who was the betrothed of Cynthia Ashburn—he saw that the matter was not one hastily to be judged and dismissed. Carefully he weighed it in the balance of his mind. On the one hand was the knowledge that did they succeed in making good their escape, Kenneth would naturally fly for shelter to his friends the Ashburns—the usurpers of Castle Marleigh. What then more natural than his taking with him the man who had helped him to escape, and who shared his own danger of recapture? And with so plausible a motive for admission to Castle Marleigh, how easy would not his vengeance become? He might at first wean himself into their good graces, and afterwards—

Before his mental eyes there unfolded itself the vista of a great revenge; one that should be worthy of him, and commensurate with the foul deed that called for it.

In the other scale the treacherous flavour of this method weighed heavily. He proposed to bind the lad to a promise, the shape of whose fulfilment he would withhold—a promise the lad would readily give, and yet, one that he must sooner die than give, did he but know what manner of fulfilment would be exacted. It amounted to betraying the lad into a betrayal of his friends—the people of his future wife. Whatever the issue for Crispin, it was odds Kenneth's prospect of wedding this Cynthia would be blighted for all time by the action into which Galliard proposed to thrust him all unconscious.

So stood the case in Galliard's mind, and the scales fell now on one side, now on the other. But against his scruples rose the memory of the treatment which the lad had meted out to him that night; the harshness of the boy's judgment; the irrevocable contempt wherein he had clearly seen that he was held by this fatuous milksop. All this aroused his rancour now, and steeled his heart against the voice of honour.

What was this boy to him, he asked himself, that he should forgo for him the accomplishing of his designs? How had this lad earned any consideration from him? What did he owe him? Naught! Still, he would not decide in haste.

It was characteristic of the man whom Kenneth held to be destitute of all honourable principles, to stand thus in the midst of perils, when every second that sped lessened their chances of escape, turning over in his mind calmly and collectedly a point of conduct.

Meanwhile Kenneth was quaking with impatient fear. Anxiously, his hands clenched and his face pale, he watched his companion, who stood with brows knit in thought, and his grey eyes staring at the ground. At length he could brook that, to him, incomprehensible and mad delay no longer.

" Sir Crispin," he whispered, plucking at his sleeve; " Sir Crispin."

The knight flashed him a glance that was almost of anger. Then the fire died out of his eyes; he signed and spoke. In that second's glance he had seen the lad's face; the fear and impatience written on it had caused the scales to fall suddenly and definitely against the boy.

" I was thinking how it might be accomplished," he said.

" There is but one way," cried the lad.

" Nay, there are two ways, and I wish to choose carefully."

" If you delay your choice much longer, none will be left you," cried Kenneth impatiently.

Noting the lad's growing fears, and resolved now upon his course, Galliard set himself to play upon them until terror should render the boy as wax in his hands.

"There speaks your callow inexperience," said he, with a pitying smile. "When you shall have lived as long as I, and endured as much; when you shall have set your wits to the saving of your life as often as have I—you'll have learnt how fatal haste can be. Failure always means the forfeiture of something; to-night it would mean the forfeiture of our lives, and it were a pity to let such good efforts as these"—and with a wave of the hand he indicated their two captures—"go wasted."

"Sir," exclaimed Kenneth, well-nigh beside himself, "if you come not with me, I go alone!"

"Whither?" asked Crispin dryly.

"Out of this."

Galliard inclined his head.

"Fare you well, sir. I'll not detain you. Your way is clear, and it is for you to choose between the door and the window."

And with that Crispin turned his back upon him and crossed to the bed, where the trooper lay glaring in mute anger. He stooped, and unbuckling the soldier's sword-belt—to which the scabbard was attached—he girt himself with it. Without raising his eyes, and keeping his back to Kenneth, who stood between him and the door, he went next to the table, and, taking up the sword that he had left there he restored it to the sheath. As the hilt clicked against the mouth of the scabbard—

"Come, Sir Crispin!" cried the lad. "Are you ready?"

Galliard wheeled sharply.

"How? Not gone yet?"

"I dare not," the lad confessed. "I dare not go alone."

Galliard laughed softly; then suddenly waxed grave.

"Before we go, Master Kenneth, I would again remind you of your assurance that were we to regain our liberty you would aid me in the task of vengeance that lies before me."

"Once already have I answered you that it is so."

"And pray, are you still of the same mind?"

"I am, I am! Anything, Sir Crispin; anything so that you come away!"

"Not so fast, Kenneth. The promise that I shall ask of you is not to be so lightly given. If we escape I may fairly claim to have saved your life, 'twixt what I have done and what I may yet do. Is it not so?"

"Oh, I acknowledge it!"

"Then, sir, in payment I shall expect your aid hereafter to help me in that which I must accomplish, that which the hope of accomplishing is the only spur to my own escape."

"You have my promise!" cried the lad.

"Do not give it lightly, Kenneth," said Crispin gravely. "It may cause you much discomfort, and may be fraught with danger even to your life."

"I promise."

Galliard bowed his head; then, turning, took the Bible from the table.

"With your hand upon this book, by your honour,

your faith, and your every hope of salvation, swear that if I bear you alive out of this house you will devote yourself to me and to my task of retribution until it shall be accomplished or until I perish ; swear that you will set aside all personal considerations and inclinations of your own, to serve me when I shall call upon you. Swear that, and, in return, I will give my life if need be to save yours to-night, in which case you will be released from your oath without more ado."

The lad paused a moment. Crispin was so impressive, the oath he imposed so solemn, that for an instant Kenneth hesitated. His cautious, timid nature whispered to him that perchance he should know more of this matter before binding himself so irrevocably. But Crispin, noting the hesitation, stifled it by appealing to the lad's fears.

"Resolve yourself. It grows light, and the time for haste is come."

"I swear !" answered Kenneth, conquered by his impatience. "I swear, by my honour, my faith, and my every hope of heaven to lend you my aid, when and how you may demand it, until your task be accomplished."

Crispin took the Bible from the boy's hands, and replaced it on the table. His lips were pressed tight, and he avoided the lad's eyes.

"You shall not find me wanting in my part of the bargain," he muttered, as he took up the soldier's cloak and hat. "Come, take that parson's steeple hat and his cloak, and let us be going."

He crossed to the door, and opening it he peered

down the passage. A moment he stood listening. All
was still. Then he turned again. In the chamber the
steely light of the breaking day was rendering more
yellow still the lanthorn's yellow flame.

"Fare you well, sir parson," he said. "Forgive
the discomfort I have been forced to put upon you,
and pray for the success of our escape. Commend me
to Oliver of the ruby nose. Fare you well, sir. Come,
Kenneth."

He held the door for the lad to pass out. As they
stood in the dimly-lighted passage he closed it softly
after them, and turned the key in the lock.

"Come," he said again, and led the way to the
stairs, Kenneth tip-toeing after him with wildly beating heart.

CHAPTER X

THE ESCAPE

TREADING softly, and with ears straining for the slightest sound, the two men descended to the first floor of the house. They heard nothing to alarm them as they crept down, and not until they paused on the first landing to reconnoitre did they even catch the murmur of voices issuing from the guard-room below. So muffled was the sound that Crispin guessed how matters stood even before he had looked over the balusters into the hall beneath. The faint grey of the dawn was the only light that penetrated the gloom of that pit.

" The Fates are kind, Kenneth," he whispered. " Those fools sit with closed doors. Come."

But Kenneth laid his hand upon Galliard's sleeve. " What if the door should open as we pass ? "

" Someone will die. But pray God that it may not. We must take the risk."

" Is there no other way ? "

" Why, yes," returned Galliard sardonically, " we can linger here until we are taken. But, oddslife, I'm not so minded. Come."

And as he spoke he drew the lad along.

His foot was upon the topmost stair of the flight, when of a sudden the stillness of the house was broken by a loud knock upon the street door. Instantly— as though they had been awaiting it—there was a stir of feet below and the bang of an overturned chair ; then a shaft of yellow light fell athwart the darkness of the hall as the guard-room door was opened.

"Back !" growled Galliard. "Back, man !"

They were but in time. Peering over the balusters, they saw two troopers pass out of the guard-room and cross the hall to the door. A bolt was drawn and a chain rattled, then followed the creak of hinges, and on the stone flags rang the footsteps and the jingling of spurs of those that entered.

"Is all well ?" came a voice, which Crispin recognized as Colonel Pride's, followed by an affirmative reply from one of the soldiers.

"Hath a minister visited the malignants ?"

"Master Toneleigh is with them even now."

In the hall Crispin could now make out the figures of Colonel Pride and of three men who came with him. But he had scant leisure to survey them, for the colonel was in haste.

"Come, sirs," he heard him say, "light me to their garret. I would see them—leastways, one of them, before he dies. They are to hang where the Moabites hanged Gives yesterday. Had I my way—— But there—lead on, fellow."

"Oh, God," gasped Kenneth, as the soldier set foot upon the stairs. Under his breath Crispin swore a terrific oath. For an instant it seemed to him there was naught left but to stand there and await recapture. Through his mind it flashed that they were five, and he but one ; for his companion was unarmed.

With that swiftness which thought alone can compass did he weigh the odds and judge his changes, and even as he considered he glanced sharply round. Dim indeed was the light, but his sight was keen, and quickened by the imminence of danger. Partly his eyes and partly his instinct told him that not six paces behind him there must be a door, and if Heaven pleased it should be unlocked, behind it they must look for shelter. It even crossed his mind in that second of crowding, galloping thought, that the room might be occupied. That was a risk he must take—the lesser risk of the two, the choice of one of which was forced upon him. He had determined all this before the soldier's foot was upon the third step of the staircase, and before the colonel had commenced the ascent. Kenneth stood palsied with fear, gazing like one fascinated at the approaching peril.

Then upon his ear fell the fierce whisper : " Tread lightly as you love your life."

In three long strides, and by steps as soft as a cat's, Crispin crossed to the door which he had rather guessed than seen. He ran his hand along until he caught the latch. Softly he tried it ; it gave, and the door opened. Kenneth was by then beside him. He paused to look back.

On the opposite wall the light of the trooper's lanthorn fell brightly. Another moment and the fellow would have reached and turned the corner of the stairs, and his light must reveal them to him. But ere that instant was passed Crispin had drawn his companion through, and closed the door as softly as he had opened it. The chamber was untenanted and almost bare of furniture, at which discovery Crispin breathed more freely.

They stood there, and heard the ascending footsteps, and the clank-clank of a sword against the stairrail. A bar of yellow light came under the door that sheltered them. Stronger it grew and farther it crept along the floor ; then stopped and receded again, as he who bore the lanthorn turned and began to climb to the second floor. An instant later and the light had vanished, eclipsed by those who followed in the fellow's wake.

" The window, Sir Crispin," cried Kenneth, in an excited whisper—" the window ! "

" No," answered Crispin calmly. " The drop is a long one, and we should but alight in the street, and be little better than we are here. Wait."

He listened. The footsteps had turned the corner leading to the floor above. He opened the door, partly at first, then wide. For an instant he stood listening again. The steps were well overhead by now ; soon they would mount the last flight, and then discovery must be swift to follow.

" Now," was all Crispin said, and, drawing his sword, he led the way swiftly, yet cautiously, to the stairs once more. In passing he glanced over the rails. The guard-room door stood ajar, and he caught the murmurs of a subdued conversation. But he did not pause. Had the door stood wide he would not have paused then. There was not a second to be lost ; to wait was to increase the already overwhelming danger. Cautiously, and leaning well upon the stout baluster, he began the descent. Kenneth followed him mechanically, with white face and a sense of suffocation in his throat.

They gained the corner, and turning, they began the perilous part of their journey. Not more than a dozen steps were there; but at the bottom stood the guard-room door, and through the chink of its opening a shaft of light fell upon the nethermost step. Once a stair creaked, and to their quickened senses it sounded like a pistol-shot. As loud to Crispin sounded the indrawn breath of apprehension from Kenneth that followed it. He had almost paused to curse the lad when, remembering how time pressed, he went on.

They were within three steps of the bottom, and they could almost distinguish what was being said in the room, when Crispin stopped, and turning his head to attract Kenneth's attention, he pointed straight across the hall to a dimly visible door. It was that of the chamber wherein he had been brought before Cromwell. Its position had occurred to him some moments before, and he had determined then upon going that way.

The lad followed the indication of his finger, and signified by a nod that he understood. Another step Galliard descended; then from the guard-room came a loud yawn, to send the boy cowering against the wall. It was followed by the sound of someone rising; a chair grated upon the floor, and there was a movement of feet within the chamber. Had Kenneth been alone, of a certainty terror would have frozen him to the wall.

But the calm, unmovable Crispin went on ; he argued that even if he who had risen were coming towards the door, there was nothing to be gained by standing still. Their only chance lay now in passing before it might be opened.

They that walk through perils in a brave man's company cannot but gain confidence from the calm of his demeanour. So was it now with Kenneth. The steady onward march of that tall, lank figure before him drew him irresistibly after it despite his tremors. And well it was for him that this was so. They gained the bottom of the staircase at length ; they stood beside the door of the guard-room, they passed it in safety. Then slowly—painfully slowly—to avoid their steps from ringing upon the stone floor, they crept across towards the door that meant safety to Sir Crispin. Slowly, step by step, they moved, and with every stride Crispin looked behind him, prepared to rush the moment he had sign they were discovered. But it was not needed. In silence and in safety they were permitted to reach the door. To Crispin's joy it was unfastened. Quietly he opened it, then with calm gallantry he motioned to his companion to go first, holding it for him as he passed in, and keeping watch with eye and ear the while.

Scarce had Kenneth entered the chamber when from above came uproar, announcing to them that their flight was discovered. It was answered by a rush of feet in the guard-room, and Crispin had but time to dart in after his companion and close the door as the troopers poured out into the hall and up the stairs, to discover what might be amiss.

Within the room that sheltered him Crispin chuckled as he ran his hand along the edge of the door until he found the bolt, and softly shot it home.

" 'Slife," he muttered, " 'twas a close thing! Ay, shout, you cuckolds," he went on. " Yell yourselves hoarse as the crows you are! You'll hang us where Gives was hanged, will you?"

Kenneth tugged at the skirts of his doublet. " What now?" he inquired.

" Now," said Crispin, " we'll leave by the window, if it please you."

They crossed the room, and a moment or two later they had dropped on to the narrow railed pathway overlooking the river, which Crispin had observed from their prison window the evening before. He had observed, too, that a small boat was moored at some steps about a hundred yards farther down the stream, and towards that spot he now sped along the footpath, followed closely by Kenneth. The path sloped in that direction, so that by the time the spot was reached the water flowed not more than six feet or so beneath them. Half a dozen steps took them down this to the moorings of that boat, which fortunately had not been removed.

"Get in, Kenneth," Crispin commanded. "There, I'll take the oars, and I'll keep under shelter of the bank lest those blunderers should think of looking out of our prison window. Oddswounds, Kenneth, I am hungry as a wolf, and as dry—ough, as dry as Dives when he begged for a sup of water. Heaven send we come upon some good malignant homestead ere we go far, where a Christian may find a meal and a stoup of ale. It's a miracle I had strength enough to crawl downstairs. 'Swounds, but an empty stomach is a craven comrade in a desperate enterprise. Hey! Have a care, boy. Now, sink me if this milksop hasn't fainted!"

CHAPTER XI

THE ASHBURNS

GREGORY ASHBURN pushed back his chair from the table at which he and his brother had but dined.

He was a tall, heavily built man, with a coarse, florid countenance set in a frame of reddish hair that hung straight and limp. In the colour of their hair lay the only point of resemblance between the brothers. For the rest Joseph was spare and of middle height, pale of face, thin-lipped, and of a cunning expression made evil by a slight cast in his colourless eyes.

In earlier life Gregory had not been unhandsome ; self-indulgence and sloth had puffed and coarsened him. Joseph, on the other hand, had never been other than ill-favoured.

" A week since the fight at Worcester," grumbled Gregory, looking lazily sideways at the mullioned windows as he spoke, " and never a word from the lad."

Joseph shrugged his narrow shoulders and sneered. It was Joseph's habit to sneer when he spoke, and his words were wont to fit the sneer.

" Need the lack of news trouble you ? " he asked, glancing across the table at his brother.

Gregory rose without meeting that glance.

" Truth to tell it does trouble me."

" And yet," quoth Joseph, " it's a natural thing enough. When battles are fought it is not uncommon for men to die."

Gregory crossed slowly to the window, and stared out at the trees of the park which autumn was already stripping.

" If he were among the fallen—if he were dead—then indeed the matter would be at an end."

" And well ended."

" You forget Cynthia," Gregory reproved him.

" Not I, man.   Listen."   And he jerked his thumb in the direction of the wainscot.

To the two men in that rich chamber of Castle Marleigh was borne the sound—softened by distance—of a girlish voice merrily singing.

Joseph uttered a cackle of contempt.

" Is that the song of a maid whose lover comes not back from the wars ? "

" If you'll remember that the child does not suspect the possibility of his having fallen."

" Gadswounds, sir, did your daughter give the fellow a thought she must be anxious. A week yesterday since the battle, and no word from him. I dare swear, Gregory, there's little in that to warrant his mistress singing."

" Cynthia is young—a child. She does not reason as you and I, nor seeks to account for his absence."

" Troubles not to account for it," Joseph amended.

" Be that as it may," returned Gregory irritably, " I would I knew."

" That which we do not know we may sometimes infer. I infer him to be dead, and there's the end of it."

" What if he should not be ? "

" Then, my good fool, he would be here."

"It is still possible that he might be a prisoner."

"Why, then, the plantations will do that which the battle hath left undone. So that, dead or captive, you see it is all one."

And, lifting his glass to the light, he closed one eye, the better to survey with the other the rich colour of the wine. Not that Joseph was curious touching that colour, but he was a juggler in gestures, and at that moment he could think of no other whereby he might so naturally convey the utter indifference of his feelings in the matter.

"Joseph, you are wrong," said Gregory, turning his back upon the window and facing his brother. "It is not all one. What if he return some day?"

"Oh, what if—what if—what if!" cried Joseph testily. "Gregory, what a casuist you might have been had not nature made you a villain! You are as full of 'what if's' as an egg of meat. Well—what if some day he should return? What if?"

"God alone knows."

"Then leave it to Him," was the flippant answer; and Joseph drained his glass.

But Gregory shook his head. "Too great a risk. I must and I will know whether Kenneth were slain or not. If he is a prisoner, then we must exert ourselves to win his freedom."

"Plague take it," Joseph burst out. "Why all this ado? Why did you ever loose that graceless whelp from his Scottish moor?"

Gregory sighed with an air of resigned patience.

"I have more reasons than one," he answered slowly. "If you need that I recite them to you, I

pity your wits. Look you, Joseph, you have more
influence with Cromwell ; more—far more—than have
I, and if you are minded to do so, you can serve me
in this."

" I wait but to learn how."

" Then go to Cromwell, at Windsor or wherever he
may be, and beg him to have inquiry made, so as
to discover if Kenneth is a prisoner. If he is not,
then clearly he is dead."

Joseph made a gesture of impatience.

" Can you not leave Fate alone ? "

" Do you think I have no conscience, Joseph ? "
cried the other with sudden vigour.

" Psh ! you are womanish."

" Nay, Joseph, I am old. I am in the autumn of
my days, and I would see these two wed before
I die."

" And are damned for a croaking, maudlin old
fool," added Joseph.

There was a moment's silence during which the
brothers eyed each other, Gregory with a sternness
before which Joseph's mocking eye was forced at
length to fall.

" Joseph, you shall go to the Lord-General."

" Well," said Joseph weakly, " we will say that I
go. But if Kenneth be a prisoner, what then ? "

" You must obtain his liberty from Cromwell. He
will not refuse you."

" Will he not ? I am none so confident."

" But you can make the attempt, and leastways we
shall have some definite knowledge of what has befallen
the boy."

" The which definite knowledge seems to me none so necessary. Moreover, Gregory, bethink you; there has been a change, and the wind carries an edge that will arouse every devil of rheumatism in my bones. I am not a lad, Gregory, and travelling at this season is no small matter for an ailing man of fifty."

Gregory approached the table, and leant his hand upon it.

" Will you go ? " he asked, squarely eyeing his brother.

Joseph fell a-pondering. He knew Gregory to be a man of fixed ideas, and he bethought him that were he now to refuse he would be hourly plagued by Gregory's speculations touching the boy's fate and recriminations touching his own selfishness. On the other hand, however, the journey daunted him. He was not a man to sacrifice his creature comforts, and to be asked to sacrifice them to a mere whim, a shadow, added weight to his inclination to refuse the undertaking.

" Since you have the matter so much at heart," he said at length, " does it occur to you that you could plead with greater fervour, and be the likelier to succeed ? "

" You know that Cromwell will lend a more willing ear to you than to me—perchance because you know so well upon occasion how to weave your stock of texts into your discourse," he added with a sneer. " Will you go, Joseph ? "

" Bethink you that we know not where he is. I may have to wander for weeks o'er the face of England."

" Will you go ? " Gregory repeated.

"Oh, a pox on it," broke out Joseph, rising suddenly. "I'll go since naught else will quiet you. I'll start to-morrow."

"Joseph, I am grateful. I shall be more grateful yet if you will start to-day."

"No, sink me, no."

"Yes, sink me, yes," returned Gregory. "You must, Joseph."

Joseph spoke of the wind again; the sky, he urged, was heavy with rain. "What signifies a day?" he whined.

But Gregory stood his ground until almost in self-defence the other consented to set out as soon as he could make ready, and cursing Master Stewart for the amount of discomfort which he was about to endure on his behoof, he went to prepare for the journey.

Gregory lingered still in the chamber where they had dined, and sat staring moodily before him at the table-linen. Anon, with a half-laugh of contempt, he filled a glass of muscadine, and drained it. As he set down the glass the door opened, and on the threshold stood a very dainty girl, whose age could not be more than twenty. Gregory looked on the fresh, oval face, with its wealth of brown hair crowning the low, broad forehead, and told himself that in his daughter he had just cause for pride. He looked again, and told himself that his brother was right; she had not the air of a maid whose lover returns not from the wars. Her lips were smiling, and the eyes—low-lidded and blue as the heavens—were bright with mirth.

"Why sit you there so glum?" she cried, "whilst my uncle, they tell me, is going on a journey?"

Gregory was minded to put her feelings to the test.

"Kenneth," he replied with significant emphasis, watching her closely.

The mirth faded from her eyes, and they took on a grave expression that added to their charm. But Gregory had looked for fear, leastways deep concern, and in this he was disappointed.

"What of him, father?" she asked, approaching.

"Naught, and that's the rub. It is time we had news, and as none comes, your uncle goes to seek it."

"Do you suppose that any ill can have befallen him?"

Gregory was silent a moment, weighing his answer. Then—

"We hope not, sweetheart," said he. "He may be a prisoner. We last had news of him from Worcester, and 'tis a week and more since the battle was fought there. Should he be a captive, your uncle has sufficient influence to obtain his enlargement."

Cynthia sighed, and moved towards the window.

"Poor Kenneth," she murmured gently. "He may be wounded."

"We shall soon learn," he answered. His disappointment grew keener; where he had looked for grief he found no more than an expression of ordinary concern. Nor was his disappointment lessened when, after a spell of thoughtful silence, she began to comment upon other things. Gregory had it in his mind to chide her for this lack of interest in the fate of her intended husband, but he let the impulse pass unheeded. After all, if Kenneth lived she should marry him. Hitherto she had been docile and willing enough to be guided by him ; she had even displayed a kindness for Kenneth ; no doubt she would do so again when Joseph returned with him—unless he were among the Worcester slain, in which case, perhaps, it would prove best that his fate was not to cause her any prostration of grief.

" The sky is heavy, father," said Cynthia from the window. " Poor uncle ! He will have rough weather for his journey."

" I rejoice that some one wastes pity on poor uncle," growled Joseph, who re-entered, " this uncle whom your father drives out of doors in all weathers to look for his daughter's truant lover."

Cynthia smiled upon him.

" It is heroic of you."

" There, there," he grumbled, " I shall do my best to find the laggard, lest those pretty eyes should weep away their beauty."

Gregory's glance reproved this sneer of Joseph's, whereupon Joseph drew close to him—

" Broken-hearted, is she not ? " he muttered, to which Gregory returned no answer.

An hour later, as Joseph climbed into his saddle, he turned to his brother again, and directing his eyes upon the girl, who stood patting the glossy neck of his nag—

" Come now," said he, " you see that matters are as I said."

"And yet," replied Gregory sternly, "I hope to see you return with the boy. It will be better so."

Joseph shrugged contemptuously. Then, taking leave of his brother and his niece, he rode out with two grooms at his heels, and took the road south.

CHAPTER XII

THE HOUSE THAT WAS ROLAND MARLEIGH'S

IT was high noon next day, and Gregory Ashburn was taking the air upon the broad terrace of Castle Marleigh, when the beat of hoofs, approaching up the avenue, arrested his attention. He stopped in his walk, and, turning, sought to discover who came. His first thought was of his brother; his second, of Kenneth. Through the half-denuded trees he made out two mounted figures, riding side by side; and from the fact of there being two, he adduced that this could not be Joseph returning.

Even as he waited he was joined by Cynthia, who came to stand beside him, and voiced the question that was in his mind. But he could do no more than answer that he hoped it might be Kenneth.

Then the horsemen passed from behind the screen of trees and came into the clearing before the terrace, and unto the waiting glances of Ashburn and his daughter was revealed a curiously bedraggled and ill-assorted pair. The one riding slightly in advance looked like a Puritan of the meaner sort, in his battered steeple-hat and cloak of rusty black. The other was closely wrapped in a red mantle, uptilted behind by a sword of prodigious length, and for all that his broad, grey hat was unadorned by any feather, it was set at a rakish, ruffling, damn-me angle that pronounced him no likely comrade for the piously-clad youth beside him.

But beneath that brave red cloak, as was presently seen when they dismounted, this gentleman was in a sorry plight. He wore a leather jerkin, so cut and soiled that any groom might have disdained it; a pair of green breeches, frayed to their utmost; and coarse boots of untanned leather, adorned by rusty spurs.

On the terrace Gregory paused a moment to call a groom to attend the new-comers, then he passed down the steps to greet Kenneth with boisterous effusion. Behind him, slow and stately as a woman of twice her years, came Cynthia. Calm was her greeting of her betrothed, contained in courteous expressions of pleasure at beholding him safe, and suffering him to kiss her hand.

In the background, his sable locks uncovered out of deference to the lady, stood Sir Crispin, his face pale and haggard, his lips parted, and his grey eyes burning as they fell again, after the lapse of years, upon the stones of this his home—the house to which he was now come, hat in hand, to beg for shelter.

Gregory was speaking, his hands resting upon Kenneth's shoulder.

" We have been anxious for you, lad," he was saying. " Almost we began to fear the worst, and yesterday Joseph left us to seek news of you at Cromwell's hands. Where have you tarried ? "

" Anon, sir ; you shall learn anon. The story is a long one."

" Well, well ! Since it has a happy ending it can wait. You'll be tired, and anxious, no doubt, to rest. Cynthia will see to it. But what scarecrow have you there? What tatterdemalion is this?" he cried, pointing to Galliard. He had imagined him a servant, but the dull flush that overspread Sir Crispin's face told him of his error.

"I'll beg your courtesy," Crispin was beginning, with some heat, when Kenneth interrupted him.

"It is to this gentleman, sir, that I owe my safety. He was my fellow-prisoner, and but for his wit and courage I should be stiff by now. Anon, sir, you shall hear the story of it, and I swear you'll desire to thank him. It is Sir Crispin Galliard, lately a captain of horse with whom I served in Middleton's Brigade."

Crispin bowed low, conscious of the keen scrutiny in which Gregory's eyes were bent upon him. In his heart there arose a fear that, perhaps after all, the years that were sped had not wrought a sufficient change in him.

"Sir Crispin Galliard," Ashburn was saying, after the manner of one who is searching his memory. "Galliard, Galliard—I remember there was one whom they called 'Rake-helly Galliard,' and who gave much trouble in the late King's time?"

Crispin breathed once more. Ashburn's scrutiny was explained.

"The same, sir," he answered, with a smile and a fresh bow. "Your servant, sir; and yours, madam."

Cynthia looked with interest at the lank, soldierly figure. She, too, had heard—as who had not?—wild stories of this man's exploits. But of no feat of his had she been told that could rival that of his escape from Worcester; and when, that same evening, Kenneth related it, after they had supped, her low-lidded eyes grew very wide, and as they fell on Crispin, admiration was blended now with interest.

Romance swayed as great a portion of her heart as it does of any woman's. She loved the poets and their songs of great deeds ; and here was one who, in the light of that which they related of him, was like an incarnation of some hero out of a romancer's ballad.

Kenneth she never yet had held in great esteem ; but of a sudden, in the presence of this harsh-featured dog of war, this grim, fierce-eyed ruffler, he seemed to fade, despite his comeliness of face and form, into a poor and puny insignificance. And when, presently, he unwisely related how when in the boat he had fainted, she found it impossible to repress a smile.

At this her father shot her a quick, uneasy glance. Kenneth stopped short, bringing his narrative abruptly to a close. Reproachfully he stared at her, turning first red, then white in his annoyance. Galliard looked on with quiet relish ; her smile had expressed that which for days he had carried in his heart. He drained his bumper slowly, and made no attempt to relieve the awkward silence that sat upon the company after that.

Truth to tell, there was emotion enough in the soul of him to hold him silent and even moody.

Here, after eighteen years, was he again in his ancestral home of Marleigh. Returned as one who came under a feigned name, to seek from usurping hands a shelter 'neath his own roof ; a beggar of that from others which it should have been his to dispense or to deny those others. As an avenger he came. For justice he came, and armed with retribution; the flame of a hate unspeakable burning in his heart, and demanding the lives of those who had destroyed him and his. For this he was content to sit a mendicant almost at that board whose head was his by every right; to sit and curb his mood, giving no outward sign of the wrath fermenting in his soul whilst mildly his eye fell upon the florid, smiling face and portly, well-fed frame of Gregory Ashburn. The time was not yet. He must wait; wait until Joseph's return, so that he might spend his vengeance upon both together.

Patient had he been for eighteen years, confident that ere he died, a just and merciful God would give him this for which he had lived and waited. Yet now that the season was at hand; now upon the very eve of that for which he had so long been patient, a frenzy of impatience fretted him.

He drank deep that night, and through deep drinking his manner thawed—for in his cups it was not his to be churlish to friend or foe. Anon Cynthia withdrew; next Kenneth, who went in quest of her. Still Crispin sat on, and drank his host's health above his breath, and his perdition under it, till in the end Gregory, who had never yet found his master at the bottle, grew numb and drowsy, and sat blinking at the tapers.

Until midnight they remained at table, talking of this and that, and each understanding little of what the other said. As the last hour of night boomed out through the great hall, Gregory spoke of bed.

"Where do I lie to-night?" asked Crispin.

"In the northern wing," answered Gregory with a hiccough.

"Nay, sir, I protest," cried Galliard, struggling to his feet, and swaying somewhat as he stood. "I'll sleep in the King's chamber."

"The King's chamber?" echoed Gregory, and his face showed the confused struggles of his brain. "What know you of the King's chamber?"

"That it faces the east and the sea, and that it is the chamber I love best."

"What can you know of it, since, I take it, you have never seen it?"

"Have I not?" he began, in a voice that was awful in its threatening calm. Then, recollecting himself, and shaking some of the drunkenness from him: "In the old days, when the Marleighs were masters here," he mumbled, "I was often within these walls. You would not know that. Roland Marleigh was my friend. The King's chamber was ever accorded me, and there, for old time's sake, I'll lay these old bones of mine to-night."

"You were Roland Marleigh's friend?" gasped Gregory. He was very white, and there was a sheen of moisture on his face. The sound of that name had wellnigh sobered him. It was almost as if the ghost of Roland Marleigh stood before him. His knees were loosened, and he sank back into the chair from which he had but risen.

"Aye, I was his friend!" assented Crispin. "Poor Roland! He married your sister, did he not, and it was thus that, having no issue and the family being extinct, Castle Marleigh passed to you?"

"He married our cousin," Gregory amended. "They were an ill-fated family."

"Oh! Your cousin was it? So. Ill-fated, indeed, if all accounts be true." Crispin's voice was maudlin. "Poor Roland! Well, for old time's sake, I'll sleep in the King's chamber, Master Ashburn."

"You shall sleep where you list, sir," answered Gregory, and they rose.

"Do you look to honour us long at Castle Marleigh, Sir Crispin?" he asked.

"Nay, sir, it is likely I shall go hence to-morrow," answered Crispin, unmindful of what he said.

"I trust not," said Gregory, in accents of relief that belied him. "A friend of Roland Marleigh's must ever be welcome in the house that was Roland Marleigh's."

"The house that *was* Roland Marleigh's," Crispin muttered. "Heigho! Life is precarious as the fall of the dice. To-night you say the house that was Roland Marleigh's; presently men will be saying the house that the Ashburns lived—ay, and died—in. Give you good night, Master Ashburn."

He staggered off, and stumbled up the broad staircase at the head of which a servant now waited, taper in hand, to conduct him to the chamber he demanded.

Gregory followed him with a dull, frightened eye. Galliard's halting, thickly uttered words had sounded like a prophecy in his ears.

CHAPTER XIII

THE METAMORPHOSIS OF KENNETH

When the morrow came, however, Sir Crispin showed no signs of carrying out his proposal of the night before, and departing from Castle Marleigh. Nor, indeed, did he so much as touch upon the subject, bearing himself rather as one whose sojourn there was to be indefinite.

Gregory offered no comment upon this; through what he had done for Kenneth they were under a debt to Galliard, and whilst he was a fugitive from the Parliament's justice it would ill become Gregory to hasten his departure. Moreover, Gregory recalled little or nothing of the words that had passed between them in their cups, save a vague memory that Crispin had said that he had once known Roland Marleigh.

Kenneth was content that Galliard should lie idle, and not call upon him to go forth again to lend him the aid he had pledged himself to render when Crispin should demand it. He marvelled, as the days wore on, that Galliard should appear to have forgotten that task of his, and that he should make no shift to set about it. For the rest, however, it troubled him but little; enough preoccupation did he find in Cynthia's manner towards him. Upon all the fine speeches that he made her she turned an idle ear, or if she replied at all it was but petulantly to interrupt them, to call him a man of great words and small deeds. Whatever he did she found ill done, and told him of it.

His sober, godly garments of sombre hue afforded her the first weapon of scorn wherewith to wound him. A crow, she dubbed him ; a canting, psalm-chanting hypocrite ; a Scripture-monger, and other contumelious epithets of like import. He heard her in amazement.

" Is it for you, Cynthia," he cried out in his surprise, " the child of a God-fearing house, to mock the outward symbols of my faith ? "

" A faith," she laughed, " that is all outward symbols and naught besides ; all texts and mournings and nose-twangings."

" Cynthia ! " he exclaimed in horror.

" Go your ways, sir," she answered, half in jest, half in earnest. " What need hath a true faith of outward symbols ? It is a matter that lies between your God and yourself, and it is your heart He will look at, not your coat. Why, then, without becoming more acceptable in His eyes, shall you but render yourself unsightly in the eyes of man ? "

Kenneth's cheeks were flushed. From the terrace where they walked he let his glance roam towards the avenue that split the park in twain. Up this at that moment, with the least suspicion of a swagger in his gait, Sir Crispin Galliard was approaching leisurely ; he wore a claret-coloured doublet edged with silver lace, and a grey hat decked with a drooping red feather —to which garments, together with the rest of his apparel, he had helped himself from the wardrobe of Gregory Ashburn. That vision of him supplied Kenneth the retort he needed. Pointing him out to Cynthia—

"Would you rather," he cried hotly, "have me such a man as that?"

"Leastways, it is a man," she taunted him.

"If, madam, a drunkard, a profligate, a brawler be your conception of a man, I would in faith that you did not account me one."

"And what, sir, would you sooner wish to be accounted?"

"A gentleman, madam," he answered pompously.

"Shall you deserve the title by slandering the man to whom you owe your life?"

"I do not slander. You yourself know of the drunken excess with which three nights ago he celebrated his coming to Castle Marleigh. Nor do I forget what I owe him. Payment is to be made in a manner you little know of. If I said of him what I did, it was but in answer to your taunts. Do you think I could endure comparison with such a man as that? Do you know what name the Royalists give him? They call him the Tavern Knight."

She looked him over with an eye of amused scorn.

"And how, sir, do they call you? The pulpit knight? Or is it the knight of the white feather? Do you know that I find you tiresome? I would have a man who with a man's failings hath also a man's redeeming virtues of honesty, chivalry, and courage, and a record of brave deeds, rather than one who has nothing of the man save the coat—that outward symbol you lay such store by."

His handsome, weak face was red.

"Since that is so, madam," he choked, "I leave you to your swaggering, ruffling Cavalier."

And, without so much as a bow, he swung round on his heel and left her. It was her turn to grow angry now, and well it was for him that he had not tarried. She dwelt with scorn upon his parting taunt, concluding that in truth she had exaggerated her opinions of Galliard's merits. Her feelings towards that ungodly gentleman were rather of pity than aught else. A brave, ready-witted man she knew him to be, as much from the story of his escape from Worcester as for the air that clung to him despite his swagger; and she deplored that one possessing those ennobling virtues should have fallen notwithstanding upon such evil ways as those which Crispin trod. Some day, perchance, when she should come to be better acquainted with him, she might even attempt to induce him into worthier courses.

Such root did the thought of this mission take in her mind that soon thereafter—and without even waiting for that riper acquaintance which at first she had held necessary—she sought to lead their talk into these delicate channels. But he as sedulously confined it to more trivial matters whenever she approached him in this mood, fencing himself about with a wall of reserve that was not lightly to be overthrown. In this his conscience was at work. In Cynthia he had discovered the flaw in the satisfaction he might have drawn from the contemplation of his vengeance. He beheld her so pure, so sweet and fresh, that he marvelled how she came to be the daughter of Gregory Ashburn. His heart smote him at the thought of how she—the innocent—must suffer with the guilty, and at the contemplation of the sorrow which he must visit upon her. Out of this sprang a constraint when in her company, for other than stiff and formal he dared not be.

During the first days he had spent at Marleigh, he had been impatient for Joseph Ashburn's return. Now he found himself hoping each morning that Joseph might not come that day.

A courier reached Gregory from Windsor with a letter wherein his brother told him that the Lord-General, not being at the castle, he was gone on to London in quest of him. And Gregory, lacking the means to inform him that the missing Kenneth was already returned, was forced to possess his soul in patience until his brother, having learnt what was to be learnt of Cromwell, should journey home.

And so the days sped on, and a week wore itself out in peace at Castle Marleigh, none dreaming of the volcano on which they stood. Each night Crispin and Gregory sat together at the board after Kenneth and Cynthia had withdrawn, and both drank deep—the one for the vice of it, the other (as he had always done) to obtain forgetfulness.

He needed it now more than ever, for he feared that the consideration of Cynthia might yet unman him. Had she scorned and avoided him—and having such evidences of his ways of life he marvelled that she did not—he might have allowed his considerations of her to weigh less heavily. As it was, she sought his company, nor seemed rebuffed at his efforts to evade her, and in every way she manifested a kindliness that drove him almost to despair.

Kenneth, knowing naught of the womanly purpose

that actuated her, and seeing but the outward signs, which, with ready jealousy, he misconstrued and magnified, grew sullen and churlish with her, with Galliard, and even with Gregory.

For hours he would mope alone, nursing his jealous mood, as though in this clownish fashion matters were to be mended. Did Cynthia but speak to Crispin, he held his breath ; did Crispin answer her, he scowled at the covert meaning wherewith his fancy invested Crispin's tones ; whilst did they chance to laugh together—a contingency that fortunately for his sanity was rare—he writhed in fury. He was a man transformed, and at times there was murder in his heart. Had he been a swordsman of more than moderate skill and dared to pit himself against the Tavern Knight, blood might well have been shed in Marleigh Park.

It seemed at last as if with his insensate jealousy all the evil humours that had lain dormant in the boy were brought to the surface, to overwhelm his erstwhile virtues—if qualities that have bigotry for a parent may truly be accounted virtues.

He cast off, not abruptly, but piecemeal, those outward symbols—his sombre clothes. First 'twas his hat he exchanged for a feather-trimmed beaver of more sightly hue ; then those stiff white bands that reeked of sanctity and cant for a collar of fine point ; next it was his coat that took on a worldly edge of silver lace. And so, little by little, step by step, was the metamorphosis effected, until by the end of the week he came forth almost a butterfly of fashion—a gallant, beribboned Cavalier. Out of a stern, forbidding

Covenanter he was transformed in a few days into a most outrageous fop. He walked in an atmosphere of musk that he himself exhaled ; his fair hair—that a while ago had hung so straight and limp—was now twisted into monstrous curls. a bunch of which were gathered by his right ear in a love-knot of pale blue silk.

Galliard observed the change in amazement, yet, knowing to what follies youth is driven when it woos, he accounted Cynthia responsible for it, and laughed in his sardonic way, whereat the boy would blush and scowl in one. Gregory, too, looked on and laughed, setting it down to the same cause. Even Cynthia smiled, whereat the Tavern Knight was driven to ponder.

With a courtier's raiment Kenneth put on, too, a courtier's ways ; he grew mincing and affected in his speech, and he—whose utterance a while ago had been marked by a scriptural flavour—now set it off with some of Galliard's less unseemly oaths.

Since it was a ruffling gallant Cynthia required, he swore that a ruffling gallant she should find him ; nor had he wit enough to see that his ribbons, his fopperies, and his capers served but to make him ridiculous in her eyes. He did indeed perceive, however, that in spite of this startling transformation, he made no progress in her favour.

" What signify these fripperies ? " she asked him, one day, " any more than did your coat of decent black ? Are these also outward symbols ? "

" You may so account them, madam," he answered sulkily. " You liked me not as I was——"

"So you flatter me by a masquerade."

"Cynthia, you mock me," he cried angrily.

"Now, Heaven forbid! I but mark the change," she answered airily. "Are not these scented clothes a masquerade, even as your coat of black and your cant were a masquerade? Then you simulated godliness; now you simulate worldliness. But now, as then, it is no more than a simulation."

He left her in a pet, and went in search of Gregory, into whose ear he poured the story of his woes that had their source in Cynthia's unkindness. From this resulted an acrid interview between Cynthia and her father, in which Cynthia at last declared that she would never be wedded to a fop.

Gregory shrugged his shoulders, replying that it was the way of young men to be fools, and that through folly lay the road to wisdom.

"Be that as it may," she answered him with spirit, "this folly leads nowhere. Master Stewart may go back to his Scottish heather; at Castle Marleigh he is wasting time."

"Cynthia!" he stormed.

"Father," she pleaded, "why be angry? You would not have me marry against my inclinations? You would not have me wedded to a man whom I despise?"

"Despise! God-'amercy! By what right do you despise him?" he demanded, his brow dark.

"By the right of the freedom of my thoughts—the only freedom that a woman knows. For the rest it seems she is but a chattel; of no more consideration to a man than his ox or his ass with which the Scriptures rank her—a thing to be given or taken, bought or sold, as others shall decree."

"Child, child, what do you know of these things?" he cried. "You are overwrought, sweetheart." And with the promise to wait until a calmer frame of mind in her should be more propitious to what he wished to say further on this score, he left her.

She went out of doors in quest of solitude among the naked trees of the park; instead she found Sir Crispin, seated in idleness upon a fallen trunk.

Through the trees she espied him as she approached, whilst the rustle of her gown announced to him her coming. He rose as she drew nigh, and, doffing his hat, made shift to pass on.

"Sir Crispin," she called, detaining him. He turned.

"Your servant, Mistress Cynthia."

"Are you afraid of me, sir?"

"Beauty, madam, is reputed to inspire courage rather than fear," he answered, with a smile.

"That, sir, is an evasion, not an answer."

"If read aright, Mistress Cynthia, it is also an answer."

"That you do not fear me?"

"It is not a habit of mine."

"Why, then, have you avoided me these three days past?"

Despite himself Crispin felt his breath quickening —quickening with a pleasure that he sought not to explain—at the thought that she should have marked his absence.

"Because perhaps if I did not," he answered slowly,

" you might come to avoid me. I am a proud man, Mistress Cynthia."

" Satan, sir, was proud, but his pride led him to perdition."

" So indeed may mine, since it leads me from you."

" Nay, sir," she laughed, " you go from me willingly enough."

" Not willingly, Cynthia. Oh, never willingly," he began. Then checked, and asked himself what he was saying. With a half-laugh, and a courtier manner he continued, " Of two evils, madam, we must choose the lesser one."

" Madam ! " she echoed, disregarding all else that he had said. " It is an ugly word, and but a moment back you called me Cynthia——"

" 'Twas a liberty that methought my grey hairs warranted, and for which you should have reproved me."

" You have not grey hairs enough to warrant it, Sir Crispin. But what if even so I account it no liberty ? "

The heavy lids were lifted from her eyes, and as their glance, frank and kindly, met his, he trembled. Then, with a polite smile, he bowed.

" I thank you for the honour."

For a moment she looked at him with a puzzled frown, then moved past him, and as he stood, stiffly erect, watching her graceful figure, he thought that she was about to leave him, and was glad of it. But before she had taken half a dozen steps—

" Sir Crispin," said she, looking back at him over her shoulder, " I am walking to the cliffs."

He could not mistake the invitation. A sad smile crept into his harsh face.

" I shall tell Kenneth if I see him," said he.

At that she frowned.

" But I do not want him. Sooner would I go alone."

" Why, then, madam, I'll tell nobody."

Was ever man so dull, she asked herself.

" There is a fine view from the cliffs," said she.

" I have always thought so," he agreed.

She desired to call him a fool ; yet she restrained herself.

" Will you not come with me ? " she asked at last, point blank.

" Why, yes, if you wish it," he answered without alacrity.

" You may remain, sir."

Her offended tone aroused him now to the understanding that he was impolite. Contrite, he stood beside her in a moment.

" With your permission, mistress, I will go with you. I am a dull fellow. Too dull to be other than poor company. Still, if you'll endure me . . ."

She interrupted him. " By no means. I do not seek the company of dull fellows." And she was gone.

He stood where she had left him, and breathed a most ungallant prayer of thanks. Next he laughed softly to himself, a laugh that was woeful with bitterness.

" 'Fore George ! " he said aloud, " it is all that was wanting ! "

(445)

He reseated himself upon the fallen tree, and there he set himself to reflect, and to realize that he, war-worn and callous, come to Castle Marleigh on such an errand as was his, should wax sick at the very thought of it for the sake of a chit of a maid, with a mind to make a mock and a toy of him. Into his thought there entered even the contemplation of flight, neglectful of the wrongs he had suffered, abandoning the vengeance he had sworn. Then with an oath he checked.

Was he a boy, beardless and green? he asked himself. Was he turned seventeen again, that to look into a pair of eyes should make him forget all things but their existence?

He rose abruptly, and set out to walk aimlessly along, until suddenly a turn in the path brought him face to face with Cynthia. She hailed him with a laugh.

"Sir laggard, I knew that willy-nilly you would follow me," she cried. And he, taken aback, could not but smile in answer, and profess that she had conjectured rightly.

CHAPTER XIV

THE HEART OF CYNTHIA ASHBURN

SIDE by side stepped that oddly assorted pair along—the maiden whose soul was as pure and fresh as the breeze that blew upon them from the sea, and the man whose life years ago had been marred by a sorrow, the quest of whose forgetfulness had led him through the mire of untold sin ; the girl upon the threshold of womanhood, her life all before her and seeming to her untainted mind a joyous, wholesome business ; the man midway on his ill-starred career, his every hope blighted save the one odious hope of vengeance, which made him cling to a life he had proved worthless and ugly, and that otherwise he had likely enough cast from him. And as they walked—

" Sir Crispin," she ventured timidly, " you are unhappy, are you not ? "

Startled by her words and the tone of them, Galliard turned his head that he might observe her.

" I, unhappy ? " he laughed ; and it was a laugh more calculated to acknowledge the fitness of her question, than to refute it as he intended. " Am I a clown, Cynthia, to own myself unhappy on such a day and while you honour me with your company ? "

She made a wry face in protest that he fenced with her.

" You are happy, then ? " she challenged him.

" What is happiness ? " quoth he, much as Pilate may have questioned what was truth. Then before she could reply he hastened to add: "I have not been quite so happy these many years."

"It is not of the present moment that I speak," she reproved him, for she scented no more than a compliment in his words, "but of your life."

Now either was he imbued with a sense of modesty touching the deeds of that life of his, or else did he wisely realize that no theme could there be less suited for the entertainment of a maid.

"Mistress Cynthia," said he, as though he had not heard her question, "I would say a word to you concerning Kenneth."

At that she turned upon him with a pout.

"But it is concerning yourself that I would have you talk. It is not nice to disobey a lady. Besides, I have little interest in Master Stewart."

"To have little interest in a future husband augurs ill for the time when he shall come to be your husband."

"I thought that you, at least, understood me. Kenneth shall never be husband of mine, Sir Crispin."

"What do you tell me?" he exclaimed.

"Oh, lackaday! Am I to wed a doll? Is he— is he a man a maid may love, Sir Crispin?"

"Indeed, had you but seen the half of life that I have seen," said he unthinkingly, "it might amaze you what manner of man a maid may love—or at least may marry. Come, Cynthia, what fault do you find in him?"

"Why, every fault."

He laughed in unbelief.

"That is too many. And whom are we to blame

for all these faults that have turned you so against him ? "

" Whom ? "

" Yourself, Cynthia. You use him ill, child. If his behaviour has been extravagant, you are to blame. You are severe with him, and he, in his rash endeavours to present himself in a guise that shall render him commendable, has overstepped discretion."

" Has my father bidden you to tell me this ? "

" Since when have I enjoyed your father's confidence ? No, no, Cynthia. I plead the boy's cause to you because—I know not because of what."

" It is ill to plead without knowing why. Let us forget the valiant Kenneth. They tell me, Sir Crispin " —and she turned her glorious eyes upon him in a manner that must have witched a statue into answering her—" that in the Royal army you were known as the Tavern Knight."

" They tell you truly. What of that ? "

" Well, what of it ? Do you blush at the very thought ? "

" *I* blush ? " He blinked, and his eyes were full of humour as they met her grave—almost sorrowful— glance. Then a full-hearted peal of laughter broke from him, and scared a flight of gulls from the rocks of Sheringham Hithe below.

" Oh, Cynthia ! " he gasped. " Picture to yourself this Crispin Galliard blushing and giggling like an embarrassed schoolgirl beset by her first lover. Picture it, I say ! As well and as easily might you picture old Lucifer warbling a psalm for the edification of a Nonconformist parson."

Her eyes were severe.

"It is always so with you. You make a mock of everything. Such I doubt not has been your way from the commencement, and it is thus that you are come to this condition."

"Nay, sweet mistress, you are wrong—you are very wrong; it was not always thus. Time was——" He paused. "Bah! 'Tis the coward cries 'time was'! Leave me the past, Cynthia. It is dead, and of the dead we should speak no ill."

"What is there in your past?" she insisted, despite his words. "What is there in it so to have warped a nature that must once have been—is, indeed, still— lofty? What is it has brought you to the level you occupy—you who were born to lead; you who——"

"Have done, child. Have done," he begged.

"Nay, tell me. Let us sit here." And taking hold of his sleeve, she sat herself upon a mound, and made room for him. With a half-laugh and a sigh he obeyed her, and there, on the cliff in the glow of the September sun, he took his seat at her side.

A silence prevailed about them, emphasized rather than broken by the droning chant of a fisherman mending his nets on the beach below, the intermittent plash of the waves on the shingle, and the scream of the gulls that circled overhead. Before the eyes of his body was stretched a wide desert of sky and water, and before the eyes of his mind the hopeless desert of his thirty-eight years.

He was almost tempted to speak. The note of warmth in her voice allured him, and was to him as drink to one who perishes of thirst. A passionate, indefinable longing impelled him to pour out the story that in Worcester he had told Kenneth, and thus to set himself better in her eyes ; to have her realize indeed that if he was come so low it was more the fault of others than his own. The temptation drew him at a headlong pace, to be checked at last by the memory that those others who had brought him to so sorry a condition were her own people. The humour passed. He laughed softly, and shook his head.

" There is nothing that I can tell you, child. Let us rather talk of Kenneth."

" I have already told you that I do not wish to talk of Kenneth."

" Nay, but you must. Willy-nilly must you. Think you it is only a war-worn, hard-drinking, swashbuckling ruffler that can err ? Does it not also occur to you that even a frail and tender little maid may do wrong ? "

" What wrong have I done ? " she cried, in consternation.

" A grievous wrong to this poor lad. Can you not realize how the only desire that governs him is the laudable one of appearing favourably in your eyes ? "

" That desire gives rise, then, to curious manifestations."

" He is mistaken in the means he adopts, that is all. In his heart his one aim is to win your esteem, and, after all, it is the sentiment that matters, not its manifestations. Why, then, are you unkind to him ? "

" But I am not unkind. Or is it unkindness to let him see that I mislike his capers ? Would it not be vastly more unkind to ignore them and encourage him to pursue them? I have no patience with him."

"As for those capers, I am endeavouring to show you that you yourself have driven him to them."

"Sir Crispin," she cried out, "you grow tiresome."

"Aye," said he, "I grow tiresome. I grow tiresome because I preach of duty. Marry, it is ever a tiresome topic."

"How duty? Of what do you talk?" And a flush of indignation spread now on her fair cheek.

"I will be clearer," said he imperturbably. "This lad is your betrothed. He is at heart a good lad, an honourable and honest lad—at times maybe over-honest and over-honourable; but let that be. To please a whim, a caprice, you set yourself to flout him, as is the way of your sex when you behold a man your utter slave. From this—being all unversed in the obliquity of woman—he conceives, poor boy, that he no longer finds favour in your eyes, and to win back this, the only thing that in the world he values, he behaves foolishly. You flout him anew, and because of it. He is as jealous with you as a hen with her brood."

"Jealous?" echoed Cynthia.

"Why, yes, jealous; and so far does he go as to be jealous even of me," he cried, with infinitely derisive relish. "Jealous of *me*! Jealous of the Tavern Knight!"

She did think of it as he bade her. And by thinking she stumbled upon a discovery that left her breathless.

The revelation began in a vague wonder at the scorn with which Crispin invested the notion that Kenneth should have cause for jealousy on his score. Was it, she asked herself, so monstrously unnatural? Then in a flash the answer came. She discovered that far from being a matter for derision, such an attitude in Kenneth was not without foundation.

In that moment she knew that it was because of Crispin, because of this man who spoke with such scorn of self, that Kenneth had become in her eyes so mean a creature. Loved him she haply never had, but leastways she had tolerated—been even flattered by—his wooing. It was, she realized, by contrasting him now with Crispin that she had grown to despise him. His weakness, his pusillanimity, his meannesses of soul, stood out in sharp relief by contrast with what she conceived the masterful strength and the broad, tolerant, spirit of Sir Crispin.

So easily may our ideals change that the very graces of face and form that a while ago had pleased her in Kenneth, seemed now effeminate attributes, well-attuned to a vacillating, purposeless mind. Far greater beauty did her eyes behold in this grim-faced soldier of fortune; the man as firm of purpose as he was upright of carriage; gloomy, proud, and reckless; still young, yet past the callow age of adolescence. Since the day of his coming to Castle Marleigh she had brought herself to look upon him as if he had stepped from some romancer's tale. The mystery that seemed to envelop him; those hints of a past that was not good—but the measure of whose evil in her pure innocence she could not guess—his very melancholy, his misfortunes, and the deeds she had heard assigned to him, all had served to fire her fancy and more besides, although, until that moment, she had not known it.

Subconsciously all this had long dwelt in her mind. And now of a sudden that self-deriding speech of Crispin's had made her aware of its presence and its meaning.

She loved him. That men said his life had not been nice, that he was a soldier of fortune, little better than an adventurer, a man of no worldly weight, were matters of no moment. She loved him. She knew it now because he had mockingly bidden her to think whether Kenneth had cause to be jealous of him, and because upon thinking of it, she found that did Kenneth know what was in her heart, he must have more than cause.

She loved him with that rare love that is ready to give and give, and seeks nothing in return ; that impels a woman to follow the man at his bidding, be his way through the world cast in places never so rugged ; cleaving to him where all besides shall have abandoned him ; and, however dire his lot, asking of God no greater blessing than that of sharing it.

And to such a love as this Crispin was blind—blind to the very possibility of its existence ; so blind that he laughed to scorn the idea of a puny milksop being jealous of him. And so, while she sat, her soul all mastered by her discovery, her face white and still for very awe of it, he to whom this wealth was given, pursued the odious task of wooing her for another.

" You have observed—you must have observed— this insensate jealousy," he was saying, " and how do you allay it ? You do not. On the contrary, you excite it at every turn. You are exciting it now by having—and I dare swear for no other purpose—lured me to walk with you, to sit here with you, and preach your duty to you. And when, through jealousy, he shall have flown to fresh absurdities, shall you regret your conduct and the fruits it has borne ? Shall you pity the lad, and by kindness induce him to be wiser ? No. You will mock and taunt him into yet worse displays. And through these displays, which are—though you may not have thought of it—of your own contriving, you will conclude that he is no fit mate for you, and there will be heart-burnings, and years hence perhaps another Tavern Knight, whose name will not be Crispin Galliard."

She had listened with bent head ; indeed, so deeply rapt by her discovery, that she had but heard the half of what he said. Now, of a sudden, she looked up, and meeting his glance—

" Is—is it a woman's fault that you are as you are?"

" No, it is not. But how does that concern the case of Kenneth ? "

" It does not. I was but curious. I was not thinking of Kenneth."

He stared at her, dumbfounded. Had he been talking of Kenneth to her with such eloquence and such fervour, that she should calmly tell him as he paused that it was not of Kenneth she had been thinking ?

" You *will* think of him, Cynthia ? " he begged. " You will bethink you too of what I have said, and by being kinder and more indulgent with this youth you shall make him grow into a man you may take pride in. Deal fairly with him, child, and if anon you find you cannot truly love him, then tell him so. But tell him kindly and frankly, instead of using him as you are doing."

She was silent a moment, and in their poignancy her feelings went very near to anger. Presently—

"I would, Sir Crispin, you could hear him talk of you," said she.

"He talks ill, not a doubt of it, and like enough he has good cause."

"Yet you saved his life."

The words awoke Crispin, the philosopher of love, to realities. He recalled the circumstances of his saving Kenneth, and the price the boy was to pay for that service ; and it suddenly came to him that it was wasted breath to plead Kenneth's cause with Cynthia, when by his own future actions he was, himself, more than likely to destroy the boy's every hope of wedding her. The irony of his attitude smote him hard, and he rose abruptly. The sun hung now a round, red globe upon the very brink of the sea.

"Hereafter he may have little cause to thank me," he muttered. "Come, Mistress Cynthia, it grows late."

She rose in mechanical obedience, and together they retraced their steps in silence, save for the stray word exchanged at intervals touching matters of no moment.

But he had not advocated Kenneth's cause in vain, for all that he little recked what his real argument had been, what influences he had evoked to urge her to make her peace with the lad. A melancholy listlessness of mind possessed her now. Crispin did not see, never would see, what was in her heart, and it might not be hers to show him. The life that might have signified was not to be lived, and since that was so it seemed to matter little what befell.

It was thus that when on the morrow her father returned to the subject, she showed herself tractable and docile out of her indifference, and to Gregory she appeared not averse to listen to what he had to advance in the boy's favour. Anon Kenneth's own humble pleading, allied to his contrite and sorrowful appearance, were received by her with that same indifference, as also with indifference did she allow him later to kiss her hand and assume the flattering belief that he was rehabilitated in her favour.

But pale grew Mistress Cynthia's cheeks, and sad her soul. Wistful she waxed, sighing at every turn, until it seemed to her—as haply it hath seemed to many a maid—that all her life must she waste in vain sighs over a man who gave no single thought to her.

CHAPTER XV

On his side Kenneth strove hard during the days that followed to right himself in her eyes. But so headlong was he in the attempt, and so misguided, that presently he overshot his mark by dropping an unflattering word concerning Crispin, whereby he attributed to the Tavern Knight's influence and example the degenerate change that had of late been wrought in him.

Cynthia's eyes grew hard as he spoke, and had he been wise he had better served his cause by talking in another vein. But jealousy had so addled what poor brains the Lord had bestowed upon him, that he floundered on, unmindful of any warning that took not the blunt shape of words. At length, however, she stemmed the flow of invective that his lips poured forth.

" Have I not told you already, Kenneth, that it better becomes a gentleman not to slander the man to whom he owes his life ? In fact, that a gentleman should scorn such an action ? "

As he had protested before so did he protest now that what he had uttered was no slander. And in his mortification at the way she used him, for which he now bitterly upbraided her, he was very near the point of tears, like the blubbering schoolboy that at heart he was.

" And as for the debt, madam," he cried, striking

the oaken table of the hall with his clenched hand, "it is a debt that shall be paid, a debt which this gentleman whom you defend would not permit me to contract until I had promised payment—aye, 'fore George!—and with interest, for in the payment I may risk my life."

"I see no interest in that, since you risk nothing more than what you owe him," she answered, with a disdain that brought the impending tears to his eyes. But if he lacked the manliness to restrain them, he possessed at least the shame to turn his back and hide them from her. "But tell me, sir," she added, her curiosity awakened, "if I am to judge, what was the nature of this bargain?"

He was silent for a moment, and took a turn in the hall—mastering himself to speak—his hands clasped behind him, and his eyes bent towards the polished floor which the evening sunlight, filtered through the gules of the leaded windows, splashed with crimson stains. She sat in the great leathern chair at the head of the board, and, watching him, waited.

He was debating whether he was bound to secrecy in the matter, and in the end he resolved that he was not. Thereupon, pausing before her, he succinctly told the story Crispin had related to him that night in Worcester—the story of a great wrong, that none but a craven could have left unavenged. He added nothing to it, subtracted nothing from it, but told the tale as it had been told to him on that dreadful night, the memory of which still had the power to draw a shudder from him.

Cynthia sat with parted lips and eager eyes, absorb-

ing that narrative of suffering that was rather as
some romancer's fabrication than a true account of
what a living man had undergone. Now with sorrow
and pity in her heart and countenance, now with anger
and loathing, she listened until he had done, and even
when he ceased, and flung himself into the nearest
chair, she sat on in silence for a spell.

Then of a sudden she turned a pair of flashing eyes
upon the boy, and in tones charged with a scorn ineffable—

"You dare," she cried, "to speak of that man as
you do, knowing this? Knowing what he has suffered,
you dare to rail against those sins to which his misfortunes have driven him? How would it have fared
with you, do you think, had you stood in the shoes
of this unfortunate? Should you have fallen on your
craven knees, and thanked the Lord for allowing you
to keep your miserable life? Should you have suc-
cumbed to the blows of fate with a whine of texts upon
your lips? Who are you?" she went on, rising,
breathless in a wrath which caused him to recoil in
sheer affright before her. "Who are you, and what
are you, that knowing what you know of this man's
life, you dare to sit in judgment upon his actions, and
condemn them. Tell me!"

But never a word had he with which to meet that
hail of angry, contemptuous questions. The answer
that had been so ready to his lips that night at Worcester, when, in a milder form, the Tavern Knight had
set him the same question, he dared not offer now.
The retort that Sir Crispin had not cause enough in
the evil of others, which had wrecked his life, to risk

the eternal damnation of his soul, he dared no longer utter. Glibly enough had he said to that stern man what he dared not say now to this sterner maid. Perhaps it was fear of her that made him dumb, perhaps that at last he knew himself for what he was by contrast with the man whose vices he had so heartily despised a while ago.

Shrinking before her anger, he racked his shallow mind for a fitting answer. Before he had found one, a heavy step sounded in the gallery that overlooked the hall, and a moment later Gregory Ashburn descended. His face was ashen, and a heavy frown made a furrow betwixt his brows.

In the fleeting glance she bestowed upon her father, Cynthia did not remark the disorder of his countenance; whilst as for Kenneth, he had enough to hold his attention for the time.

Gregory's entrance set an awkward constraint upon them ; nor had he any word to say as he came heavily up the hall.

At the lower end of the long table he paused, and resting his hand upon the board, he seemed on the point of speaking. But suddenly a sound reached him that caused him to draw a sharp breath ; it was the rumble of wheels and the crack of a whip.

" It is Joseph ! " he cried, in a voice the relief of which was so marked that Cynthia noticed it. And with that exclamation he flung past them, and out through the doorway to meet his brother so opportunely returned.

He reached the terrace steps as the coach pulled up and the lean figure of Joseph Ashburn emerged from it.

" So, Gregory," he grumbled for greeting, " it was on a fool's errand you sent me, after all. That knave, your messenger, found me in London at last when I had outworn my welcome at Whitehall. But, 'swounds, man," he cried, remarking the pallor of his brother's face, " are you ill ? "

" I have news for you, Joseph," answered Gregory in a voice that shook.

" It is not Cynthia ? Nay, for there she stands— and her pretty lover by her side. 'Slife, what a cox-comb the lad's grown."

And with that he hastened forward to kiss his niece, and congratulate Kenneth upon being restored to her.

" I heard of it, lad, in London," quoth he, a leer upon his sallow face—" the story of how a fire-eater named Galliard befriended you, trussed a parson and a trooper, and dragged you out of jail a short hour before hanging-time."

Kenneth flushed. He felt the sneer in Joseph's words like a stab. He thought that the man's tone implied that another had done for him that which he could never have done for himself, and Kenneth felt that this was so said in Cynthia's presence with malicious purpose.

He was right. It was Joseph's nature to be spiteful and venomous whenever chance afforded him the opportunity. And he had been particularly soured at present by his recent discomforts, suffered in a cause wherewith he had no sympathy—that of the union Gregory desired of Cynthia and Kenneth.

There was an unpleasant smile on his thin lips, and

his crooked eyes rested tormentingly upon the young
man when Gregory plucked at the skirts of his coat,
drew him aside, and beckoned him away. They entered
the chamber where they had held their last interview
before Joseph had set out for news of Kenneth. With
an air of mystery Gregory closed the door, and turned
to face his brother. He stayed him in the act of unbuckling his sword-belt.

"Wait, Joseph!" he cried dramatically. "This is
not the moment to disarm. Keep your sword on your
thigh, man; you will need it as you never yet have
needed it." He paused, took a deep breath, and
hurled the news at his brother.

"Roland Marleigh is alive, and he is here." And he
sat down like a man exhausted.

Joseph did not start; he did not cry out; he did
not so much as change countenance. A slight quiver
of the eyelids was the only sign he gave of the shock
that his brother's announcement had occasioned. The
hand that had rested on the buckle of his sword-belt
slipped quietly to his side, and he deliberately stepped
up to Gregory, his eyes set searchingly upon the pale,
flabby face before him. A sudden suspicion darting
through his mind, he took his brother by the shoulders
and shook him.

"Gregory, you fool, you have drunk overdeep in
my absence."

"I have, I have," wailed Gregory, "and my God,
it was he was my table-fellow, and set me the example."

"Like enough, like enough," returned Joseph, with
contempt. "My poor Gregory, the wine has so fouled
your worthless wits at last, that they conjure up

phantoms to sit at the table with you. Come, man, what petticoat business is this? Bestir yourself."

At that Gregory caught the drift of Joseph's suspicions.

He lumbered to his feet, and stood towering above his brother. "It was no ghost sat with me, but Roland Marleigh himself, in the flesh, and strangely changed by time. So changed that I knew him not, nor should I know him now but for that which, not ten minutes ago, I overheard."

His angry earnestness was so impressive, his sanity so obvious, that Joseph's suspicions were all scattered.

He caught Gregory's wrist in a grip that made his brother wince, and forced him back into his seat.

"Gadslife, man, what is it you mean?" he demanded through set teeth. "Tell me."

And Gregory told him of the manner of Kenneth's coming to Sheringham and to Castle Marleigh, accompanied by one Crispin Galliard, the same that had been known for his mad exploits in the late wars as "Rake-Helly Galliard," and that was now known to the malignants as "The Tavern Knight" for his drunken ways. Crispin's mention of Roland Marleigh on the night of his arrival now returned vividly to Gregory's mind, and he repeated it, ending with the story which that very evening he had overheard Kenneth telling Cynthia.

"And this Galliard, then, is none other than that pup of insolence, Roland Marleigh, grown into a dog of war?" quoth Joseph.

He was calm—singularly calm considering what such news meant to him.

" There remains no doubt of it."

" And you saw this man day by day, sat with him night by night over your damned sack, and knew him not ? Oddswounds, man, where were your eyes ? "

" You may suppose me blind. But he is so changed that I would defy you, Joseph, to have recognized him."

Joseph sneered, and the flash of his eyes told of the contempt wherein he held his brother's judgment.

" Think not that, Gregory. I have cause enough to remember him." Then suddenly changing his tone for one of eager anxiety—

" But the lad, Gregory, does he suspect, do you think ? "

" Not a whit. In that lies this fellow's diabolical cunning. Learning of Kenneth's relations with us, he seized the opportunity Fate offered him that night at Worcester, and bound the lad on oath to help him when he should demand it, without disclosing the names of those against whom he should require his services. The boy expects at any moment to be bidden to go forth with him upon his mission of revenge, little dreaming that it is here that this tragedy is to be played out."

" This comes of your fine matrimonial project for Cynthia," muttered Joseph acridly. He laughed his unpleasant laugh, and for some moments there was silence.

" To think, Gregory," he broke out at last, " that for a fortnight he should have been beneath this roof, and you should have found no means of doing more effectively that which was done too carelessly eighteen years ago."

He spoke so coldly of it that Gregory shuddered and looked at his brother in alarm.

"What now, fool?" cried Joseph, scowling. "Are you as weak as you are blind? Damn me, sir, it seems well that I am returned. I'll have no Marleigh plague my old age for me." Then he went on in a quieter voice, whose ring was sinister: "To-morrow I shall find a way to draw this your dog of war to some secluded ground. I have some skill." He tapped his hilt as he spoke. "Besides, you shall be there, Gregory." And his smile was darkly significant.

"Is there no other way?" asked Gregory, in distress.

"There was," answered Joseph. "There was the Parliament. At Whitehall I met a man—one Colonel Pride—a bloodthirsty old Puritan soldier, who would give his right hand to see this Galliard hanged. Galliard, it seems, slew the fellow's son at Worcester. Had I but known," he added regretfully—"had your wits been keener, and you had discovered it and sent me word, I had found means to help Colonel Pride to his revenge. As it is"—he shrugged his shoulders—"there is not time."

"It may be——" began Gregory, then stopped abruptly with an exclamation that caused Joseph to wheel sharply. The door had opened, and on the threshold Sir Crispin Galliard stood, deferentially, hat in hand.

Joseph's astonished glance played rapidly over him for a second. Then—

"Who the devil may you be?" he blurted out.

Despite his anxiety, Gregory almost laughed at the question. The Tavern Knight came forward.

"I am Crispin Galliard, at your service," said he, bowing. "I was told that the master of Marleigh was returned, and that I should find you here. So I hastened, sir, to proffer you my thanks for the generous shelter this house has given me this fortnight past."

Whilst he spoke he measured Joseph with his eyes, and his glance was as baleful as his words were civil. Joseph was lost in amazement. Little trace was there in this fellow of the Roland Marleigh he had known. Moreover, he had looked to find an older man, forgetting that Roland's years could not yet amount to forty. Then, again, the fading light, whilst revealing the straight, supple lines of his lank figure, softened the haggardness of the face and made him appear yet younger than the light of noon would have shown him.

In an instant Joseph had recovered, and for all that his mind misgave him—tortured by a desire to learn whether Crispin was aware of their knowledge concerning him—his smile was serene, and his tones level and pleasant, as he made answer—

"Sir, you are very welcome. You have valiantly served one dear to us, and the entertainment of our poor house, for as long as you may deign to honour it, is but the paltriest of returns."

CHAPTER XVI

THE RECKONING

SIR CRISPIN had heard nothing of what was being said as he entered the room, and he had no suspicion that his identity was discovered. He had but hastened to perform that which, under ordinary circumstances, would have been a natural enough duty towards the master of the house. He had been actuated also by an impatience again to behold this Joseph Ashburn —this man who had dealt him that murderous sword-thrust eighteen years ago. He observed him attentively, and gathering from his scrutiny that here was a dangerous, subtle fellow, different, indeed, from his heavy-witted brother, he took the resolve to act at once.

And so when he appeared in the hall at supper-time, he came armed and booted and equipped as for a journey.

Joseph was standing alone by the huge fire-place, his face to the burning logs, and his foot resting upon one of the andirons. Gregory and his daughter were together in the embrasure of a window. By the other window, across the hall, stood Kenneth, alone and disconsolate, gazing out at the drizzling rain that had begun to fall.

As Galliard descended, Joseph turned his head, and his eyebrows shot up and wrinkled his forehead at beholding the knight's equipment.

"How is this, Sir Crispin?" said he. "You are going a journey?"

"Too long already have I imposed myself upon the hospitality of Castle Marleigh," Crispin answered as he came and stood before the blazing logs. "To-night, Mr. Ashburn, I go hence."

A curious expression flitted across Joseph's face. The next moment, his brows, still knit as he sought to fathom this sudden action, he was muttering the formal regrets that courtesy dictated. But Crispin had remarked that change of countenance, fleeting though it had been, and it flashed into his mind that Joseph knew him. As he moved away towards Cynthia and her father, he thanked Heaven that he had taken such measures as he had thought wise and prudent for the carrying out of his resolve.

Following him with a glance, Joseph asked himself whether Crispin had discovered that he was recognized, and had determined to withdraw, leaving the reckoning for another and more propitious season. In answer—little knowing the measure of the man he dealt with—he told himself it must be so, and having arrived at this conclusion, he there and then determined that Crispin must not depart free to return and plague them when he listed. Since Galliard shrank from forcing matters to an issue, he himself would do it that very night, and thereby settle for all time this business. And so before he sat down to sup Joseph looked to it that his sword lay at hand behind his chair at the table-head.

The meal was a quiet one enough. Kenneth was sulking under the fresh ill-usage—as he deemed it—

that he had endured at Cynthia's hands. Cynthia, in
her turn, was grave and silent. That story of Sir
Crispin's sufferings gave her much to think of, as did
also his departure, and more than once did Galliard
find her eyes fixed upon him with a look half of pity,
half of some other feeling that he was at a loss to
interpret. Gregory's big voice was little heard. The
sinister glitter in his brother's eye made him appre-
hensive and ill at ease. For him the hour was indeed
in travail and like to bring forth strange doings—but
not half so much as it was for Crispin and Joseph,
each bent upon forcing matters to a head ere he
quitted that board. And yet but for these two the
meal would have passed off in dismal silence. Joseph
was at pains to keep suspicion from his guest, and
with that intent he talked gaily of this and that, told
of slight matters that had befallen him on his recent
journey, and of the doings that in London he had
witnessed, investing each trifling incident with a
garb of wit that rendered it entertaining.

And Galliard—actuated by the same motives—
grew reminiscent whenever Joseph paused and let
his nimble tongue—ever nimblest at a table—amuse
those present or seem to amuse them, by a score of
drolleries.

He drank deeply too, and this Joseph observed with
satisfaction. But here again he misjudged his man.
Kenneth, who ate but little, seemed also to have
developed an unusual thirst, and Crispin grew at
length alarmed at that ever empty goblet so often
filled. He would have need of Kenneth before the
hour was out, and he rightly feared that did matters

thus continue, the lad's aid was not to be reckoned with. Had Kenneth sat beside him he might have whispered a word of restraint in his ear, but the lad was on the other side of the board.

At one moment Crispin fancied that a look of intelligence passed from Joseph to Gregory, and when presently Gregory set himself to ply both him and the boy with wine, his suspicions deepened, and he grew watchful and wary.

Anon Cynthia rose. Upon the instant Galliard was also on his feet. He escorted her to the foot of the staircase, and there—

"Permit me, Mistress Cynthia," said he, "to take my leave of you. In an hour or so I shall be riding."

Her eyes were wistful, and he might have noticed that she lost some colour.

"Fare you well, sir," she said in a low voice, to add in a tone that lent sincerity to the formal words : "May good fortune attend you."

"Mistress, I thank you. Fare you well."

He bowed low. She dropped him a slight curtsy, and ascended the stairs. Once as she reached the gallery above, she turned. He had resumed his seat at table, and was in the act of filling his glass. The servants had withdrawn, and for half an hour thereafter they sat on, sipping their wine, and making conversation—while Crispin grew every instant more boisterous, until at length his boisterousness passed into incoherence. His eyelids drooped heavily, and his chin kept ever and anon sinking forward on to his breast.

Kenneth, flushed with wine, yet master of his wits, watched him with contempt. This was the man Cynthia preferred to him! Contempt was there also in Joseph Ashburn's eye, mingled with satisfaction. He had not looked to find the task so easy. At length he deemed the season ripe.

" My brother tells me that you were once acquainted with Roland Marleigh," said he.

" Aye," he answered thickly. " I knew the dog— a merry, reckless soul, d——n me. 'Twas his reckless-ness killed him, poor devil—that and your hand, Mr. Ashburn, so the story goes."

" What story ? "

" What story ? " echoed Crispin. " The story that I heard. Do you say I lie ? " And, swaying in his chair, he sought to assume an air of defiance.

Joseph laughed in a fashion that made Kenneth's blood run cold.

" Why, no, I don't deny it. It was in fair fight he fell. Moreover, he brought the duel upon him-self."

Crispin spoke no word in answer, but rose unsteadily to his feet, so unsteadily that his chair was overset and fell with a crash behind him. For a moment he surveyed it with a drunken leer, then went lurching across the hall towards the door that led to the ser-vants' quarters. The three men sat on, watching his antics in contempt, curiosity, and amusement. They saw him gain the heavy oaken door and close it. They heard the bolts rasp as he shot them home, and the lock click ; and they saw him withdraw the key and slip it into his pocket.

The cold smile still played round Joseph's lips as Crispin turned to face them again, and on Joseph's lips did that same smile freeze as he saw him standing there, erect and firm, his drunkenness all vanished, and his eyes keen and fierce ; as he heard the ring of his metallic voice—

"You lie, you murderer. It was no fair fight. It was no duel. It was a foul, murderous stroke you dealt him in the back, thinking to butcher him as you butchered his wife and his babe. But there is a God, Master Ashburn," he went on in an ever-swelling voice, "and I lived. Like a salamander I came through the flames in which you sought to destroy all trace of your crime. I lived, and I, Crispin Galliard, the debauched Tavern Knight that was once Roland Marleigh, am now to call the reckoning. It is not thus that I had looked to come home again, nor thus I had hoped for justice. The common hangman should have had the handling of you, and in that hope I rode with the King. But since the King has not prevailed, since I am still an outcast, I must do what I can with my own hands."

The very incarnation was he then of an avenger, as he stood towering before them, his grim face livid with the passion into which he had lashed himself, his blazing eyes watching them in that cunning, half-closed way that was his when his mood was dangerous. And yet the only one that quailed was Kenneth, his ally, upon whom comprehension burst with the suddenness of a blow.

Joseph recovered from the surprise of Crispin's suddenly resumed sobriety. He understood the trick that Galliard had played upon them so that he might cut off their retreat in the only direction in which they might have sought assistance, and he blamed himself for not having foreseen it. Still, anxiety he felt none ; his sword was to his hand, and Gregory was armed ; at the very worst they were two calm and able men opposed to a half-intoxicated boy, and a man whom fury, he thought, must strip of half his power. Probably, indeed, the lad would side with them, despite his plighted word. Again, he had but to raise his voice, and, though the door that Crispin had fastened was a stout one, he never doubted but that his call would penetrate it and bring servants to his aid.

And so, a smile of cynical unconcern on his lips, his answer came in a cold, incisive voice.

" The reckoning you have come to call shall be met in full, sir. Rake-helly Galliard is the hero of many a reckless deed, but my judgment is at fault if this prove not his crowning recklessness and his last one. Gadswounds, sir, it's a rashness to come single-handed to beard the lion in his den ? "

" Say the cur in his kennel," Crispin flung back. " Blood and wounds, Master Joseph, will you frighten me with words ? "

Still Joseph smiled, deeming himself master of the situation.

" Were help needed, the raising of my voice would bring it me. But it is not. We are three to one."

" You reckon wrongly. Mr. Stewart belongs to me to-night—bound by an oath that it would damn his soul to break, to help me when and where I may call upon him ; and I call upon him now. Draw your sword."

Kenneth stood pale and limp, clasping and unclasping his hands.

"God's curse on you," he burst out. "You have tricked me, you have cheated me."

"Bear your oath in mind," was the cold answer. "If you deem yourself wronged by me, hereafter we can settle that. But first fulfil me what you have sworn. Out with your blade, man."

Still Kenneth hesitated, and but for Gregory's rash action at this critical juncture, it is possible that he would have elected to break his plighted word. But Gregory, fearing that he might determine otherwise, resolved there and then to remove the chance of it. Whipping out his sword, he made a vicious pass at the lad's breast. Kenneth avoided it by leaping backwards, but in an instant Gregory had sprung after him, and seeing himself thus beset, Kenneth was forced to draw that he might defend himself.

They stood in the space between the table and that part of the hall that abutted on to the terrace ; opposite to them, by the door which he had closed, stood Crispin. At the table-head Joseph still sat—cool, self-contained, even amused.

He realized the rashness of Gregory's attack upon one who might yet have been won over to their side ; but he never doubted that a few passes would dispose of the lad's opposition, and he saw no need to interfere. Not until Crispin was advancing upon him slowly, his rapier naked in his hand, was he forced to look to himself. He caught at the sword that stood behind him, and leaping to his feet he sprang forward to meet his grim antagonist. Galliard's eyes flashed, he raised his rapier, and their blades met.

To the clash of their meeting came an echoing clash from beyond the table.

"Hold, sir!" Kenneth had cried, as Gregory bore down upon him. But Gregory's answer had been a lunge which the boy had instinctively parried. Taking that crossing of blades for a sign of opposition, Gregory thrust again more viciously. Kenneth parried again, narrowly, his blade pointing straight at his aggressor. He saw the opening, and both instinct and the desire to repel Gregory's onslaught drew him into venturing a riposte, which drove Gregory back until his shoulders touched the panels of the wall. Simultaneously the boy's foot struck the back of the chair which in rising Crispin had overset, and he stumbled. How it happened he scarcely knew, but as he hurtled forward his blade slid along his opponent's, and entering Gregory's right shoulder pinned him to the wainscot.

Joseph heard the tinkle of a falling blade, and assumed it to be Kenneth's. For the rest he was just then too busy to dare withdraw for a second his eyes from Crispin's. Until that hour Joseph Ashburn had accounted himself something of a swordsman, and more than a match for most masters of the weapon. But in Crispin he found a fencer of a quality such as he had never yet encountered. Every feint, every trick in his catalogue, had he paraded, yet ever with the same result—his point was foiled and put aside with ease.

Desperately he fought now, darting that point of his hither and thither in and out whenever the slightest opening offered ; yet ever did it meet the gentle averting pressure of Crispin's blade. He fought on and began to wonder as the seconds went by that Gregory did not come to his aid. Then the dreadful thought that perhaps Gregory was overcome occurred to him. In such a case he must reckon upon himself alone. He cursed the over-confidence that had led him into that ever-fatal error of under-estimating his adversary. He might have known that one who had acquired Sir Crispin's fame was no ordinary man, but one accustomed to face great odds and master them. He might call for help. He marvelled as the thought occurred to him that the clatter of their blades had not drawn his servants from their quarters. Fencing still, he raised his voice—

" Ho there ! John, Stephen ! "

" Spare your breath," growled the knight. " You'll need it. None will hear you, call as you will. I gave your four henchmen a flagon of canary laced with brandy so that they should drink to my safe journey hence. They have emptied it ere this, I make no doubt, and a single glass of it would set the hardest toper asleep for the round of the clock."

An oath was Joseph's only answer—a curse it was upon his own folly and assurance. A little while ago he had thought to have drawn so tight a net about this ruffler, and here was he now taken in its very toils, well-nigh exhausted and in his enemy's power.

It occurred to him at last that Crispin deliberately

stayed his hand ; that he fenced only on the defensive ; and he wondered what might his motive be. He realized that he was mastered, and that at any moment Galliard might send home his point. He was bathed from head to foot in a sweat that was at once of exertion and despair. A frenzy seized him. He would yet turn to advantage this hesitancy of Crispin's to strike the final blow.

He braced himself for a supreme effort, and turning his wrist from a simulated thrust in the first position, he doubled, and stretching out, lunged vigorously in quarte. As he lengthened his arm in the stroke there came a sudden twitch at his wrist ; the weapon was twisted from his grasp, and he stood disarmed at Crispin's mercy.

A gurgling cry broke despite him from his lips, and his eyes grew wide in terror as they encountered the knight's sinister glance. Not three paces behind him was the wall, and on it, within the hand's easy reach, hung many a trophied weapon that might have served him then. But the fascination of fear was upon him, numbing his wits and his limbs, with the thought that the next pulsation of his tumultuous heart would prove its last. The calm, unflinching courage that had been Joseph's only virtue was shattered, and his iron will that had unscrupulously held hitherto his very conscience in bondage was turned to water now that he stood face to face with death.

Æons of time it seemed to him were sped since the sword was wrenched from his hand, and still the stroke he awaited did not come ; still Crispin stood, sinister and silent before him, watching him, as the snake watches the bird, with eyes from which Joseph could not withdraw his own, and yet before which it seemed to him that he shrivelled.

The candles were burning low in their sconces, and the corners of that ample, gloomy hall were filled with shadows that formed a setting well suited to the grim picture made by those two figures—the one towering stern and vengeful, the other crouching palsied and livid.

Beyond the table, and with the wounded Gregory—lying unconscious and bleeding—at his feet, stood Kenneth looking on in silence, in wonder and in horror.

To him also, as he watched, the seconds seemed minutes from the time when Crispin had disarmed his opponent until with a laugh—short and sudden as a stab—he dropped his sword and caught his victim by the throat.

However fierce the passion that had actuated Crispin, it had been held hitherto in strong subjection. But now at last it suddenly welled up and mastered him, causing him to cast all restraint to the winds, to abandon reason and to give way to the lust of rage that rendered ungovernable his mood.

Like a burst of flame from embers that have been smouldering was the upleaping of his madness, transfiguring his face and transforming his whole being. A new, unconquerable strength possessed him ; his pulses throbbed with the quickened coursing of his blood, and his soul was filled with the cruel elation that attends a lust about to be indulged—the elation of the beast about to rend its prey.

He was pervaded by the desire to wreak slowly and with his hands the destruction of his broken enemy. To have passed his sword through him would have been too swiftly done ; the man would have died, and Crispin would have known nothing of his sufferings. But to take him thus by the throat ; slowly to choke the life's breath out of him ; to feel his desperate, writhing struggles ; to be conscious of every agonized twitch of his sinews ; to watch the purpling face, the swelling veins, the protruding eyes filled with the dumb horror of his agony ; to hold him thus—each second becoming a distinct, appreciable measure of time— and thus to take what payment he could for all the blighted years that lay behind him—this he felt would be something to be savoured.

Meanwhile the shock of surprise at the unexpected action had awakened again the man in Joseph. For a second even hope knocked at his heart. He was sinewy and active, and perchance he might yet make Galliard repent that he had discarded his rapier. The knight's reason for doing so he thought he had in Crispin's contemptuous words :

" Good steel were too great an honour for you, Mr. Ashburn."

And as he spoke, his lean, sinewy fingers tightened about Joseph's throat in a grip that crushed the breath from him, and with it the new-born hope of proving master in his fresh combat. He had not reckoned with this galley-weaned strength of Crispin's, a strength that was a revelation to Joseph as he felt himself almost lifted from the ground, and swung this way and that, like a babe in the hands of a grown man.

Vain were his struggles. His strength ebbed fast; the blood, held overlong in his head, was already obscuring his vision, when at last the grip relaxed, and his breathing was freed. As his sight cleared again he found himself back in his chair at the table-head, and beside him Sir Crispin, his left hand resting upon the board, his right grasping once more the sword and his eyes bent mockingly and evilly upon his victim.

Kenneth, looking on, could not repress a shudder. He had known Crispin for a tempestuous man, quickly moved to wrath, and he had oftentimes seen anger make terrible his face and glance. But never had he seen aught in him to rival this present frenzy; it rendered satanical the baleful glance of his eyes and the awful smile of hate and mockery with which he gazed at last upon the helpless quarry that he had waited eighteen years to bring down.

" I would," said Crispin, in a harsh, deliberate voice, " that you had a score of lives, Joseph. As it is, I have done what I could. Two agonies have you undergone already, and I am inclined to mercy. The end is at hand— If you have prayers to say, say them, though I doubt it will be wasted breath—you are over-ripe for hell."

" You mean to kill me," gasped Joseph, growing yet a shade more livid.

" What else were you supposing ? Twice already have I given you a foretaste of death. Did you think I merely jested ? "

Joseph's teeth clicked together in a snap of determination. That sneer of Crispin's acted upon him as a blow—but as a blow that stimulates. He braced himself for fresh resistance ; not of action, for that he realized were futile, but of argument.

" It is murder that you do," he said.

" No ; it is justice. It has been long on the way, but it has come at last."

" Bethink you, Mr. Marleigh——"

" Call me not by that name," cried the other harshly, fearfully. " I have not borne it these eighteen years, and thanks to what you have made me, it is not meet that I should bear it now."

There was a pause. Then Joseph spoke again with great calm and earnestness.

" Consider well, Sir Crispin, what you are about to do. It can benefit you in naught."

" Oddslife, do you say so ? Do you think it will not benefit me to see you receive at last your wages ? "

" You may have to pay dearly for what at best must prove a fleeting satisfaction."

" Not fleeting, Joseph. The memory of it shall send me rejoicing through what years or days of life be left me. A satisfaction that for eighteen years I have been waiting to taste, though the moment after it be mine should find me stark and cold."

" Sir Crispin, you are in enmity with the Parliament —an outlaw almost. I have some influence—much influence. By exerting it——"

Crispin laughed.

" Have done, sir ! You talk in vain. What to me is life, or aught that life can give ? If I have so long endured the burden of it, it has been so that I might draw from it this hour. Do you think there is any bribe would turn me from my purpose ? "

A groan from Gregory, who was regaining consciousness, drew his attention aside.

" Truss him up, Kenneth," he commanded, pointing to the recumbent figure. " How ? Do you hesitate ? Now, as God lives, I'll be obeyed ; or you shall have an unpleasant reminder of the oath you swore me ! "

With a look of loathing the lad dropped on his knees to do as he was bidden— Then of a sudden—

" I have not the means," he announced.

" Fool, does he not wear a sword-belt and a sash ! Attend to it ! "

" Why do you force me ? " the lad still protested passionately. " You have tricked and cheated me, yet I have kept my oath and rendered you the assistance you required. They are in your power now, can you not do the rest of your foul work yourself ? "

" On my soul, Master Stewart, I am over-patient with you ! Are we to wrangle at every step before you'll take it ? I will have your assistance through this matter as you swore to give it. Come, truss me that fellow, and have done with words."

His fierceness overthrew the boy's outburst of resistance. Kenneth had wit enough to see that his mood was dangerous, and so, with an oath and groan, he went to work to pinion Gregory.

Then Joseph spoke again, his voice miraculously steady.

" Weigh well this act of yours, Sir Crispin. You are still young ; much of life lies yet before you.

Do not wantonly destroy it by an act that cannot repair the past."

"But it can square the account, Joseph. As for my life, you destroyed that years ago. The future has nothing to offer; the present has this." And he drew back his sword to strike.

CHAPTER XVII

JOSEPH DRIVES A BARGAIN

TERROR leapt afresh into Joseph's eyes at that movement of Crispin's, and for the third time that night did he taste the agony that is Death's forerunner. Yet Galliard delayed the stroke. He held his sword poised, the point aimed at Joseph's breast, and holding, he watched him, marking each phase of the emotion reflected upon his livid countenance. He was reluctant to strike, for to strike would mean to end this exquisite torture of horror.

Broken Joseph had been before and passive; now of a sudden he became violent again, but in a different way. He flung himself upon his knees before Sir Crispin, and passionately pleaded for the sparing of his miserable life.

Crispin looked on with an eye at once of scorn and of cold relish. It was thus he wished to see him, broken and anguished, suffering thus something of all that which he himself had suffered through despair in the years that were sped. With satisfaction then he watched his victim's agony; he watched it too with loathing—for a craven was in his eyes an ugly sight, and a craven Joseph in that moment was become. His parchment-like face was grey and mottled, his brow gleaming with sweat; his lips were blue and quivering, his eyes distraught.

In the silence of one who waits stood Crispin, listening, calm and unmoved, as though he heard not, until

Joseph's whining prayers culminated in an offer to make reparation. Then Crispin broke in at length.

"What reparation can you make, you murderer? Can you restore to me the wife and child you butchered eighteen years ago?"

"I can restore your child at least," cried the other frenziedly. "I can and will restore him to you if you but stay your hand. That and much more will I do to repair the past."

Crispin lowered his sword-arm, and for a full minute stood and stared at Joseph. His jaw was fallen and the grim firmness all gone from his face, and replaced by amazement, then unbelief followed by question; then unbelief again. The pallor of his cheeks was deepened. At last, however, he broke into a hard laugh.

"What lie is this you offer me?"

"It is no lie," Joseph cried, in accents so earnest that some of the unbelief passed again from Galliard's face. "It is the truth—God's truth. Your son lives."

"Hell-hound, it is a lie! On that fell night, as I swooned under your cowardly thrust, I heard you calling to your brother to slit the squalling bastard's throat. Those were your very words, Joseph."

"It is true. Yes. But I was not obeyed. Gregory swore we should give the babe a chance of life. He should never know whose he was, he said, and I agreed. We took the boy away. He has lived and thrived."

The knight stared at him for a moment; then he sank into a chair as if bereft of strength. He strove to think, but think coherently he could not. At last—

"Where is the proof of this?" he demanded hoarsely.

"I swear that what I have told you is true. I swear it on the Cross of our Redeemer!" protested Joseph with a solemnity that was not to be ignored. Nevertheless Crispin sneered.

"I ask for proofs, man, not oaths. What proofs can you afford me?"

"There are the man and the woman by whom the lad was reared."

"And where shall I find them?"

Joseph parted his lips to answer, then closed them again. In his eagerness he had almost given away the information which he now proposed to make the price of his life. He was recovering confidence at Crispin's tone and questions, gathering from both that the knight was willing to believe if proof were set before him. He rose to his feet, and when next he spoke his voice had won back some of its calm.

"That," said he, "I will tell you when I have your word that you will depart, leaving Gregory and me unharmed. I will supply you with what money you may need, and I will give you a letter to those people, so couched that what they tell you by virtue of it shall be a corroboration of my words."

His elbow resting upon the table, and his hand to his brow so that it shaded his eyes, Crispin sat a while in thought, swayed by emotions and doubts, the like of which he had never yet known in all his chequered life. Was Joseph lying? That was the question that repeatedly arose, and oddly enough, for all his mistrust of the man, he was inclined to believe him. Joseph watched him with much anxiety and some hope.

At length Crispin withdrew his hands from eyes that were grown haggard, and rose.

" Let us see the letter that you will write," said he. " There you have pen, ink, and paper. Write."

" You consent ? " asked Joseph.

" I will tell you when you have written."

In a hand that trembled Joseph wrote a few lines, then handed Crispin the sheet, whereon he read—

" The bearer of this is Sir Crispin Galliard, who is intimately interested in the matter that lies betwixt us, and whom I pray you answer fully and accurately the questions he may put you."

" I understand," said Crispin slowly. " Yes, it will serve. Now the superscription." And he returned the paper.

Ashburn was himself again by now. He realized the advantage he had gained, and he would not easily relinquish it.

" I shall add the superscription," said he calmly, " when you swear to depart without further molesting us."

Crispin paused yet, considering. If Joseph lied to him now, he would find means to return, he told himself. And so he took the oath demanded.

Joseph dipped his pen, and paused meditatively to watch a drop of ink, wherewith it was overladen, fall back into the horn. The briefest of pauses was it, yet it was not the accident it appeared to be. Hitherto Joseph had been as sincere as he had been earnest, intent only upon saving his life at all costs, and forgetting in his fear of the present the dangers that the future might hold for him were Crispin Galliard still at large. But in that second of dipping his quill, assured that the peril of the moment was overcome, and that Crispin would go forth as he said, his evil cunning resumed sway. As he watched the drop of ink roll from his pen-point, he remembered that in London there dwelt at the sign of " The Anchor," in Thames Street, one Colonel Pride, whose son this Galliard had slain, and who, did he once lay hands upon him, was not like to let him go again. In a second was the thought conceived and the determination taken, and, as he folded the letter and set upon it the superscription, Joseph could have laughed aloud in his exultation at the craft with which he was outwitting his enemy.

Crispin took the package and read thereon—

" This is to Mr. Henry Lane, at the sign of ' The Anchor,' in Thames Street, London."

The name was fictitious—one that Joseph set down upon the spur of the moment, his intention being to send a messenger that should outstrip Sir Crispin, and warn Colonel Pride of his coming.

" It is well," was Crispin's only comment. He, too, was grown calm again and fully master of himself. He placed the letter carefully within the breast of his doublet.

" If you have lied to me, if this is but a shift to win your miserable life, rest assured, Master Ashburn, that you have but put off the day of reckoning for a very little while."

It was on Joseph's lips to answer that none of us is immortal, but he bethought him that the pleasantry might be ill-timed.

Galliard took his hat and cloak from the chair on which he had placed them upon descending that evening. Then he turned to Joseph again.

" You spoke of money a moment ago," he said, in the tones of one demanding what is his own—the tones of a gentleman speaking to his steward. " I will take a hundred Caroluses. More I cannot carry in comfort."

Joseph gasped at the amount. For a second it even entered his mind to resist the demand. Then he remembered that there was a brace of pistols in his study ; if he could get those he would settle matters there and then without the aid of Colonel Pride.

" I will fetch the money," said he, betraying his purpose by his alacrity.

" By your leave, Master Ashburn, I will come with you."

Joseph's eyes flashed him a quick look of baffled hate.

" As you will," said he, with an ill grace.

As they passed out, Crispin turned to admonish Kenneth.

" You will remember, sir, you are still in my service. See that you keep good watch."

Kenneth bent his head without replying. But Master Gregory required little watching. He lay a helpless, half-swooning heap upon the floor, in the blood that oozed from his wounded shoulder. Even were he untrussed, there was little to be feared from him.

During the brief while they were alone together, Kenneth did not so much as attempt to speak to him. He sat down upon the nearest chair, and with his chin in his hands and his elbows on his knees he pondered the miserable predicament into which Sir Crispin had got him, and more bitter than ever it had been was now his hatred of the knight. That Galliard should be upon the eve of finding his son, and a sequel to the story he had heard from him that night in Worcester, was to Kenneth a thing of no account. Galliard had ruined him with the Ashburns. He could never now hope to win the hand of Cynthia, to achieve which he had been willing to turn both fool and knave—aye, had turned both. There was naught left him but to return to the paltry Scottish estate of his father, there to meet the sneers of those who no doubt had heard that he was gone South to marry a great English heiress.

He cursed the luck that had brought Crispin into his life. He cursed Crispin for the evil he had suffered from him, forgetting that but for Crispin he would have been carrion a month ago and more.

Deep at his bitter musings was he when Joseph returned, followed by Galliard. The knight came across the hall and stopped to look at Gregory.

" You may untruss him when I am gone," said he. " And in a quarter of an hour from now you are released from your oath to me. Fare you well," he added with unusual gentleness, and turning a glance that was almost regretful upon the lad. " We are not like to meet again, but should we, I trust it may be in happier times. If I have harmed you in this business, remember that I also served you and that my need was great. Fare you well." And he held out his hand.

" Take yourself to hell, sir ! " answered Kenneth, turning his back upon him. The ghost of a smile played round Joseph Ashburn's lips as he watched them.

CHAPTER XVIII

COUNTER-PLOT

So soon as Sir Crispin had taken his departure, and whilst yet the beat of his horse's hoofs was to be distinguished above the driving storm of rain and wind without, Joseph hastened across the hall to the servants' quarters. There he found his four grooms slumbering deeply, their faces white and clammy, and their limbs asprawl in odd, helpless attitudes. Vainly did he kick and curse them; arouse them he could not from their stupor.

And so, finding a lanthorn, he went out, himself, to the stables, whence Crispin had lately taken his best nag, and with his own hands saddled a horse. His lips were screwed into a wicked smile—a smile that still lingered upon them when presently he retraced his steps to the room where his brother sat with Kenneth.

In his absence the lad had dressed Gregory's wound; he had induced him to take a little wine, and had set him upon a chair, in which he now lay back, white and exhausted.

" The quarter of an hour is passed, sir," said Joseph coldly, as he entered.

Kenneth made no sign that he heard. He sat on like a man in a dream. His eyes that saw nothing were bent upon Gregory's pale, flabby face.

" The quarter of an hour is passed," Joseph repeated in a louder voice.

Kenneth looked up, then rose and sighed, passing his hand wearily across his brow.

" I understand," he replied in a low voice. " You mean that I must go ? "

Joseph waited a moment before replying. Then—

" It is past midnight," he said slowly, " and the weather is wild. You may lie here until morning, if you are so minded. But go then you must," he added sternly. " I need scarce say, sir, that you will have no speech with my niece, nor ever again set foot in Castle Marleigh."

" I understand, sir ; I understand. And yet . . ." He left the sentence unfinished.

Joseph raised his eyebrows. " And yet ? " he asked.

" I was the victim of an oath, given when I did not know against whom my hand was to be lifted. Oh, sir, am I to suffer all my life because this trick was put upon me ? You, Master Gregory," he cried, turning passionately to Cynthia's father, " you understand my position how I was forced into it."

Gregory opened his eyes. " Go to the devil," he groaned. " I understand that you have given me a wound that will take a month to heal."

" Not by intent, sir. I swear it was an accident ! "

" To swear this and that appears to be your chief purpose in life," growled Gregory for answer. " You had best go ; we are not likely to listen to excuses."

" Did you rather suggest a remedy now," Joseph put in quietly.

Kenneth swung round.

"What remedy is there? How can I undo what I have done? Show me but the way, and I'll follow it, no matter where it leads!"

Some such protestations Joseph had hoped to hear. For a while he was silent, making pretence to ponder. At length—

"Kenneth," he said, "if you are really sincere, it is possible that you may repair the evil you have done. If you are ready to do as I ask, we shall be willing on our side to forget this night."

Eagerly he was answered: "You have but to give me your commands, sir, and whatever the cost I will perform them!"

"It is a matter that will cost you little," answered Joseph. "One, indeed, that I could entrust to one of my grooms."

That whilst his grooms lay drugged the matter was so pressing that his messenger must set out that very night, Joseph did not think of adding.

"I would, sir," answered the boy, "that the task were great and difficult."

"Yes, yes." Joseph was sarcastic. "We are acquainted with both your courage and your resource." After that he was again silent and thoughtful for a moment; then with a sudden sharp glance at the lad—

"You shall have this chance of setting yourself right with us," he said. "Go make ready for a journey. You will set out at once for London. Take what you may require and arm yourself; then return to me here."

Gregory, who, despite his sluggish wits, divined—

partly, at least—what was afoot, made shift to speak. But his brother silenced him by a gesture.

"Go," Joseph said to the boy. And, without comment, Kenneth rose and left them.

"What would you do?" asked Gregory when the door had closed.

"Make doubly sure of that ruffian," answered Joseph coldly. "Colonel Pride might be absent when he arrives, and Marleigh might learn that none of the name of Lane dwells at 'The Anchor' in Thames Street. It would be fatal to awaken his suspicions and bring him back to us."

"But surely Richard or Stephen might carry your errand?"

"They might if they were not so drugged that they cannot be aroused. I might even go myself, but it is better so. There is even comedy in it. Kenneth shall outride our bloodthirsty knight to warn Pride of his coming, and when he comes he will walk into the hands of the hangman. It will be a surprise for him. For the rest, I shall keep my promise concerning his son. He shall have news of him from Pride. But it will come a little late."

Gregory shuddered.

"'Fore God, Joseph, it's a foul thing to do," he cried. "Sooner would I never set eyes on the lad again. Let him go his ways as you intended."

"I never did intend it. What trustier messenger could I find now that I have lent him zest by fear? To win Cynthia, we may rely upon him safely to do that in which another might fail."

"Joseph, you will roast in hell for it."

Joseph laughed him to scorn.

"Come, let me get you to bed, you canting hypocrite; your wound makes you light-headed."

It was a half-hour before Kenneth returned, booted, cloaked, and ready for his journey. He found Joseph alone, busily writing, and in obedience to a sign he sat down to wait, until, at last, with a final scratch and splutter Joseph flung down his pen. With the pounce-box tilted in the air, like a dicer about to make his throw, he looked at the lad.

"You will spare neither whip nor spur until you reach London, Kenneth. You must ride night and day; the matter is of the greatest urgency."

Kenneth nodded that he understood, and Joseph sprinkled the sand over the written page.

"I know not when you should reach London so that you may be in time, but," he continued, and as he spoke he creased the paper and poured the superfluous sand back into the box, "I should say that by midnight to-morrow your message should be delivered. Aye," he continued, in answer to the lad's gasp of surprise, "it is hard riding, I know, but if you would still win Cynthia you must do it. Spare neither money nor horseflesh, and keep to the saddle until you are in Thames Street."

He folded the letter, sealed it, and wrote the superscription, "These to Colonel Pride, at the sign of 'The Anchor' in Thames Street."

He rose and handed the package to Kenneth, to whom the superscription meant nothing, since he had not seen that borne by the letter which Crispin had received.

"You will deliver this intact, and with your own hands, to Colonel Pride in person—none other. Should he be absent from Thames Street upon your arrival, seek him out instantly wherever he may be. Upon your faithful observance of these conditions remember that your future depends. If you are in time, as indeed I trust and think you will be, you may account yourself as good as Cynthia's husband. Fail and—well, you need not return."

"I shall not fail, sir," Kenneth promised. "What man can do to make the journey within twenty-four hours, I will do."

He would have stayed to thank Joseph for the signal favour of this chance of rehabilitation, but Joseph cut him short.

"Take this purse. You will find a horse ready saddled in the stables. It will bear you to Norton at least. There get you a fresh one, and when that is done, another. Now be off."

CHAPTER XIX

THE INTERRUPTED JOURNEY

WHEN the Tavern Knight left the gates of Marleigh Park behind him on that wild October night, he drove deep the rowels of his spurs, and set his horse at a perilous gallop along the road to Norwich. The action was of instinct rather than of thought. In the turbulence of his mind, one clear current there was, and one only—the knowledge that he was bound for London for news of this son of his whom Joseph had told him lived. He did not even speculate what manner of man his child was grown, nor yet what walk of life he had been reared to tread. He lived: he was somewhere in the world; that for the time sufficed him. The Ashburns had not, it seemed, destroyed quite everything that made his life worth enduring—the life that so often and so wantonly he had exposed.

His son lived, and in London he should have news of him. To London then must he get himself with all dispatch, and he swore to take no rest until he reached it. And with that firm resolve to urge him, he ploughed his horse's flanks, and sped on through the night. The rain beat in his face, yet he scarce remarked it, as—again more by instinct than by reason—he buried his countenance to the eyes in the folds of his cloak.

Later the rain ceased, and clearer grew the line of light betwixt the hedgerows, by which he had steered his desperate career. Fitfully a crescent moon peered out from among ragged wind-driven clouds. The poor ruffler was fallen into meditation, and scarcely noticed that his nag did no more than amble. He roused himself of a sudden when half-way down a gentle slope some five miles from Norwich, and out of temper at discovering the sluggishness of the pace, he again gave the horse a taste of the spurs. The action was fatal. The incline was become a bed of sodden clay, and he had not observed with what misgivings his horse pursued the treacherous footing. The sting of the spur made the animal bound forward, and the next instant a raucous oath broke from Crispin as the nag floundered forward on to its knees. Like a stone from a catapult Galliard flew over its head and rolled down the few remaining yards of the slope into a very bog of slime at the bottom.

Down this same hill, some twenty minutes later, came Kenneth Stewart with infinite precautions. He was in haste—a haste more desperate far than even Crispin's. But his character held none of Galliard's recklessness, nor were his wits bemused by such news as Crispin had received that night. He realized that to be swift he must be cautious in this night-riding. And so, carefully he came, with a firm hand on the reins, yet leaving it to his horse to find safe footing.

He had reached the level ground in safety, and was about to put his nag to a smarter pace, when of a sudden from the darkness of the hedge he was hailed by a harsh, metallic voice, the sound of which sent a tremor through him.

" Sir, you are choicely met, whoever you may be.

I have suffered a mischance down that cursed hill, and my horse has gone lame."

Kenneth kept his cloak over his mouth, trusting that the muffling would sufficiently disguise his accents as he made answer.

" I am in haste, my master. What is your will ? "

" Why, marry, so am I in haste." It was years since any scruple had troubled him ; and none was likely to trouble him to-night. " My will is your horse, sir. Oh, I'm no robber. I'll pay you for it, and handsomely. But have it I must. 'Twill be no great discomfort for you to walk to Norwich. You may do it in an hour."

" My horse, sir, is not for sale," was Kenneth's brief answer. " Give you good night."

" Hold, man ! Blood and hell, stop ! If you'll not sell the beast to serve a gentleman, I'll shoot it under you."

Kenneth caught the gleam of a pistol-barrel levelled at close quarters, and he shivered in indecision. Every instant was precious to him. As in a flash it came to him that perhaps Sir Crispin also rode to London, and that it was expected of him to arrive there first if he were to be in time. Swiftly he weighed the odds in his mind, and took the determination to dash past Sir Crispin, risking his aim and trusting to the dark to befriend him.

But even as he determined thus, what moon there was became unveiled, and the light of it fell upon his face from which the cloak was lowered. An exclamation of surprise escaped Sir Crispin, who was now at the horse's head.

"'Slife, Master Stewart, I did not know your voice. Whither do you ride?"

"What is it to you? Have you not played enough havoc with me? Am I never to be rid of you? Castle Marleigh," he added, with well-feigned anger, "has closed its doors upon me. What does it signify to you whither I ride? Suffer me at least to go my ways."

The passionate reproach cut Galliard keenly. He held himself at that moment a very knave for having used this boy, and thereby cast a blight upon his life. He sought words in which to express something of what he felt; then, realizing how futile all words must prove, he stepped aside.

"Ride on, Master Stewart," he said. "Your way is clear."

And Kenneth, waiting for no second invitation, rode on and left him. He rode in gratitude to the Providence that had caused him so easily to overcome an obstacle that at first he had supposed impassable. Stronger grew in his mind the conviction that to fulfil the mission Joseph required of him, he must reach London ahead of Sir Crispin. The knowledge that he was ahead of him, and that he must derive an ample start from Galliard's mishap, warmed him like wine.

Thus relieved from his weight of anxiety, he little recked fatigue, and such excellent use did he make of his horse that he reached Newmarket on it an hour before the morrow's noon.

An hour he rested there, and broke his fast. Then on a fresh horse—a powerful and willing animal—he set out once more.

By half-past two he was at Newport. But so hard

had he ridden that man and beast alike were in a lather, and whilst he himself felt sick and tired, the horse was utterly unfit to bear him further. For half an hour he rested there, and made a meal washed down with a pint of claret laced with brandy. Then on a third horse he started upon the last stage of his journey.

The wind was damp and penetrating; the roads morasses of mud, and overhead gloomy banks of dark grey clouds moved sluggishly, the light that was filtered through them giving the flat landscape a bleak and dreary aspect. In his jaded condition Kenneth soon became a prey to the depression of it. His lightness of heart of some dozen hours ago was now all gone, and not even the knowledge that his mission was well-nigh accomplished sufficed to cheer him. To add to his discomfort a fine rain set in towards four o'clock, and when a couple of hours later he clattered along the road cut through a wooded slope in the direction of Waltham, he was become a very limp and sorry individual.

He did not so much as notice the horsemen moving cautiously among the closely-set trees on either side of the road. It was growing prematurely dark, and objects were none too distinct. And thus it befell that when from the reverie of dejection into which he had fallen he was suddenly aroused by the thud of hoofs, he looked up to find two mounted men barring the road some ten yards in front of him. Their attitude was unmistakable, and it crossed poor Kenneth's mind that he was beset by robbers. But a second glance showed him their red cloaks and military steel caps, and he knew them for soldiers of the Parliament.

Hearing the beat of hoofs behind him, he looked over his shoulder to see four other troopers closing rapidly down upon him. Clearly he was the object of their attention. He had been a fool not to have perceived this earlier, and his heart misgave him, for all that had he paused to think he must have realized that he had nothing to fear, and that in this some mistake must lie.

" Halt ! " came the deep voice of the sergeant, who, with a trooper, held the road in front.

Kenneth drew up within a yard of them, conscious that the man's dark eyes were scanning him sharply from beneath his morion.

" Who are you, sir ? " the bass voice demanded.

Alas for human vanity ! Even Kenneth, who never yet had achieved aught for the cause he served, grew of a sudden chill to think that this sergeant might recognize his name for one that he had heard before associated with deeds performed on the King's behalf.

For a second he hesitated ; then—

" Blount," he stammered, " Jasper Blount."

" Verily," sneered the sergeant, " it almost seemed you had forgotten it." And from that sneer Kenneth gathered with fresh dread that the fellow mistrusted him.

" Whence are you, Master Blount ? "

Again Kenneth hesitated. Then, recalling Ashburn's high favour with the Parliament, and seeing that it could but advance his cause to state the true sum of his journey—

" From Castle Marleigh," he replied.

" Faith, sir, you seem still in doubt. Whither are you travelling ? "

" To London."

" On what errand ? " The sergeant's questions fell swift as sword-strokes.

" With letters for Colonel Pride."

The reply, delivered more boldly than Kenneth had spoken hitherto, was not without effect.

" From whom are these letters ? "

" From Mr. Joseph Ashburn, of Castle Marleigh."

" Produce them."

With trembling fingers Kenneth complied. This the sergeant observed as he took the package.

" What ails you, man ? " quoth he.

" Naught, sir—'tis the cold."

The sergeant scanned the package and its seal. In a measure it was a passport, and he was brought to the conclusion that this man was indeed the messenger he represented himself. Certainly he had not the air nor the bearing of him for whom they waited, nor did the sergeant think that their quarry would have armed himself with a dummy package against such a chance. And yet the sergeant was not master after all, and did he let this fellow pursue his journey, he might reap trouble for it hereafter ; whilst likewise if he detained him, Colonel Pride, he knew, was not an over-patient man. He was still debating what course to take, and had turned to his companion with the muttered question—

" What think you, Peter ? " when by his precipitancy Kenneth ruined his slender chance of being permitted to depart.

" I pray you, sir, now that you know my errand, suffer me to pass on."

There was an eager tremor in his voice that the sergeant mistook for fear. He noted it, and remembering the boy's hesitancy in answering his earlier questions, he decided upon his course of action.

" We shall not delay your journey, sir," he answered, eyeing Kenneth sharply, " and as your way must lie through Waltham, I will but ask you to ride with us thus far, so that there you may answer any questions our captain may have to ask."

" But, sir——"

" No more, master courier." The sergeant beckoned a trooper to his side, and muttered an order.

As the man withdrew they wheeled their horses, and at a sharp word of command Kenneth rode on towards Waltham between the sergeant and a trooper.

CHAPTER XX

THE CONVERTED HOGAN

Night black and impenetrable had set in ere Kenneth and his escort clattered over the greasy stones of Waltham's High Street, and drew up in front of "The Crusader Inn."

The door stood wide and hospitable, and a warm shaft of light fell from it and set a glitter upon the wet street. Avoiding the common-room, the sergeant led Kenneth through the inn-yard, and into the hostelry by a side entrance. He urged the youth along a dimly-lighted passage. On a door at the end of this he knocked, then, lifting the latch, he ushered Kenneth into a roomy, oak-panelled chamber.

At the far end a huge fire burnt cheerfully, and with his back to it, his feet planted wide apart upon the hearth, stood a powerfully built man of medium height, whose youthful face and uprightness of carriage assorted ill with the grey of his hair, pronouncing that greyness premature. He seemed all clad in leather, for where his jerkin stopped his boots began. A cuirass and feathered headpiece lay in a corner, whilst on the table Kenneth espied a broad-brimmed hat, a sword, and a brace of pistols.

As the boy's eyes came back to the burly figure on the hearth, he was puzzled by a familiar, intangible something in the fellow's face.

He was racking his mind to recall where last he had seen it, when with slightly elevated eyebrows and a

look of recognition in his somewhat prominent blue
eyes—

" Soul of my body," exclaimed the man in surprise,
" Master Stewart, as I live."

" Stuart ! " cried both sergeant and trooper in a
gasp, starting to scan their prisoner's face.

At that the burly captain broke into a laugh.

" Not the young man Charles Stuart," said he ;
" no, no. Your captive is none so precious. It is only
Master Kenneth Stewart, of Bailienochy."

" Then it is not even our man," grumbled the
soldier.

" But Stewart is not the name he gave," cried the
sergeant. " Jasper Blount he told me he was called.
That needs explaining, Captain. It seems that I was
well advised to bring him along."

The captain made a gesture of disdain. In that
moment Kenneth recognized him. He was Harry
Hogan—the man whose life Galliard had saved in
Penrith.

" Bah, a worthless capture, Beddoes," he said.

" Maybe not," retorted the sergeant. " He carries
papers which he states are from Joseph Ashburn of
Castle Marleigh, to Colonel Pride. Colonel Pride's
name is on the package, but may not that be to make
game of us ? Why else did he say he was called
Blount ? "

Hogan's brows were knit.

" So, so ! Ha ! Remove his weapons, and search
him."

With affected calm Kenneth suffered them to carry
out this order. Inwardly he boiled at the delay, and

cursed himself for having so needlessly given the name
of Blount. But for that Hogan must have straightway dismissed him. However, it was not likely that
they would long detain him. Finding nothing upon
him but Ashburn's letter, surely they would let him
go at once.

But their search was a very thorough one. They
drew off his boots, and wellnigh stripped him naked,
submitting each article of his apparel to careful
examination. At length it was over, and Hogan held
Ashburn's package, turning it over in his hands, his
brow thoughtful.

"Surely, sir, you will now allow me to leave," cried
Kenneth. "I assure you my business is of the greatest
urgency, and unless I am in London by midnight I
shall be too late."

"Too late for what?" quoth Hogan.

"I—I don't know."

"Oh?" The Irishman's laugh was not quite
pleasant.

Now it happened that Colonel Pride and he were
on anything but the best of terms. The colonel
accounted him—with reason—a godless soldier of
fortune bound to the Parliament's cause by no interest
beyond that of gain; and, himself a zealot, Colonel
Pride had with distasteful frequency shown Hogan
the quality of his feelings. That Hogan did not fear
him was because it was not in Hogan's nature to
fear any man. But he realized that it might be useful
as well as sweet to find a flaw in the old Puritan's
armour. If the package were harmless, his having
opened it was still a matter that the discharge of his

duty would sanction. Thus he reasoned, and he resolved to break the seal and make himself master of the contents of that letter.

Hogan's unpleasant laugh startled Kenneth, suggesting that perhaps, after all, the delay was by no means at an end, that Hogan suspected him of something—he could not think of what.

Then in a flash an idea came to him.

"May I speak to you privately for a moment, Captain Hogan?" He spoke in such a tone of importance—imperiousness, almost—that the Irishman was impressed. He scented disclosures.

"Faith, you may if you have aught to tell me," and he signed to Beddoes and his companion to withdraw.

"Now, Master Hogan," Kenneth began resolutely as soon as they were alone, "I ask you to let me go my way unmolested. Too long already has the stupidity of your followers unjustly detained me. That I reach London by midnight is to me a matter of the gravest moment, and you shall let me."

"Soul of my body, Mr. Stewart, it's the fierce spirit ye've acquired since last we parted."

"In your place I should leave our last parting unmentioned, master turncoat."

The Irishman's eyebrows went up.

"Like that, is it? Faith, now, I don't care for your tone——"

"You'll care for it less before all's done if you detain me." He was rashly confident that he held the whip. "What would your saintly, crop-eared friends say if they knew as much of your past history as I do?"

"Sure now, it's a matter for conjecture," said Hogan.

"How do you think they would welcome the story of the roystering rake and profligate who deserted the army of King Charles because they were about to hang him for murder?"

"Ah! How, indeed?" sighed Hogan.

"What manner of reputation, think you that, for a captain of the godly army of the Parliament?"

"Och! The devil of a reputation, to be sure," confessed Hogan with humility.

"And now, Captain Hogan," Kenneth wound up loftily, "if you'll return me that package you can be rid of me before I sow the mischief that'll bring you a crop of hemp."

Hogan stared into the lad's flushed face with a look of whimsical astonishment, and for a brief spell there was silence between them. Slowly then, with his eyes still fixed upon Kenneth's, the captain unsheathed a dagger. The boy drew back, with a sudden cry of alarm. Hogan's laugh was like the neigh of a horse as he ran the blade under the seal of Ashburn's letter.

"Och! Don't be afraid, now," he said pleasantly. "There's no thought of hurting you in my mind at all." He paused in the act of raising the seal. "Lest you should treasure uncomfortable delusions, dear Master Stewart, let me be reminding you that I am an Irishman—not a fool. Were ye thinking my fame so poor a thing that when I left the beggarly army of King Charles for that of the Parliament, I wasn't after realizing how at any moment I might come face to face with someone who had heard of my old exploits, and would denounce me ? You don't find me masquerading under a false name. I am here, sir, as Harry Hogan, a sometime follower of the Egyptian Pharaoh, Charles Stuart ; an erstwhile besotted, blinded soldier in the army of the Amalekite ; a whilom erring malignant, but converted by a crowning mercy into a zealous, faithful servant of Israel. There were vouchsafings and upliftings, and the devil knows what else, when this stray lamb was gathered to the fold.

" Now, Mr. Stewart, you may tell them what you will, and, faith, it'll be nothing to what they'll tell you in return, to show you how signally the light of grace hath been shed upon a scoundrel."

He laughed again, and broke the seal at last. Kenneth, crestfallen and abashed, watched him, without attempting further interference.

" It's better advised you would have been, young sir, had you been less hasty and anxious. It is a fatal fault of youth's. But time—if, indeed, you live—will be curing you. Your anxiety about this package is my warrant for opening it."

Kenneth sneered at the man's conclusions, and, shrugging his shoulders, turned away.

" Perhaps when you have read it, you will realize how conceit may also lead a man into fatal errors. Perhaps, too, you will be able to satisfy Colonel Pride for tampering with his letters."

But Hogan never heeded him. He had unfolded the sheet, and at the first words he beheld, a frown contracted his brows. As he read on the frown deepened, and when he had done, an oath escaped him.

"God's life!" He raised his eyes, and let them rest long and searchingly upon Kenneth, who gave him back stare for stare.

"What—what is it?" the lad asked at last.

But Hogan never answered him. He strode past him to the door, and flung it wide.

"Beddoes!" he called. A step sounded in the passage, and the sergeant appeared. "Have you a trooper there?"

"There is Peter, who rode with me."

"Let him look to this fellow. Tell him to set him under lock and bolt here in the inn until I shall want him, and tell him that he shall answer for him with his neck."

Kenneth drew back in alarm.

"Sir—Captain Hogan—will you explain——"

"Explain, is it? Marry, you shall have explanations to spare before morning, or I'm a fool. But ye've no cause for fear. There's no harm intended you. Take him away, Beddoes; then come back to me, here."

When Beddoes returned, he found Hogan seated in the leathern arm-chair, with Ashburn's letter spread before him on the table.

"Was I right after all in my suspicions, Captain?" ventured the sergeant complacently.

"It's more than right you were, Beddoes; you were heaven-inspired. It is no State matter that you have chanced upon, but one that closely touches a man in whom I am interested."

The sergeant's eyes were full of questions, but Hogan enlightened him no further.

"You will ride back to your post at once," he ordered. "Should Lord Oriel fall into your hands, as we hope, you will send him to me. But you will continue to patrol the road, and demand the business of all comers. There's a man named Sir Crispin Galliard, who should be riding this way soon. You'll detain him and bring him to me. He is a tall, lank man——"

"Faith, I know him, sir," Beddoes interrupted. "The Tavern Knight they called him in the malignant army—a roaring, dissolute brawler. I saw him in Worcester when he was taken after the fight."

Hogan frowned. The righteous Beddoes knew more than was convenient. "That is the man," he answered shortly. "Go now, and see that he does not slip past you. I have great and urgent need of him."

Beddoes' eyes were opened in surprise.

"He may be possessed of information I'm needing," Hogan explained. "Away with you, man."

When alone, Harry Hogan turned his arm-chair sideways towards the fire. He filled a pipe—for in his foreign campaigning he had acquired the habit of tobacco smoking—stretched his sinewy legs across a second chair, and composed himself for meditation. An hour went by; the host looked in to see if the captain required anything. Another hour sped on, and the captain dozed.

He awoke with a start. The fire had burned low, and the hands of the huge clock in the corner pointed to midnight. From the passage came to him the sound of steps and raised voices.

Before he could rise, the door was flung wide, and a tall, gaunt man was hustled across the threshold by two soldiers. His head was bare, and his hair wet and dishevelled. His doublet was torn and his shoulder bleeding, whilst his empty scabbard hung like a limp tail behind him.

"We have brought him, Captain," one of the men announced.

"Aye, you crop-eared, psalm-whining cuckolds, you've brought me, damn you," said Sir Crispin, and his eyes rolled fiercely.

As they came to rest on Hogan's impassive face, he abruptly stemmed his invective.

The Irishman rose, and looked past him at the troopers. "Leave us," he commanded shortly.

He remained standing by the hearth until the footsteps of his men had died away. Then he crossed the chamber, passed Crispin without a word, and quietly locked the door. That done, he turned, a broad smile on his tanned face, holding out his hand.

"Glory be, Cris! At last I may thank you and maybe repay some of the service you did me on a night at Penrith."

CHAPTER XXI

THE MESSAGE KENNETH BORE

In amazement Crispin took the outstretched hand of his old fellow-roysterer.

" Oddslife," he said, " if to have me waylaid, dragged from my horse, and pricked by those lobster-coated sons of dogs of yours be your manner of expressing gratitude, I'd as lief you had let me go unthanked."

But Hogan was solemn. " And yet, Cris, I dare swear you'll not think so before another hour is sped. Ough, man, how cold you are ! There's a bottle of strong waters yonder——"

The Roundhead captain turned aside, took up the black-jack and poured half a glass of its contents.

" Drink, man," he said briefly, and Crispin, nothing loath, obeyed him.

Next Hogan drew the torn and sodden doublet from his guest's back, pushed a chair over to the table, and bade him sit. Again, nothing loath, Crispin did as he was bidden. He was stiff from cold and riding, and so with a sigh of satisfaction he settled himself down and stretched his long legs.

Hogan slowly took the seat opposite to him, and coughed. He was at a loss how to open the parlous subject, how to communicate to Crispin the amazing news upon which he had stumbled.

" 'Slife, Hogan," laughed Crispin dreamily, " I little thought it was to you those mannerless crop-ears carried me with such rudeness. I little thought, indeed, ever to see you again. But it seems you've prospered, you knave, since the night you left Penrith."

And he turned his head the better to survey the Irishman.

"Och! After a fashion," Hogan agreed. "My life's just a version of the parable of the fatted son and the prodigal calf, so it is. They tell me, now, there is greater joy in heaven over the repentance of a sinner than—than—— Plague on it! How does it go?"

"Than over the downfall of a saint?" suggested Crispin.

"I'll swear that's never the text, but any of my troopers could quote it you; there's never a man of them that isn't an incarnate Church militant." He paused, whilst Crispin laughed softly. Then abruptly: "And so you are riding to London, are you?" said he.

"How should you know that?"

"Faith, it's nothing to what else I know. I can even tell you to what house you ride, and on what errand. You are for the sign of 'The Anchor' in Thames Street, for news of your son, whom Joseph Ashburn tells you is alive."

Crispin sat bolt upright, in amazement and suspicion.

"You are well informed, you gentlemen of the Parliament."

"On the matter of your errand," the Irishman returned quietly, "it's much better informed I am than yourself. Shall I tell you who it is lives at the sign of 'The Anchor'—not whom you have been told lives there, but who really dwells in that house?"

Hogan paused as though awaiting some reply; then softly he answered his own question—" Colonel Pride."

For the moment the name awoke no recollection, conveyed no meaning to Crispin.

" And who the devil may Colonel Pride be ? "

Hogan was visibly disappointed.

" A certain powerful and vindictive member of the Rump, whose son you killed at Worcester."

This time the shaft went home. Galliard sat forward in his chair, his colour darkening.

" 'Slife, Hogan, you'll not mean that Joseph Ashburn was betraying me into that man's hands ? "

" You have said it."

" But——"

Crispin stopped short. His face had become ashen. He sank back again in his chair, and setting both hands upon the table before him, looked straight at Hogan.

" But, my son, Hogan, my son ? " His voice was piteous. " Oh, God in heaven ! " he cried in sudden passion. " What hell's work is this ? "

Behind his pale lips his teeth were chattering. His hands shook as he held them, still clenched, before him. Then, in a dull, concentrated voice—

" Hogan," he vowed, his face distorted, " I'll kill him for it. Fool, blind, pitiful fool that I am."

" Wait, Cris," said Hogan, laying a hand upon his arm. " It is not all false. Joseph Ashburn sought, it is true, to betray you into the hands of Colonel Pride, sending you to the sign of ' The Anchor ' with the assurance that there you should have news of your son. That was false; yet not all false. Your son does live; and at the sign of 'The Anchor' it is likely you would have had the news of him you sought. But that news would have come too late to profit you."

Mastering himself by an effort, and in a voice that was oddly shaken—

"Hogan," cried Crispin, "you are torturing me! What is that you really know?"

The Irishman brought out Ashburn's letter.

"My men," said he, "are patrolling the roads in wait for a malignant that's wanted by the Parliament. We had news that he is making for Harwich, in the hope maybe of finding a vessel to carry him to France, and we expect that he will ride this way. Three hours ago a young man unable clearly to account for himself rode into our patrol, and was brought to me. He was the bearer of a letter to Colonel Pride from Joseph Ashburn. He had given my sergeant a wrong name, and betrayed such anxiety to be gone that I accounted his errand suspicious, and broke the seal of that letter. You may be after thanking God, Cris, every night of your life that I did."

"Was this young man Kenneth Stewart?" asked Crispin.

"It was."

"Damn the lad," he began. Then he checked. "No, no. I've little cause to curse him. I have done him harm enough. I can hardly blame him for seeking to be quits."

"The lad," returned Hogan, "must be himself a dupe. He can have had no suspicion of the message he carried. Let me be reading it to you ; it will make all clear."

Hogan drew a taper nearer, spread the paper upon the table, smoothed it out, and read—

" ' HONOURED SIR,—The bearer of the present should, if he rides well, outstrip another messenger I have despatched to you upon a fool's errand, with a letter addressed to one Mr. Lane at the sign of "The Anchor." The bearer of that other letter is the notorious malignant, Crispin Galliard, by whose hand your son was slain under your very eyes at Worcester, whose capture I know that you warmly desire and with whom I doubt not you will know how to deal. To us he has been a source of no little molestation ; his liberty, in fact, is a perpetual menace to our lives. For some eighteen years this Galliard has believed dead a son that my cousin bore him. News of this son, whom I have just informed him lives—as indeed he does—is the lure by which I am drawing him into your net. Fore-warned by the present, I make no doubt you will prepare to receive him fittingly. But before that justice which he escaped at Worcester be meted out to him at Tyburn or on Tower Hill, I would have you give him that news touching his son which I am sending him to you to receive. Inform him, sir, that his son, Jocelyn Marleigh——' "

Hogan paused, and shot a furtive glance at Galliard. The knight was leaning forward now, his eyes strained, his forehead beaded with perspiration, and his breathing heavy.

" Read on," he begged hoarsely.

" ' His son, Jocelyn Marleigh,' " Hogan resumed, " ' is the bearer of this letter, the man whom he has injured and who detests him, the man with whom he has, by a curious chance, been in much close association, and whom he has known as Kenneth Stewart.' "

" What ! " gasped Crispin. Then with sudden vigour, " Oh, 'tis a lie," he cried, " a fresh invention of that lying scoundrel, a device to torture me."

Hogan held up his hand.

" There is a little more," he said, and continued—

" ' Should he doubt this, bid him look closely into the lad's face, and ask him, after he has scrutinized it, what image it evokes. Should he still doubt thereafter, thinking the likeness to which he has been singularly blind to be no more than a freak of chance, bid them show him the lad's right foot. It bears a mark that I think should convince him. For the rest, honoured sir, I beg you to keep all information touching his parentage from the boy himself, wherein I have weighty ends to serve. Within a day or two of your receipt of this letter, I look to have the honour of waiting upon you. In the meanwhile, honoured sir, believe me that while I am, I am your obedient servant,

JOSEPH ASHBURN.' "

Across the narrow table the two men's glances met —Hogan's full of concern and pity, Crispin's charged

with horror. A little while they sat without speech
or movement, then Crispin rose slowly to his feet,
and with steps uncertain as a drunkard's crossed to
the window. He pushed it open, and let the icy wind
upon his face and head, unconscious of its sting.
Moments passed, during which the knight went over
the last few months of his turbulent life, since his
first meeting at Perth with Kenneth Stewart. He
recalled how strangely and unaccountably he had been
drawn to the boy when first he beheld him in the castle
yard, and how, owing to a feeling for which he could
not account, since the lad's character had little that
might commend him to such a man as Crispin, he had
contrived that Kenneth should serve in his company.
He recalled how at first—and often afterwards even
—he had sought to win the boy's affection, despite
the fact that there was naught in the boy that he
truly admired, and much that he deplored. Was it
possible that these his feelings were dictated by
Nature to his unconscious mind? It must indeed be
so, and the written words of Joseph Ashburn to
Colonel Pride were true. Kenneth was indeed his son.
The conviction was upon him. He conjured up the
lad's face, and a cry of discovery escaped him. How
blind he had been not to have seen before the likeness
of Alice—his poor, butchered girl-wife of eighteen
years ago. How dull never before to have realized
that this likeness it was which had drawn him to the
boy.

He was calm again, and in his calm he sought to
analyse his thoughts, and he was shocked to find how
far they were from glad. He yearned—as he had

yearned that night in Worcester—for the lad's affection, and yet, for all his yearning, he realized that with the conviction that Kenneth was his offspring came a sense of bitter disappointment. He was not such a son as the knight would have had him. In horror he put the thought aside. The craven hands that had reared the lad had warped his nature ; he would guide it henceforth ; he would straighten it out into a nobler shape. Then he smiled bitterly to himself. What manner of man was he to train a youth to lofty and noble ways ?—he, a debauched ruffler with a nickname for which, had he any sense of shame, he would have blushed ! Again he remembered the lad's disposition towards himself ; but this, he thought, he hoped, he knew that he would now be able to overcome.

He closed the window, and turned to face his companion. He was himself again, and calm, for all that his face was haggard.

" Where is the boy ? "

" I have detained him here. Will you see him ? "

" At once, Hogan. At once. I am convinced."

The Irishman went to open the door, and called an order to the trooper waiting in the passage.

Whilst they waited they stood with no word uttered between them. At last steps sounded in the corridor, and Kenneth was rudely thrust into the room. Hogan signed to the trooper, who closed the door and withdrew.

Crispin advanced a step and paused, his eyes devouring the lad and receiving in exchange a glance charged with a malevolence that at once found expression.

"I might have known, sir, that you were not far away," he exclaimed bitterly, forgetting for the moment how he had left Crispin behind him on the previous night. "I might have guessed that my detention was your work."

"Why should you?" asked Crispin quietly, his eyes scanning the lad's face with a hungry look.

"Because it is your cursed way to work my ruin in all things. Not content with involving me in your foul schemes at Castle Marleigh, you must needs cross my path again when I am about to make amends, and so blight my last chance. My God, sir, am I never to be rid of you? What harm have I done you?"

A spasm of pain, like a ripple over water, crossed the knight's swart face.

"If you but consider, Kenneth," he said, speaking very humbly, "you will see how unjust you are. Since when have I, Galliard, served the Parliament, that Roundhead troopers should do my bidding? As for what happened at Sheringham you are over-hard with me. It was a compact we made, and but for which, you forget that you had been hanged three weeks ago."

"Would to Heaven that I had been," the boy burst out, "sooner than pay such a price for keeping my wretched life!"

"As for my presence here," Crispin continued, leaving the outburst unheeded, "it has naught to do with your detention."

"You lie!"

Hogan caught his breath with a sharp hiss, and a

dead silence followed. That silence struck terror into Kenneth's heart. He encountered Crispin's eye bent upon him with a look he could not fathom, and much would he now have given to recall the two words that had burst from him in the heat of his rage. He remembered the unscrupulous, deadly character attributed to the man at whom he had flung them, and in his timid fancy he already saw payment demanded. Already he pictured himself lying cold and stark in the streets of Waltham with a sword-wound through his middle. His face went grey and his lips trembled.

When Galliard spoke at last, the mildness of his tone filled Kenneth with a new dread. In his experience of Crispin's ways he had come to look upon mildness as the man's most dangerous phase.

"You are mistaken. I spoke the truth; it is a habit of mine—perhaps the only gentlemanly habit left me. I tell you again that I am not accountable for your detention. I arrived here half an hour ago, as the Captain will inform you, and I was conducted hither by force, having been seized by his men, even as you were seized. No," he added, with a sigh, "it was not my hand that detained you; it was the hand of Fate." Then suddenly changing his voice to a more vehement key, "Do you know on what errand you rode to London?" he demanded. "To betray your father into the hands of his enemies; to deliver him up to the hangman."

Kenneth's eyes grew wide; his mouth fell open. Dully, uncomprehendingly, he met Sir Crispin's sad gaze.

"My father!" he said at last in a hushed voice. "Sir, what is it you mean? My father has been dead these ten years. I scarce remember him."

Crispin's lips moved, but no word did he utter. Then with a gesture of despair he turned to Hogan, who stood apart, a silent witness.

"My God, Hogan," he cried. "How shall I tell him?"

The Irishman answered the appeal by turning to Kenneth.

"The fact is, sir, you've been misled in the matter of your parentage," he bluntly told him. "Alan Stewart, of Bailienochy, was not your father."

Kenneth looked from one to the other of them.

"Not my father? Sirs, is this a jest?" Remarking at length the solemnity of their countenances, he stopped short. Crispin came close up to him, and placed a hand upon his shoulder. The boy shrank under the touch, and again an expression of pain crossed the ruffler's face.

"Do you recall, Kenneth," he said slowly, almost sorrowfully, "the story that I told you that night in Worcester, when we sat waiting for dawn and the hangman?"

"What's that to the matter?"

"Do you remember its details? Do you remember that I told you how, when I swooned under the stroke of Joseph Ashburn's sword, the last words I heard were those in which he bade his brother slit the throat of the babe in the cradle? You were, yourself, present yesternight at Castle Marleigh when Joseph Ashburn told me that Gregory had been mercifully inclined;

that my child had not died ; that if I gave him his life he would restore him to me. You remember ? "

Kenneth nodded. " I remember. Yes." A vague, numbing fear was creeping round his heart. With fascinated eyes he watched the knight's face—drawn and haggard.

" It was a trap that Joseph Ashburn set for me. Yet he did not altogether lie. The child Gregory had indeed spared, and it seems from what I have learned within the last half-hour that he had entrusted his rearing to Alan Stewart, of Bailienochy, seeking afterwards—I take it—to wed the boy to his daughter, so as to make themselves doubly safe ; so that should ever the King come to his own again, they should have the protection of a Marleigh who had served his King."

" You mean," the lad almost whispered, and his accents were unmistakably of horror, " you mean that I am your—— Oh, God, I'll not believe it ! " he cried out, with such sudden passion that Crispin recoiled as if he had been struck. A dull flush crept into his cheeks to fade upon the instant and give place to a pallor, if possible, deeper than before.

" I'll not believe it. I'll not believe it," the boy repeated, as if seeking by that reiteration to shut out a conviction by which he was beset. " I'll not believe it ! " And now his voice had lost its passionate vehemence, and was sunk almost to a moan.

" I found it hard to believe, myself," was Crispin's answer, not entirely without bitterness. " But I have a proof here that seems incontestable, even had I not the proof of your face to which I have been blind these months. Blind with the eyes of my body, at least. The eyes of my soul must have recognized you when first they saw you in Perth. The voice of the blood ordered me then to your side, and though I heard its call, I understood not what it meant. Read this letter, boy—the letter that you were to have carried to Colonel Pride."

With his eyes still fixed in a gaze of stupefaction upon Galliard's face, Kenneth took the paper. Then slowly, involuntarily almost it seemed, he dropped his glance and read. He was long in reading, as though the writing presented difficulties, and his two companions watched him the while, and waited. At last he turned the paper over, and examined seal and superscription as if suspicious that he held a forgery.

But in some subtle mysterious way—that voice of the blood perchance to which Crispin had alluded—he felt conviction stealing down upon his soul. Mechanically he moved across to the table, and sat down. Without a word, and still holding the crumpled letter in his clenched hand, he set his elbows on the table, and, pressing his temples to his palms, he sat there dumb. Within him a volcano raged, and its fires were fed with loathing—loathing for this man whom he had ever hated, yet never as he hated him now, knowing him to be his father. It seemed as if to all the wrongs which Crispin had done him during the months of their acquaintance, he had now added a fresh and culminating wrong by discovering this parentage.

He sat and thought, and his soul grew sick. He

probed for some flaw, sought for some mistake that
might have been made. And yet the more he thought,
the more he dwelt upon his youth in Scotland, the
more convinced was he that Crispin had told him the
truth. Pre-eminent argument of conviction to him
was the desire of the Ashburns that he should marry
Cynthia. Oft he had marvelled that they, wealthy,
and even powerful, selfish and ambitious, should have
chosen him, the scion of an obscure and impoverished
Scottish house, as a bridegroom for their daughter.
The news now before him made their motives clear ;
indeed, no other motive could exist, no other explanation could there be. He was the heir of Castle Marleigh, and the usurpers sought to provide against the
day when another revolution might oust them and
restore the rightful owners.

Some elation his shallow nature felt at realizing this,
but that elation was short-lived, and dashed by the
thought that this ruffler, this debauchee, this drunken,
swearing, roaring Tavern Knight was his father ;
dashed by the knowledge that meanwhile the Parliament was master, and that whilst matters stood so,
the Ashburns could defy—could even destroy him,
did they learn how much he knew ; dashed by the
memory that Cynthia, whom in his poor way—out
of his love for himself—he loved, was lost to him for
all time.

And here, swinging in a circle, his thoughts reverted
to the cause of this—Crispin Galliard, the man who
had betrayed him into yesternight's foul business and
destroyed his every chance of happiness ; the man
whom he hated, and whom, had he possessed the

courage as he was possessed by the desire, he had risen up and slain ; the man that now announced himself his father.

And thinking thus, he sat on in silent, bitter resentment. He started, to feel a hand upon his shoulder, and to hear the voice of Galliard evidently addressing him, yet using a name that was new to him.

" Jocelyn, my boy," the voice trembled. " You have thought, and you have realized—is it not so ? I too thought, and thought brought me conviction that what that paper tells is true."

Vaguely then the boy remembered that Jocelyn was the name the letter gave him. He rose abruptly, and brushed the caressing hand from his shoulder. His voice was hard—possibly the knowledge he had gained told him that he had nothing to fear from this man, and in that assurance his weak soul grew brave and bold and arrogant.

" What I must realize is that I owe you nothing but unhappiness and ruin. By a trick, by a low fraud, you enlisted me into a service that has proved my undoing. Once a cheat always a cheat. What credit in the face of that can I give this paper ? To me it is incredible, nor do I wish to credit it, for though it were true, what then ? What then ? " he repeated, raising his voice into accents of defiance.

Misery and amazement were blended in Galliard's glance.

Hogan, standing squarely upon the hearth, was aware of a desire to kick Master Kenneth, or Master Jocelyn, into the street. His lip curled in ineffable contempt, for his shrewd eyes read to the bottom of the lad's mean soul and saw there clearly writ the confidence that emboldened him to voice that insult to the man he must know for his father. Standing there, he compared the two, marvelling deeply how they came to be sire and son. A likeness he saw now between them, yet a likeness that seemed but to mark the difference. The one harsh, resolute, and manly, for all his reckless living and his misfortunes; the other mild, effeminate, hypocritical, and shifty. He read it not in their countenances alone, but in every line of their figures as they stood, and in his heart he cursed himself for having been the instrument to disclose the relationship in which they stood.

The youth's insolent question was followed by a spell of silence. Crispin could not believe that he had heard aright. At last he stretched out his hands in a gesture almost of supplication—he who throughout his thirty-eight years of life, and despite the misfortunes that had been his, had never yet stooped to plead from any man.

" Jocelyn," he cried, and the pain in his voice must have melted a heart of steel, " try to be less hard. Have you forgotten the story of my miserable life, the story that I told you in Worcester ? Can you not understand how suffering may destroy all that is worthy in a man ; how the forgetfulness of the wine-cup may come to be his only consolation ; the hope of vengeance his only motive for living on, withholding him from self-destruction ? Can you not picture such a life, and can you not pity and forgive much of the wreck that it may make of a man once honourable ? "

Pleadingly he looked into the lad's face. It remained cold and unmoved.

"I understand," he continued brokenly, "that I am not such a man as any lad might welcome for a father. But you who know what my life has been, Jocelyn, you can surely find some gentleness for me in your heart. I had naught that was good or wholesome to live for, Jocelyn ; naught to curb the moods that sent me along evil ways to seek forgetfulness and reparation.

"But from to-night, Jocelyn, my life in you must find a new interest, a new motive. For your sake, Jocelyn, I shall strive again to become what I was, so that you may have no cause to blush for your father."

Still the lad stood silent.

"Jocelyn ! My God, do I talk in vain ? " cried the wretched man. "Have you no heart, boy ? "

At last the youth spoke. He was not moved. The agony of this strong man, the broken pleading of one whom he had ever known arrogant and strong had no power to touch a mind, consumed as it was by the contemplation of his undoing—magnified a hundredfold—which this man had wrought.

"You have ruined my life," was all he said.

"I will rebuild it, Jocelyn. I have friends in France —friends high in power who lack neither the means nor the will to aid me. You are a soldier, Jocelyn."

"As much a soldier as I'm a saint," said Hogan to himself.

"Together we will find service in the armies of King Louis," Crispin pursued. "I promise it. Service in which there is honour to be won. There we will abide until this England shakes herself out of her rebellious nightmare. Then, when the King shall come to his own, Castle Marleigh will be ours again. Trust me, Jocelyn." Again his arms went out appealingly—" Jocelyn—my son ! "

But the boy made no move to take the outstretched hands, gave no sign of relenting. His mind nurtured its resentment—cherished it indeed.

" And Cynthia ? " he asked coldly.

Crispin's hands fell to his sides ; they grew clenched and his eyes lighted of a sudden.

" I had forgotten ! I understand you now. Yes, I dealt sorely with you there, and you have the right to be resentful. What, after all, am I to you—what can I be to you compared with her whose image fills your soul ? What is aught in the world to a man, compared with the woman on whom his heart is set ? Do I not know it ? Have I not suffered for it ?

" But mark me, Jocelyn "—and he straightened himself suddenly—" even in this, that which I have done I will undo. As I have robbed you of your mistress, so will I win her back for you. I swear it. And when that is done, when thus every harm I have caused you is repaired, then, Jocelyn, perhaps you will come to look upon me with less repugnance and less resentment."

" You promise much, sir," quoth the boy, with an ill-repressed sneer. " Too much. Far more than you can accomplish."

Hogan grunted audibly. Crispin drew himself up, erect, lithe, and supple—a figure to inspire confidence in the most despairing. He placed a hand, nervous, and strong as steel, upon the boy's shoulder, and the clutch of his fingers made Jocelyn wince.

"Low though your father be fallen," said he sternly, "you may believe that he has never yet broken his word. I have pledged you mine, and to-morrow I shall set out to perform what I have promised. I shall see you before I start. You will sleep here, will you not?"

Jocelyn shrugged his shoulders.

"It signifies little where I lie."

Crispin smiled sadly, and sighed.

"You have no faith in me yet. But I shall earn it. Be sure I shall. Hogan, can you find him quarters?"

Hogan replied gruffly that there was the room the boy had already been confined in, and that he could lie in it for the night if he so chose. And deeming that there was nothing to be gained by waiting, he at once led the youth from the room and down the passage. At the foot of the stairs the Irishman paused, and raised the taper aloft so that its light might fall full upon the face of his companion.

"Were I your father," said he grimly, "I would kick you from one end of Waltham to the other by way of teaching you filial piety! And were you not his son, I would be doing the same by you this minute. You despise your father for a roysterer, for a man of loose ways. Let me, who have seen something of men, and who read you to-night to the very dregs of your contemptible soul, tell you that though you may be his son, you compare with him as an earthworm to a god. Come ! " he ended abruptly. " I will light you to your chamber."

When presently Hogan returned to Crispin, he found the Tavern Knight—that man of iron in whom none had ever seen a trace of fear or weakness—seated with his arms before him on the table, and his face buried in them, sobbing like some poor, weak woman.

CHAPTER XXII

SIR CRISPIN'S UNDERTAKING

THROUGH the long October night Crispin and Hogan sat on, and neither sought his bed. Crispin's quick wits—his burst of grief once over—had been at work to find a way to accomplish that which he had undertaken.

One difficulty confronted him, and until he had mentioned it to Hogan, seemed unsurmountable—he had need of a ship. But in this the Irishman could assist him. He knew of a vessel then at Harwich, whose master was in his debt, which should suit his purpose. Money, however, would be needed. But when Crispin announced that he was master of some hundred Caroluses, Hogan, with a wave of the hand, declared the matter settled. Less than a quarter of that sum would hire the man he knew. This determined, Crispin unfolded his project to Hogan, who laughed at the simplicity of it, for all that inwardly he deplored the risk Sir Crispin must run for the sake of one so unworthy.

"If the maid loves him, the thing is as good as done."

"The maid does not love him; leastways, I fear not."

Hogan was not surprised.

"Why, then, faith, I don't see how it's to be done at all." And the Irishman became grave.

Crispin laughed unpleasantly. Years and misfortune had made him cynical.

" What after all is the love of a maid ? A caprice, a fancy, a thing that may be guided, overcome or compelled as the occasion shall demand. Opportunity is love's parent, Hogan, and given that, any maid may love any man. Cynthia shall love my son."

" To be sure ! But if she doesn't ? If she should be saying nay to your proposals ? There are such women."

" What then ? I shall know how to compel her, and as I find her, so shall I carry her away. It will be none so poor a vengeance on the Ashburns after all." His brow grew clouded. " But not what I had dreamed of, or should have taken had that dog Joseph not cheated me. To forgo it now—after all these years of waiting—is another sacrifice I make to Jocelyn. To serve him I must go cautiously. The girl may fret and fume and stamp, but willy-nilly she shall come away. Once I have her in France, friendless, alone, I make no doubt that she will see the convenience of loving Jocelyn—leastways of marrying him—and thus shall I have more than repaired the injuries I have done him."

The Irishman's broad face was grave ; his reckless, merry eye fixed Galliard with a look of sorrow, and this grey-haired, sinning soldier of fortune, who had never known a conscience, muttered softly—

" It is not a nice thing you contemplate, Cris."

Galliard winced, and his glance fell.

" There is my son," he grumbled, " and in this lies the only way to his heart."

Hogan stretched a hand across the table, to set it upon Crispin's arm.

" Is he worth such a stain upon your honour, Crispin ? "

There was a pause.

" It's a little late in the day, Hogan, for you and me to prate of honour. God knows my honour has worn rather ragged. What matter another splash, another rent in that which is tattered beyond all semblance of its original condition ? "

" I asked you," the Irishman persisted, " whether your son was worth the sacrifice that this ugly deed entails ? "

Crispin shook his arm from the other's grip, and rose abruptly. He crossed to the window, and drew back the curtain.

" Day is breaking," said he gruffly. Then, turning and facing Hogan across the room, " I have pledged my word to Jocelyn," he said. " The way I have chosen is the only one, and I shall follow it. But if your conscience cries out against it, Hogan, I give you back your promise of assistance, and I shall shift alone. I have done so all my life."

Hogan shrugged his massive shoulders, and reached for the bottle of strong waters.

" If it's resolved you are, there is an end to it. My conscience shall not trouble me, and upon what aid I have promised and what more I can give, you may depend. I drink to your undertaking."

Thereafter they discussed the matter of the vessel that Crispin would require, and it was arranged between them that Hogan should send a message to the skipper, bidding him come to Harwich, and there await and place himself at Sir Crispin's orders. For

twenty pounds Hogan thought that he would under-
take to land Sir Crispin in France. The messenger
might be dispatched forthwith, and the *Lady Jane*
should be ready for sea in a couple of days' time.

Before this was determined, the inmates of the
hostelry were astir, and from the inn-yard came to
them the noise of bustle and preparation for the day.

Presently they left the chamber where they had
sat so long, and at the yard pump the Tavern Knight
performed a rude morning toilet. Thereafter, on a
simple fare of herrings and brown ale, they broke their
fast ; and before the meal was done, Kenneth, pale
and worn, with dark circles round the eyes, entered
the common-room, to sit moodily apart. But when
later Hogan went to see to the dispatching of his
messenger, Crispin rose and crossed to him.

Kenneth watched him furtively, without pausing in
his meal. He had spent a very miserable night pondering the future, which looked gloomy enough, and
debating whether—forgetting and ignoring what had
passed—he should return to the genteel poverty of his
Scottish home, or accept the proffered service of this
man who announced himself—and whom he now believed—to be his father. He had considered, but he
was far from having chosen between Scotland and
France, when Crispin now broke in upon him.

" Jocelyn," he said, speaking slowly, almost humbly.
" In an hour's time I shall set out to return to Marleigh
to fulfil my last night's promise to you. How I shall
accomplish it I scarce know as yet ; but be sure that
accomplish it I shall. I have arranged to have a
vessel awaiting me, and within five days—or a week

at the most—I look to cross to France, bearing Cynthia with me."

He paused for some reply, but none came. The boy sat on with an impassive face, his eyes glued to the table but his mind busy enough upon that which his father was pouring into his ear. Presently Crispin continued.

" You will hardly refuse to do as I suggest, Jocelyn. I shall make you the fullest amends if you but obey my directions. You must quit this place as soon as possible, and proceed on your way to London. There you must find a ship to carry you to France, and you will await me at the ' Auberge du Soleil ' at Calais. Is it agreed, Jocelyn ? "

There was a slight pause, and Jocelyn took his resolution. Yet there was still a sullen look in the eyes he lifted to his father's face.

" I have little choice, sir," he made answer. " If you accomplish what you promise, I own that you will have made amends, and I may ask your pardon for my yesternight's want of faith. I shall be at Calais to await you."

Crispin sighed, and for a second his face hardened. That cold, curt acceptance was not the answer for which he had hoped, and for a moment it rose to the lips of this man of fierce and sudden moods to draw back and let the son whom, at the moment he found himself beginning to detest, go his own way, which assuredly would lead him to perdition. But a second's thought was enough to quell that mood.

" I shall not fail you," he said coldly. " Have you money for the journey ? "

The boy flushed as he remembered that little was left of what Joseph Ashburn had given him. Crispin saw the flush, and reading aright its meaning, he drew from his pocket a purse that he had been fingering, and placed it quietly upon the table. "There are twenty Caroluses in that bag. That should suffice to carry you to France. Fare you well until we meet at Calais."

And without giving the boy time to utter thanks that might be unwilling, he turned and quickly left the room.

Within the hour he was in the saddle, and his horse's head was turned northwards once more.

He rode through Newport some three hours later without drawing rein. By the door of " The Raven Inn " stood a travelling carriage, upon which he did not so much as bestow a look.

By the merest thread hangs at times the whole of a man's future life, the destinies even of men as yet unborn. So much may depend indeed upon a glance, that had not Crispin kept his eyes that morning upon the grey road before him, had he chanced to look sideways as he passed " The Raven Inn " at Newport, and seen the Ashburn arms displayed upon the panels of that coach, he would of a certainty have paused. And had he done so, his whole destiny would assuredly have shaped a different course from that which it was unconsciously pursuing.

CHAPTER XXIII

GREGORY'S PENITENCE

JOSEPH'S journey to London was occasioned by a very natural anxiety to assure himself that Crispin was taken in the toils he had so cunningly prepared for him, and that at Castle Marleigh he would trouble them no more. To this end he quitted Sheringham on the day after Crispin's departure.

Not a little perplexed was Cynthia at the topsy-turvydom in which that morning she had found her father's house. Kenneth was gone; he had left in the dead of night, and seemingly in haste and suddenness, since on the previous evening there had been no talk of his departing. Her father was abed with a wound that made him feverish, by which none could tell her how he had come. Their grooms were all sick, and wandered in a dazed and witless fashion about the castle, their faces deadly pale and their eyes lustreless. In the hall she had found a chaotic disorder upon descending, and one of the panels of the wainscot she saw was freshly cracked.

Slowly the idea forced itself upon her mind that there had been brawling the night before, yet was she very far from surmising what could have led to it. Her conclusion was that the men had drunk deep, that in their cups they had waxed quarrelsome, and that swords had been drawn.

Of Joseph then she sought enlightenment, and Joseph lied right handsomely, like the ready-witted knave he was. He offered her a plausible story; a story that played cunningly upon her knowledge of the compact between Kenneth and Sir Crispin.

"You may not know," said he—full well aware that she did know—"that when Galliard saved Kenneth's life at Worcester he exacted from the lad a promise that in return Kenneth should aid him in some vengeful business he had on hand."

Cynthia nodded that she understood or that she knew, and glibly Joseph pursued—

"Last night, when on the point of departing, Sir Crispin, who had drunk over-freely, as is his custom, reminded Kenneth of his plighted word, and demanded of the boy that he should upon the instant go forth with him. Kenneth replied that the hour was over-late to be setting out upon a journey, and he requested Galliard to wait until to-day, when he would be ready to fulfil what he had promised. But Sir Crispin retorted that Kenneth was bound by his oath to go with him when he should require it, and again bade the boy make ready at once. Words ensued between them, the boy insisting upon waiting until to-day, and Sir Crispin insisting upon his getting his boots and cloak and coming with him there and then. More heated grew the argument, till in the end Galliard, being put out of temper, snatched at his sword, and would have spitted the boy had not your father interposed, thereby getting himself wounded. Thereafter, in his drunken lust Sir Crispin went the length of wantonly cracking that panel by way of showing Kenneth what he had to expect unless he obeyed him. At that I intervened, and using my influence, I prevailed upon Kenneth to go with Galliard as he demanded. To this, for all his reluctance, Kenneth ended by consenting, and so they are gone."

By that most glib and specious explanation Cynthia was only half convinced. True, she added a question touching the amazing condition of the grooms, in reply to which Joseph afforded her a part of the truth.

" Sir Crispin sent them some wine, and they drank to his departure so heartily that they are not rightly sober yet."

Wondering, Cynthia repaired to her father.

Now Gregory had not agreed with Joseph what tale they were to offer Cynthia, for it had never crossed his dull mind that in the disorder of the hall and the absence of Kenneth she might find matter for explanation. And so when she touched upon his wound, like the blundering fool he was, he must needs let his tongue wag upon a tale which if no less imaginative than Joseph's, was vastly its inferior in plausibility and had yet the quality of differing from it totally in substance.

" Plague on that dog, your lover, Cynthia," he growled from the mountain of pillows that propped him. " If he should come to wed my daughter after pinning me to the wainscot of my own hall may I be for ever damned."

" How ? " quoth she. " Do you say that Kenneth did it ? "

" Aye, did he. He ran at me ere I could draw, like the coward he is, sink him, and had me through the shoulder in the twinkling of an eye."

Here was something beyond her understanding. What were they concealing from her? She set her wits to the discovery and plied her father with another question.

"How came you to quarrel?"

"How? 'Twas—'twas concerning you, child," replied Gregory at random, and unable to think of a likelier motive.

"How, concerning me?"

"Leave me, Cynthia," he groaned in despair. "Go, child, I am sorely wounded. I have the fever, girl. Go; let me sleep."

"But tell me, father, what passed."

"Unnatural child," whined Gregory feebly, "will you plague a sick man with questions? Would you keep him from the sleep that may means recovery to him?"

"Father, dear," she murmured softly, "if I thought it was as you say, I would leave you. But you make it plain that you are but attempting to conceal something from me—something that I should know, that I must know. Bethink you that it is of the man I am to marry that you have spoken."

By a stupendous effort Gregory shaped a story that to him seemed likely.

"Well, then, since know you must," he answered, "this is what befell: we had all drunk overdeep—to our shame do I confess it—and growing tender-hearted for you and bethinking me of your professed distaste to Kenneth's suit, I told him that for all the results that were likely to attend his sojourn at Castle Marleigh, he might as well bear Sir Crispin company

in his departure. He flared up at that, and demanded
of me that I should read him my riddle. Faith, I
did, by telling him that we were like to have snow
on midsummer's day ere he became your husband.
That so angered him, being as he was all addled with
wine and ripe for any madness, that he sprang up
and drew on me there and then. The others sought to
get between us, but he was over-quick, and before I
could do more than rise from the table his sword was
through my shoulder and into the wainscot at my
back. After that it was clear he could not remain
here, and I demanded that he should leave upon the
instant. Himself he was nothing loath, for he realized
his folly, and he misliked the gleam of Joseph's eye—
which can be very wicked upon occasion. Indeed,
but for my intercession Joseph had laid him stark."

That both her uncle and her father were lying to
her—the one cunningly, the other stupidly—was now
plain enough, and vaguely uneasy was Cynthia to
learn the truth. Later that day the castle was busy
with the bustle of Joseph's departure, and this again
was a matter that puzzled her.

" Whither do you journey, uncle ? " she asked of
him as he was in the act of leaving.

" To London, sweet cousin," was his brisk reply.
" I am, it seems, becoming a very vagrant in my old
age. Have you commands for me ? "

" What is it you look to do in London ? "

" There, child, let that be for the present. I will
tell you perhaps when I return. The door, Stephen."

She watched his departure with uneasy eyes and
uneasy heart. A fear pervaded her that in all that

had befallen, in all that was befalling still—whatever it might be—some evil was at work, and an evil that had Sir Crispin for its scope. She had neither reason nor evidence from which to draw this inference. It was no more than instinct, a presage of ill.

Her apprehensions urged her to seek what information she could on every hand, but without success. From none could she cull the merest scrap of evidence to assist her.

On the morrow, however, she had information as prodigal as it was unexpected, and from the unlikeliest of sources—her father himself. Chafing at his inaction and lured into indiscretions by the subsiding of the pain of his wound, Gregory quitted his bed and came below that night to sup with his daughter. As his wont had been for years, he drank freely. That done, alive to the voice of his conscience, and seeking to drown its loud-tongued cry, he drank more freely still, so that in the end his henchman, Stephen, was forced to carry him to bed.

This Stephen had grown grey in the service of the Ashburns, and amongst much valuable knowledge that he had amassed was a skill in dealing with wounds and a wide understanding of the ways of healing them. This knowledge made him realize how unwise at such a season was Gregory's debauch, and he reproachfully wagged his head over his master's state of stupor.

Stephen's fears concerning him were realized when upon the morrow Gregory awoke on fire with the fever. They summoned a leech from Sheringham, and this cunning knave, with a view to adding importance to the cure he was come to effect, and which in reality presented no alarming difficulty, shook his head with ominous gravity, and whilst promising to do all that his skill permitted, spoke of a clergyman to help Gregory make his peace with God. For the leech had no cause to suspect that the whole of the Sacred College might have found the task beyond its powers.

At this sudden prospect of death terror took Gregory in its grip. How could he die with such a load as that which he carried upon his soul? And the leech, seeing how the matter preyed upon his patient's mind, made shift—but too late—to tranquillize him with assurances that he was not really like to die, and that he had but mentioned a parson so that Gregory in any case should be prepared.

The storm once raised, however, was not so easily to be allayed, and the conviction remained with Gregory that his sands were running out, and that the end could be but a matter of days in coming.

Realizing as he did how richly he had earned damnation, his terror grew, and all that day he tossed and turned, now blaspheming, now praying, now weeping. His life had been indeed one protracted course of wrong-doing, and many had suffered by Gregory's evil ways—many a man and many a woman. But as the stars pale and fade when the sun mounts the sky, so too were the lesser wrongs that marked his earthly pilgrimage of sin rendered pale by the greater wrong he had done Roland Marleigh—a wrong which was not ended yet, but whose completion Joseph was

even then working to effect. If only he could save
Roland Marleigh even now in the eleventh hour; if
by some means he could warn him not to repair to
the sign of "The Anchor" in Thames Street. His dis-
ordered mind took no account of the fact that in the
time that was sped since the knight's departure he
should already have reached London.

And so it came about that, consumed at once by the
desire to make confession to whomsoever it might be,
and the wish to attempt yet to avert the crowning
evil of whose planning he was partly guilty inasmuch
as he had tacitly consented to Joseph's schemes,
Gregory called for his daughter. She came readily
enough, hoping for exactly that which was about to
take place, yet fearing sorely that her hopes would
suffer frustration, and that she would learn nothing
from her father.

"Cynthia," he cried, in mingled dread and sorrow,
"Cynthia, my child, I am about to die."

She knew both from Stephen and from the leech
that this was far from his condition. Nevertheless her
filial piety was at that moment a touching sight. She
smoothed his pillows with a gentle grace that was in
itself a caress, even as her soft sympathetic voice
was a caress. She took his hand, and spoke to him
endearingly, seeking to relieve the sombre mood whose
prey he was become, assuring him that the leech had
told her his danger was none so imminent, and that
with quiet and a little care he would be up and about
again ere many days were sped. But Gregory rejected
hopelessly all efforts at consolation.

"I am on my death-bed, Cynthia," he insisted,

"and when I am gone I know not whom there may be to cheer and comfort your lot in life. Kenneth is away on an errand of Joseph's, and it may well betide that he will never again cross the threshold of Castle Marleigh. Unnatural though I may seem, sweetheart, my dying wish is that this may be so."

She looked up in some surprise.

"Father, if that be all that grieves you, I can reassure you. I do not love Kenneth."

"You apprehend me amiss," said he tartly. "Do you recall the story of Sir Crispin Galliard's life that you had from Kenneth on the night of Joseph's return?" His voice shook as he put the question.

"Why, yes. I am not like to forget it, and nightly do I pray," she went on, her tongue outrunning discretion and betraying her feelings for Galliard, "that God may punish those murderers who wrecked his existence."

"Hush, girl," he whispered in a quavering voice. "You know not what you say."

"Indeed I do; and as there is a just God my prayer shall be answered."

"Cynthia," he wailed. His eyes were wild, and the hand that rested in hers trembled violently. In that moment of horror and panic the whole truth burst out of him. "It is against your father and your father's brother that you invoke God's vengeance."

She had been kneeling at his bedside; but now she rose slowly and stood silent for a spell, her eyes seeking his with an awful look that he dared not meet. At last—

"Oh, you rave," she protested, "it is the fever."

"Nay, child, my mind is clear enough, and what I say is true."

"True?" she echoed, no louder than a whisper, her eyes round with horror. "True that you and my uncle are the butchers who slew their cousin, this man's wife, and sought to murder him as well—leaving him for dead? True that you are the thieves who, claiming kinship by virtue of that very marriage, have usurped his estates and this his house during all these years, whilst he himself went outcast, homeless, and destitute? Is that what you ask me to believe?"

A feeble sob was his only answer.

Her face was white to the very lips, and her blue eyes smouldered behind the shelter of her drooping lids. She put her hand to her breast, then to her brow, pushing back the brown hair by a mechanical gesture that was pathetic in the tale of pain it told. For support she was leaning against the wall by the head of his couch. In silence she stood so while you might count to twenty; then with a sudden vehemence revealing the passion of anger and grief that swayed her—

"Why," she cried, "why in God's name do you tell me this?"

"Why?" His utterance was thick, and his eyes, that were grown dull as a snake's, stared straight before him, daring not to meet his daughter's glance. "I tell it you," he said, "because I am dying." And he hoped that the consideration of that dread fact might melt her, and might by pity win her back to him. That she was lost to him he realized.

" I tell you because I am dying," he repeated. " I tell it you because in such an hour I must make confession and repent, that God may have mercy upon my soul. I tell it you, too, because the tragedy begun eighteen years ago is not yet played out, and it may yet be mine to avert the end we had prepared—Joseph and I. Thus perhaps a merciful God will place it in my power to make some reparation. Listen, child. It was against us, as you will have guessed, that Galliard enlisted Kenneth's services, and here on the night of Joseph's return he called upon the boy to fulfil him what he had sworn. The lad had no choice but to obey ; indeed, I forced him to it by attacking him and compelling him to draw, which is how I came by this wound.

" Sir Crispin had of a certainty killed Joseph, but that your uncle stayed his hand by telling him that his son still lives."

" He saved his life by a lie ! That was worthy of him."

" Nay, child, he spoke the truth, and when Joseph offered to restore the boy to him, he had every intention of doing so. But in the moment of writing the superscription to the letter Sir Crispin was to bear to those who had reared the child, Joseph bethought him of a foul scheme for Galliard's final destruction. And so he has sent him to London instead, to a house in Thames Street, where dwells one Colonel Pride, who bears Sir Crispin a heavy grudge, and into whose hands he will be thus delivered. Can anything still be done, Cynthia, to arrest this—to save Sir Crispin from Joseph's snare ? "

" As well might you seek to restore the breath to a dead man," she answered, and her voice was so oddly calm, so cold and bare of expression, that Gregory shuddered to hear it.

" Do not delude yourself," she added. " Sir Crispin will have reached London long before this, and by now Joseph will be well on his way to see that there is no mistake made, and that the life you ruined hopelessly years ago is plucked at last from this unfortunate man. Merciful God ! And I am your daughter ! " she cried. " I have been reared upon the lands that by crime you gained ? Lands that by crime you hold—for they are his ; every stone, every stick that goes to make the place belongs to him, and now he has gone to his death by your contriving."

A moan escaped her, and she covered her face with her hands. A moment she stood rocking there —a fair, lissom plant swept by a gale of ineffable emotion. Then the breath seemed to go all out of her in one great sigh, and Gregory, who dared not look her way, heard the swish of her gown, followed by a thud as she collapsed and lay swooning on the ground.

So disturbed at this was Gregory's spirit that, forgetting his wound, his fever, and the death which he had believed impending, he lowered himself from his couch, and throwing wide the door, bellowed for Stephen. In frightened haste came his henchman to answer the petulant summons, and then went off again as quickly in quest of Cynthia's woman.

Between them they bore the unconscious girl to her chamber, leaving Gregory to curse himself for having been cheated of a confession that it now seemed to him had been unnecessary, since in his newly-found vitality he suspected that death was none so near a thing as that fool of a leech had led him to believe.

CHAPTER XXIV

THE WOOING OF CYNTHIA

CYNTHIA'S swoon was after all but brief. Upon recovering her first act was to dismiss her woman. She had need to be alone—the need of the wounded animal to creep away and hide from its kind. And so alone with her sorrow she remained through that long day.

That her father's condition was grievous she knew to be untrue; so that concerning him there was not even the pity that she might have felt had she believed —as he would have had her believe—that he was dying.

As she pondered the monstrous disclosure he had made, her heart hardened against him, and even as she had asked him whether indeed she was his daughter, so now she vowed to herself that she would be his daughter no longer. She would leave Castle Marleigh, never again to set eyes upon her father, and she hoped that during the little time she must yet remain there —a day, or two at most—she might be spared the ordeal of again meeting a parent for whom not only was respect dead, but who inspired her with just that feeling of horror she must have for any man who confessed himself a murderer and a thief.

She resolved to repair to London to a sister of her mother's, where for her dead mother's sake she would find a haven extended readily when all was disclosed.

At eventide she came at last from her chamber.

She had need of air, need of the balm that nature alone can offer in solitude to poor wounded human souls.

It was a mild and sunny evening, that seemed rather of August than of October, and aimlessly Mistress Cynthia wandered towards the cliffs overlooking Sheringham Hithe. She came to seat herself at last in sad dejection upon the turf, and gazed wistfully seaward, her mind straying now from the sorry theme that had held dominion in it, to the memories this very spot evoked.

It was there, sitting as she sat now, her eyes upon the shimmering waste of sea, and the gulls circling overhead, that she had awakened to the knowledge of her love for Crispin. And so to him strayed now her thoughts, and to the fate to which her father had sent him ; and thus back again to her father and the evil he had wrought. It is matter for conjecture whether her present horror of Gregory would have been as deep and unfilial as it was, had another than Crispin Galliard been his victim.

Her life seemed at an end as she sat that October evening on the cliffs. No remaining interest linked her to existence ; nothing, it seemed, was left her to hope for till the end should come—and no doubt it would be long in coming, for time moves slowly when we wait.

Wistful she sat and thought, and every thought begat a sigh, and then of a sudden—surely it was a trick of fancy of her enslaved imagination—a crisp, metallic voice rang out close behind her.

" Give you good evening, Mistress Cynthia."

There was a catch in her breath as she turned her head. Her cheeks took fire, and for a second were aflame. Then they went deadly white, and it seemed that time and life and the very world had paused in its relentless progress towards eternity. For there stood he who was the object of her thoughts and sighs, sudden and unexpected, as though the earth had cast him up on to her surface.

His thin lips were parted in a smile that softened the harshness of his face, and his eyes seemed then to her alight with kindness. A moment's pause there was, during which she sought her voice, and when she had found it, all that she could falter was—

" Sir Crispin, how come you here ? They told me that you rode to London."

" Why, so I did. But on the road it happened that I halted, and having halted I discovered reason why I should return."

He had discovered a reason. She asked herself in panic what might that reason be, and finding herself no answer to the question, she put it next to him.

He drew near to her before replying.

" May I sit with you awhile, Cynthia ? "

She moved aside to make room for him, as though the broad cliff had been a narrow ledge, and with the sigh of a weary man finding a resting-place at last, he sank down beside her.

There was a tenderness in his voice that set her pulses stirring. Did she guess aright the reason that had caused him to break his journey and return ? That he had done so—no matter what the reason— she thanked God from her inmost heart, as for a miracle that had saved him from the doom awaiting him in London town.

" Am I foolish, child, to think that perhaps the meditation in which I found you rapt was for one, unworthy though he be, who went hence but some few days ago ? "

The ambiguous question drove every speculation from her mind.

" Have I conjectured rightly ? " he asked, since she kept silence.

" Maybe you have," she murmured in return, and then, marvelling at her boldness, felt herself on fire. He glanced sharply at her from narrowing eyes. It was scarcely the answer he had looked to receive.

As a father might have done he took the slender hand that rested upon the grass beside him, and she, poor child, mistaking the promptings of that action, suffered it to lie in his strong grasp. With averted head she gazed upon the sea below, until a mist of tears rose up to blot it out. The breeze seemed full of melody and gladness. God was very good to her, and sent her in her hour of need this great consolation —a consolation indeed that must have served to efface whatever sorrow could have beset her.

" Why then, sweet lady, is my task, which I had feared to find all fraught with difficulty, grown easy indeed."

And hearing him pause—

" What task is that, Sir Crispin ? " she asked, intent on helping him.

He did not reply at once. He found it difficult to devise an answer. To tell her brutally that he was come to bear her away, willing or unwilling, on behalf of another, was not easy. Indeed, it was impossible, and he was glad that inclinations in her, which he had been far from suspecting, put all harsh necessity aside.

" My task, Mistress Cynthia, is to bear you hence. To ask you to resign this peaceful life, this quiet home in a little corner of the world, and to go forth to bear life's hardships with one who, whatever be his short-comings, has the all-redeeming virtue of loving you beyond aught else in life."

He gazed intently at her as he spoke, and her eyes fell before his glance. He noted the warm, red blood suffusing her cheeks, her brow, her very neck ; and he could have laughed aloud for joy at finding so simple that which he had feared would prove so hard. Some pity, too, crept unaccountably into his stern heart, fathered by the little faith which he reposed in Jocelyn. And where, had she resisted him, he would have grown harsh and compelling, her acquiescence struck the weapons from his hands, and he caught himself wellnigh warning her against accompanying him.

" It is much to ask," he said. " But love is selfish, and love asks much."

" No, no," she protested softly, " it is not much to ask. Rather is it much to offer."

His amazement grew. Yet he continued—

" Bethink you, Cynthia, I have ridden back to Sheringham to ask you to come with me into France, where my son awaits us ? "

He forgot for the moment that she was in ignorance of his relationship to the man he looked upon as her lover, whilst on her side she gave little thought to this mention of a son, of whose existence she had already heard from her father, but whose identity she had no reason to suspect. The hour was too full of other things that touched her more nearly.

" I ask you to abandon the ease in which you dwell for a life as a soldier's bride. It may be rough and precarious for a while, though, truth to tell, I command abroad some good friends upon whose assistance I can safely count to find your husband honourable employment and set him on the road to more. And how, guided by so sweet a saint, could he fail to mount to fame and honour ? "

She spoke no word, but the hand resting in his entwined his fingers in an answering pressure.

" Dare I then ask so much ? " cried he. And as if the ambiguity which had marked his speech were not enough, he must needs, as he put this question, bend in his eagerness towards her until her brown tresses touched his swart cheek. So that it was not strange that the eagerness wherewith he urged another's suit should have been by her interpreted as her heart would have had it.

She set her hands upon his shoulders, and meeting his eager gaze with the frank glance of the maid who, out of trust, is fearless in her surrender—

" Throughout my life I shall thank God that you have dared it," she softly answered him.

Something in that answer he accounted odd ; yet, pondering it, he took her meaning to be that since Jocelyn had lacked the courage to woo boldly, she was glad that he had sent an ambassador less timid.

A pause followed, and for a spell they sat silent, he thinking of how to frame his next words ; she happy and content to sit beside him without speech. She may have marvelled a little at the restraint of his wooing which was like unto no wooing in her romancer's tales, but then she reflected how unlike he was to other men, and in this perceived the explanation.

" I wish," he mused, " that matters were easier ; that it might be mine boldly to sue your hand from your father, but it may not be. Even had events not fallen out as they have done, it had been difficult. As it is, it is impossible."

Again his meaning was ambiguous. When he spoke of suing for her hand from her father, he did not think of adding that he would have sued it for his son.

" I do not think I have a father any longer," she replied, and observing the question with which his eyes were of a sudden charged—" Would you, to whom so much is known, have me own a thief, a murderer, my father ? " She displayed the fierceness of defiant shame.

" Ah ! you have learnt then ? "

" Yes," she answered miserably, " I know all there is to be known. I learnt it all this morning. All day have I pondered it in my shame and I had taken the resolve to leave Sheringham. I had intended going to London to my mother's sister. So that you see how very opportunely you are come." She smiled up at him through the tears that were glistening in her eyes. " You come even as I was despairing—nay, when already I had despaired."

He was no longer puzzled by the readiness of her acquiescence. Here was the explanation. Forced by the honesty of her pure soul to abandon the house of a father she knew at last for what he was, the refuge Crispin offered her was as welcome as it was opportune. She had determined before he came, to quit Castle Marleigh, and timely indeed was his offer of the means of escape from surroundings that were grown impossible. A great pity filled his heart. She was selling herself, he thought ; accepting the proposal which, on his son's behalf, he made, and from which at any other season, he feared, she might well have shrunk.

That pity was reflected on his countenance now, and noting its solemnity, and misconstruing it, she smiled, despite herself. He did not ask her why she smiled, he did not notice it ; his thoughts were busy already upon another matter.

When next he spoke, it was to describe to her the hollow of the road where on the night of his departure from the castle he had been flung from his horse. She knew the spot, she told him, and there at dusk upon the following day she would come to him. Her woman must accompany her, and for all that he feared such an addition to the party might retard their flight, yet he could not gainsay her resolution. Her uncle, he learnt from her, was absent from Sheringham ; he had set out four days ago for London. For her father she would leave a letter, and in this matter Crispin urged her to observe circumspection, giving no indication of the direction of her journey.

In all he said, now that matters were arranged, he was calm, practical, and unloverlike, and for all that she would he had been less self-possessed, her faith in him caused her, upon reflection, even to admire this which she conceived to be restraint. Yet, when at parting he did no more than courteously bend before her and kiss her fingers as any simpering gallant might have done, she was all but vexed, and not to be outdone in coldness, grew frigid. But it was lost upon him. He had not a lover's discernment, quickened by anxious eyes that watch for each flitting change upon his mistress's face.

They parted thus, and into the heart of Mistress Cynthia there crept that night a doubt that banished sleep. Was she wise in entrusting herself so utterly to a man of whom, after all, she knew but little, and this learnt from rumours which had not been good? But scarcely was it because of this that doubts assailed her. Rather was it because of his cool deliberateness which argued anything but the ardent love with which she would have him inspired.

For consolation she recalled a line that had it that great fires were soon burnt out, and she sought to reassure herself that the flame of his love, if not all-consuming, would at least burn bright and steadfastly until the end of life. And so she fell asleep, betwixt hope and fear, yet no longer with any hesitancy touching the morrow's course.

In the morning she took her woman into her confidence, and scared her with it out of what little sense the creature owned. Yet to such purpose did she talk, that when that evening, as Crispin waited by the coach he had brought, in the hollow of the road, he saw approaching him a portly, middle-aged

dame, with a valise. This was Cynthia's woman, and
Cynthia herself was not long in following muffled in a
long, black cloak.

There was no lack of warm affection in his greeting.
But neither was there any of that rapture to which
she held herself entitled as some little recompense for
all that on his behalf she abandoned.

Urbanely he handed her into the coach, and, after
her, her woman. Then seeing that he made shift to
close the door—

"How is this?" she asked. "Do you not ride
with us?"

He pointed to a saddled horse standing by the
roadside, which she had not noticed.

"It will be better so. You will be more at comfort
in the carriage without me. Besides, it will travel the
lighter and the swifter, and speed will prove our best
friend."

He closed the door, and stepped back with a word
of command to the driver. The whip cracked, and
Cynthia flung herself back in tears. What manner
of lover, she asked herself, was this, and what manner
of woman she, to let herself be borne away by one
who made so little use of the arts and wiles of sweet
persuasion? To carry her off, and yet not so much
as sit beside her, was worthy only of a man who
described such a journey as tedious. She marvelled
greatly at it, yet more she marvelled at herself that
she did not abandon so mad an undertaking.

The coach moved on and the flight from Sheringham
was begun.

CHAPTER XXV

CYNTHIA'S FLIGHT

THROUGHOUT the night they went rumbling on their way at a pace whose sluggishness elicited a deal of grumbling from Crispin as he rode a few yards in the rear, ever watchful of the possibility of pursuit. But there was none, nor none need he have feared, since whilst he rode through the cold night, Gregory Ashburn slept as peacefully as a man may with the fever and an evil conscience, imagining his dutiful daughter safely abed.

With the first streaks of steely light came a thin rain to heighten Crispin's discomfort, for of late he had been overmuch in the saddle, and strong though he was, he was yet flesh and blood, and subject to its ills. Towards ten o'clock they passed through Denham. When they were clear of it Cynthia put her head from the window. She had slept soundly, and, being rested, her mood was lighter and happier. As Crispin rode a yard or so behind, he caught sight of her fresh, smiling face, and it affected him curiously. The tenderness that two days ago had been his as he talked to her upon the cliffs was again upon him, and the thought that soon she would be linked to him by the ties of kinship was pleasant. She gave him good morrow prettily, and he, spurring his horse to the carriage door, was solicitous to know of her comfort. Nor did he again fall behind until Stafford was reached. Here, at the sign of " The Suffolk

Arms," he called a halt, and they broke their fast on the best the house could give them.

Cynthia was almost gay, and so indeed was Crispin, yet when she had noted in him that coolness which she accounted restraint, her spirits gradually sank again.

To Crispin's chagrin there were no horses to be had. Someone in great haste had ridden through ahead of them, and taken what relays the hostelry could give, leaving four jaded beasts in the stable. It seemed, indeed, that they must remain there until the following day, and in coming to this conclusion, Sir Crispin's temper suffered sorely.

" Why need it put you so about," wondered Cynthia, " since I am with you ? "

" Blood and fire, madam," she was answered, " it is precisely for that reason that I am vexed. What if your father came upon us here ? "

" My father, sir, is abed with a sword-wound and a fever," she replied, and so reminded him of how Kenneth had spitted Gregory through the shoulder.

" Still," he returned, " he will have discovered your flight, and I dare swear we shall have his myrmidons upon our heels. Should they come up with us we shall hardly find them more gentle than he would be."

That startled her, and for a second there was silence. Then her hand stole forth upon his arm, and she looked at him with tightened lips and a defiant air.

" What, indeed, if they do ? Are you not with me ? "

A king had praised his daring, and for his valour had dubbed him knight upon a field of stricken battle ;

yet the honour of it had not brought him the elation those words—expressing her utter faith in him and his prowess—awakened in his heart. Upon the instant the delay ceased to fret him.

"Why, since you put it so," he laughed, "I care not who comes. The Lord Protector himself shall not drag you from me."

It was the nearest he had gone to a lover's speech since they had left Sheringham, and it pleased her ; yet in uttering it he had stood a full two yards away, and this had pleased her less.

Bidding her remain and get what rest she might, he left her, and she, following his straight, lank figure —so eloquent of strength—and the familiar poise of his left hand upon the pummel of his sword, felt proud indeed that he belonged to her, and secure in his protection. She sat herself at the window when he was gone, and whilst she awaited his return her thoughts were with him. Her eyes were bright, and there was a flush upon her cheeks. Not even in the wet, greasy street could she find any unsightliness that afternoon. But as she waited, and the minutes grew to hours, the flush faded, and the sparkle died gradually from her eyes. Her shapely mouth took on a pout of impatience, which anon grew into a tighter mould, as he continued absent.

A frown drew her brows together, and Mistress Cynthia's thoughts were much as they had been the night before she left Castle Marleigh. Where was he ? Why came he not ? She took up a book that lay upon the table, and sought to while away the time by reading. The afternoon faded into dusk, and still he did not come. Her woman appeared, to ask whether she could call for lights, and at that Cynthia became almost violent.

" Where is Sir Crispin ? " she demanded. And to the dame's quavering answer that she knew not, she angrily bade her go ascertain.

In a pet, Cynthia paced the chamber whilst Catherine was gone upon that errand. Did this man account her a toy to while away the hours for which he could find no more profitable diversion, and to leave her to perish of tedium when aught else offered ? Was it a small thing that he had asked of her, to go with him into a strange land, that he should show himself so little sensible of the honour done him ?

Then she checked the unkindly assumptions in sudden fear for him. What if some evil chance were answerable for this absence ? What if harm should have overtaken him ? The dread thought was growing to certainty when the door opened and her woman appeared.

" Well ? " cried Cynthia, seeing her alone. " Where is Sir Crispin ? "

" Below, madam."

" Below ? " echoed she. " And what, pray, doth he below ? "

" He is at dice with a gentleman from London."

In the dim light of the October twilight the woman saw not the sudden pallor of her mistress's cheeks, but she heard the gasp of pain that was almost a cry. In her mortification, Cynthia could have wept had she given way to her feelings. The man who had induced her to elope with him sat at dice with a gentleman from London ! Oh, it was monstrous ! She broke into a laugh that appalled her tiring-woman ; then, mastering her hysteria, she took a sudden determination.

" Call me the host," she cried, and the frightened Catherine obeyed her at a run.

When the landlord came, bearing lights, and bending his aged back obsequiously—

" Have you a pillion ? " she asked abruptly. " Well, fool, why do you stare ? Have you a pillion ? "

" I have, madam."

" And a knave to ride with me, and a couple more as escort ? "

" I might procure them, but——"

" How soon ? "

" Within half an hour, but——"

" Then go see to it," she broke in, her foot beating the ground impatiently.

" But, madam——"

" Go, go, go ! " she cried, her voice rising at each utterance of that imperative.

" But, madam," the host persisted despairingly, and speaking quickly so that he might get the words out, " I have no horses fit to travel ten miles."

" I need to go but five," she answered him, her only thought being to get the beasts, no matter what their condition. " Now, go, and come not back until all is ready. Use dispatch and I will pay you well, and above all, not a word to the gentleman who came hither with me."

The sorely puzzled host withdrew to do her bidding, won to it by her promise of good payment.

Alone she sat for half an hour, vainly fostering the

hope that ere the landlord returned to announce the conclusion of his preparations, Crispin might have remembered her and come. But he did not appear, and in her solitude this poor little maid was very miserable, and shed some tears that had still more of anger than sorrow in their source. At length the landlord came. She summoned her woman, and bade her follow by post on the morrow. The landlord she rewarded with some gold pieces, and was led by him through a side door into the inn-yard.

Here she found three horses, one equipped with the pillion on which she was to ride behind a burly stable-boy. The other two were mounted by a couple of stalwart and well-armed men, one of whom carried a funnel-mouthed musketoon with a swagger that promised prodigies of valour.

Wrapped in her cloak, she mounted behind the stable-boy, and bade him set out and take the road to Denham. Her dream was at an end.

Master Quinn, the landlord, watched her departure with eyes that were charged with doubt and concern. As he made fast the door of the stable-yard after she had passed out, he ominously shook his hoary head and muttered to himself humble, hostelry-flavoured philosophies touching the strange ways of men with women, and the stranger ways of women with men. Then, taking up his lanthorn, he slowly retraced his steps to the buttery where his wife was awaiting him.

With sleeves rolled high above her pink and deeply dimpled elbows stood Mistress Quinn at work upon the fashioning of a pasty, when her husband entered and set down his lanthorn with a sigh.

" To be so plagued," he growled. " To be brow-beaten by a slip of a wench—a fine gentleman's baggage with the airs and vapours of a lady of quality. Am I not a fool to have endured it ? "

" Certainly you are a fool," his wife agreed, knead-ing diligently, " whatever you may have endured. What now ? "

His fat face was puckered into a thousand wrinkles. His little eyes gazed at her with long-suffering malice.

" You are my wife," he answered pregnantly, as who would say : Thus is my folly clearly proven ! and seeing that the assertion was not one that admitted of dispute, Mistress Quinn was silent.

" Oh, 'tis ill done ! " he broke out a moment later. " Shame on me for it ; it is ill done ! "

" If you have done it it's sure to be ill done, and shame on you in good sooth—but for what ? " put in his wife.

" For sending those poor jaded beasts upon the road."

" What beasts ? "

" What beasts ? Do I keep turtles ? My horses, woman."

" And whither have you sent them ? "

" To Denham with the baggage that came hither this morning in the company of that very fierce gentle-man who was in such a pet because we had no horses."

" Where is *he* ? " inquired the hostess.

" At dice with those other gallants from town."

" At dice quotha ? And she's gone, you say ? " Mrs. Quinn paused in her labours squarely to face her husband.

"Ay," said he.

"Stupid!" rejoined his docile spouse, vexed by his laconic assent. "Do you mean that she has run away?"

"'Tis what anyone might suppose from what I have told you," he answered sweetly.

"And you have lent her horses and helped her to get away, and you leave her husband at play in there?"

"You have seen her marriage lines, I make no doubt."

"You dolt! If the gentleman horsewhips you, you will have richly earned it."

"Eh? What?" gasped he, and his rubicund cheeks lost something of their high colour, for here was something that had not entered into his calculations. But Mistress Quinn stayed not to answer him. Already she was making for the door, wiping the dough from her hands on to her apron as she went. A suspicion of her purpose flashed through her husband's mind.

"What would you do?" he asked her nervously.

"Tell the gentleman what has taken place."

"Nay," he cried, resolutely barring her way. "Nay. That you shall not. Would you—would you ruin me?"

She gave him a look of contempt, and dodging his grasp she gained the door and was half-way down the passage towards the common-room before he had overtaken her and caught her round the middle.

"Are you mad, woman?" he shouted. "Will you undo me?"

" Do you undo me," she bade him, snatching at his hands. But he clutched with the tightness of despair.

" You shall not go," he swore. " Come back and leave the gentleman to make the discovery for himself. I dare swear it will not afflict him overmuch. He has abandoned her sorely since they came ; not a doubt of it but that he is weary of her. At least he need not know I lent her horses. Let him think she fled a-foot when he finds her gone."

" I *will* go," she answered stubbornly, dragging him with her a yard or two nearer the door. " The gentleman shall be warned. Is a woman to run away from her husband in my house, and the husband never be told of it ? "

" I promised her," he began.

" What care I for your promises ? I will tell him, so that he may yet go after her if he chooses."

" You shall not," he insisted, gripping her more closely. But at that moment a delicately mocking voice greeted their ears.

" Marry, 'tis vastly diverting to hear you," it said. They looked round, to find one of the party of town sparks that had halted at the inn standing arms akimbo in the narrow passage, clearly waiting for them to make room. " A touching sight, sir," said he sardonically to the landlord. " A wondrous touching sight to behold a man of your years playing the turtle-dove to his good wife like the merest fledgeling. It grieves me to intrude myself so harshly upon your cooing, though if you'll but let me pass you may resume your chaste embrace without uneasiness, for I give you my word I'll never look behind me."

Abashed, the landlord and his dame fell apart. Then, ere the gentleman could pass her, Mistress Quinn, like a true opportunist, sped swiftly down the passage and into the common-room before her husband could again detain her.

Now, within the common-room of " The Suffolk Arms " Sir Crispin sat face to face with a very pretty fellow, all musk and ribbons, and surrounded by some half-dozen gentlemen on their way to London who had halted to rest at Stafford.

The pretty gentleman swore lustily, affected a monstrous wicked look, assured that he was impressing all who stood about with some conceit of the wicked ways he pursued in town.

A game started with crowns to while away the tedium of the enforced sojourn at the inn had grown to monstrous proportions. Fortune had favoured the youth at first, but as the stakes grew her favours to him diminished, and at the moment that Cynthia rode out of the inn-yard, Mr. Harry Foster flung a gold piece with an oath upon the table.

" Rat me," he swore, " there's the end of a hundred."

He toyed gloomily with the red ribbon in his black hair, and Crispin, seeing that no fresh stake was forthcoming, made shift to rise. But the coxcomb detained him.

" Tarry, sir," he cried, " I've not yet done. 'Slife, we'll make a night of it."

He drew a ring from his finger, and with a superb gesture of disdain pushed it across the board.

" What'll ye stake ? " And, in the same breath, " Boy, another stoup," he cried.

Crispin eyed the gem carelessly.

" Twenty Caroluses," he muttered.

" Rat me, sir, that nose of yours proclaims you a Jew, without more. Say twenty-five, and I'll throw."

With a tolerant smile, and the shrug of a man to whom twenty-five or a hundred are of like account, Crispin consented. They threw ; they threw again ; Crispin passed and won.

" What'll ye stake ? " cried Mr. Foster, and a second ring followed the first.

It was at this moment that the door leading from the interior of the inn was flung open, and Mrs. Quinn, breathless with exertion and excitement, came scurrying across the room. In the doorway, behind her, stood the host in hesitancy and fear. Bending to Crispin's ear, Mrs. Quinn delivered her message in a whisper that was heard by most of those who were about.

" Gone ! " cried Crispin in consternation.

The woman pointed to her husband, and Crispin, understanding from this that she referred him to the host, called to him.

" What's this, landlord ? " he shouted. " Come hither, and tell me whither is the lady gone ! "

" I know not," replied the quaking host, adding the particulars of Cynthia's departure, and the information that she seemed in great anger.

" Saddle me a horse," cried Crispin, leaping to his feet, and pitching Mr. Foster's trinket upon the table as though it were a thing of no value. " Towards Denham you say they rode ? Haste, man ! " And as the host departed he swept the gold and the ring he had won into his pockets, preparing to depart.

"Hoity, toity!" cried Mr. Foster. "What sudden haste is this?"

"I am sorry, sir, that fortune has been unkind to you, but I must go. Circumstances have arisen which——"

"D——n your circumstances!" roared Foster, getting on his feet. "You'll not leave me thus!"

"With your permission, sir, I will."

"But you shall not have my permission!"

"Then I shall be so unfortunate as to go without it. But I shall return."

"Sir, 'tis an old legend, that!"

Crispin turned about in despair. To be embroiled now might ruin everything, and by a miracle he kept his temper. He had a moment to spare while his horse was being saddled.

"Sir," he said, "if you have upon your pretty person trinkets to half the value of what I have won from you, I'll stake the whole against them on one throw, after which, no matter what the result, I take my departure. Are you agreed?"

There was a murmur of wonder from those present at the reckless generosity of the proposal, and Foster was forced to accept it. Two more rings he drew forth, a diamond from the ruffles at his throat, and a pearl that he wore in his ear. The lot he set upon the board, and Crispin threw the winning cast as the host entered to say that his horse was ready.

He gathered the trinkets up, and with a polite word of regret he was gone, leaving Mr. Harry Foster to meditate upon the pledging of one of his horses to the landlord in discharge of his lodging.

And so it fell out that before Cynthia had gone six miles along the road to Denham, one of her attendants caught a rapid beat of hoofs behind them, and drew her attention to it, suggesting that they were being followed. Faster Cynthia bade them travel, but the pursuer gained upon them at every stride. Again the man drew her attention to it, and proposed that they should halt and face him who followed. The possession of the musketoon gave him confidence touching the issue. But Cynthia shuddered at the thought, and again, with promises of reward, urged them to go faster. Another mile they went, but every moment brought the pursuing hoof-beats nearer and nearer, until at last a hoarse challenge rang out behind them, and they knew that to go farther would be vain ; within the next half-mile, ride as they might, their pursuer would be upon them.

The night was moonless, yet sufficiently clear for objects to be perceived against the sky, and presently the black shadow of him who rode behind loomed up upon the road, not a hundred paces off.

Despite Cynthia's orders not to fire, he of the musketoon raised his weapon under cover of the darkness and blazed at the approaching shadow.

Cynthia cried out—a shriek of dismay it was ; the horses plunged, and Sir Crispin bore down on them. He of the musketoon heard the swish of a sword being drawn, and saw the glitter of the blade in the dark. A second later there was a shock as Crispin's horse dashed into his, and a blow across the forehead,

which Galliard delivered with the hilt of his rapier,
sent the fellow hurtling from the saddle.   His comrade
clapped spurs to his horse at that and was running
a race with the night wind in the direction of
Denham.

Before Cynthia on the pillion quite knew what had
happened the seat in front of her was empty, and she
was riding back to Stafford with Crispin beside her,
his hand upon the bridle of her horse.

"You little fool!" he said angrily, half gibingly;
and thereafter they rode in silence—she too mortified
with shame and anger to venture upon words.

The journey back to Stafford was a speedy one,
and soon they stood again in the inn-yard out of
which she had ridden but an hour ago.   Avoiding
the common-room, Crispin ushered her through the
side door by which she had quitted the house.   The
landlord met them in the passage, and looking at
Crispin's face the pallor and fierceness of it drove
him back without a word.

Together they ascended to the chamber where in
solitude she had spent the day.   Her feelings were
those of a child caught in an act of disobedience, and
she was angry with herself and her weakness that it
should be so.   Yet within the room she stood with
bent head, never glancing at her companion, in whose
eyes there was a look of blended anger and amazement as he observed her.   At length in calm, level
tones—

"Why did you run away?" he asked.

The question was to her anger as a gust of wind
to a smouldering fire.   She threw back her head

defiantly, and fixed him with a glance as fierce as his own.

" I will tell you," she cried, and suddenly stopped short. The fire died from her eyes, and they grew wide in wonder—in fascinated wonder—to see a deep stain overspreading one side of his grey doublet, from the left shoulder downwards. Her wonder turned to horror as she realized the nature of that stain and remembered that one of her men had fired upon him.

" You are wounded ? " she faltered.

A twisted smile overspread his face, and seemed to accentuate its pallor. He made a deprecatory gesture. Then, as if in that gesture he had expended his last grain of strength, he swayed suddenly as he stood. He made as if to reach a chair, but at the second step he stumbled, and without further warning he fell supine at her feet, his left hand upon his heart, his right outstretched straight from the shoulder. The loss of blood he had sustained, following upon the fatigue and sleeplessness that had been his of late, had demanded its due from him, man of iron though he was.

Upon the instant her anger vanished. A great fear that he was dead descended upon her, and to heighten the horror of it came the thought that he had received his death-wound through her agency. With a moan of anguish she went down upon her knees beside him. She raised his head and pillowed it in her lap, calling to him by name, as though her voice alone must suffice to bring him back to life and conscious-ness. Instinctively she unfastened his doublet at the

neck, and sought to draw it away that she might see
the nature of his hurt and staunch the wound if
possible, but her strength ebbed away from her, and
she abandoned her task, unable to do more than
murmur his name.

"Crispin, Crispin, Crispin!"

She stooped and kissed the white, clammy forehead,
then his lips, and as she did so a tremor ran through
him, and he opened his eyes. A moment they looked
dull and lifeless, then they waxed questioning.

A second ago these two had stood in anger with
the width of the room betwixt them; now, in a
flash, he found his head on her lap, her lips on his.
How came he there? What did it mean?

"Crispin, Crispin," she cried, "thank God you did
but swoon!"

Then the awakening of his soul came swift upon
the awakening of his body. He lay there, oblivious
of his wound, oblivious of his mission, oblivious of
his son. He lay with senses still half dormant and
comprehension dulled, but with a soul alert he lay,
and was supremely happy with a happiness such as
he had never known in all his ill-starred life.

In a feeble voice he asked—

"Why did you run away?"

"Let us forget it," she answered softly.

"Nay—tell me first."

"I thought—I thought——" she stammered; then,
gathering courage, "I thought you did not really care,
that you made a toy of me," said she. "When they
told me that you sat at dice with a gentleman from
London I was angry at your neglect. If you loved

me, I told myself, you would not have used me so, and left me to mope alone."

For a moment Crispin let his grey eyes devour her blushing face. Then he closed them and pondered what she had said, realization breaking upon him now like a great flood. A hundred things that had puzzled him in the last two days grew of a sudden clear, and filled him with a joy unspeakable. He dared scarce believe that he was awake, and Cynthia by him—that he had indeed heard aright what she had said. How blind he had been, how nescient of himself !

Then, as his thoughts travelled on to the source of the misapprehension, he remembered his son, and the memory was like an icy hand upon his temples to chill him through and through. Lying there with eyes still closed he groaned. Happiness was within his grasp at last. Love might be his again did he but ask it, and the love of as pure and good a creature as ever God sent to sweeten a man's life. A great tenderness possessed him. A burning temptation to cast to the winds his plighted word, to make a mock of faith, to deride honour, and to take this woman for his own.

She loved him—he knew it now ; he loved her— the knowledge had come as suddenly upon him. Compared with this what could his faith, his word, his honour give him ? What to him, in the face of this, was that paltry fellow, his son, who had spurned him !

The hardest fight he ever fought, he fought there, supine upon the ground, his head in her lap.

Had he fought it out with closed eyes, perchance honour and his plighted word had won the day; but he opened them, and they met Cynthia's.

A while they stayed thus; the hungry glance of his grey eyes peering into the clear blue depths of hers; and in those depths his soul was drowned, his honour stifled.

"Cynthia," he cried, "God pity me, I love you!" And he swooned again.

CHAPTER XXVI

TO FRANCE

THAT cry, which she but half understood, was still ringing in her ears, when the door was of a sudden flung open, and across the threshold a very daintily arrayed young gentleman stepped briskly, the expostulating landlord following close upon his heels.

"I tell thee, lying dog," he cried, "I saw him ride into the yard, and, 'fore George, he shall give me the chance of mending my losses. Be off to your father, you devil's natural."

Cynthia looked up in alarm, whereupon that merry blood catching sight of her, halted in some confusion at what he saw.

"Rat me, madam," he cried, "I did not know—I had not looked to——" He stopped, and remembering at last his manners he made her a low bow.

"Your servant, madam," said he, "your servant, Harry Foster."

She gazed at him, her eyes full of inquiry, but said nothing, whereat the pretty gentleman plucked awkwardly at his ruffles and wished himself elsewhere.

"I did not know, madam, that your husband was hurt."

"He is not my husband, sir," she answered, scarce knowing what she said.

"Gadso!" he ejaculated. "Yet you ran away from him?"

Her cheeks grew crimson.

261

"The door, sir, is behind you."

'So, madam, is that thief the landlord," he made answer, no whit abashed. "Come hither, you bladder of fat, the gentleman is hurt."

Thus courteously summoned, the landlord shuffled forward, and Mr. Foster begged Cynthia to allow him with the fellow's aid to see to the gentleman's wound. Between them they laid Crispin on a couch, and the town spark went to work with a dexterity little to have been expected from his flippant exterior. He dressed the wound, which was in the shoulder and not in itself dangerous. It was the loss of blood that had brought some gravity to the knight's condition. They propped his head upon a pillow, and presently he sighed and, opening his eyes, complained of thirst, and was manifestly surprised at seeing the coxcomb turned leech.

"I came in search of you to pursue our game," Foster explained when they had ministered to him, "and, 'fore George, I am vastly grieved to find you in this condition."

"Pish, sir, my condition is none so grievous—a scratch, no more, and were my heart itself pierced the knowledge that I have gained——" He stopped short. "But there, sir," he added presently, "I am grateful beyond words for your timely help."

His glance met Cynthia's and he smiled. The host coughed significantly, and shuffled towards the door. But Master Foster made no shift to move; he stood instead beside Galliard, though in apparent hesitation.

"I should like a word with you ere I go," he said

at length. Then turning and perceiving the land-lord standing by the door in an attitude of waiting—

" Take yourself off," he cried to him. " Crush me, may not one gentleman say a word to another without being forced to speak into your inquisitive ears as well. You will forgive my heat, madam, but, God a'mercy, that greasy rascal tries me sorely.

" Now, sir," he resumed, when the host was gone. " I stand thus : I have lost to you to-day a sum of money which, though some might account consider-able, is in itself no more than a trifle.

" I am, however, greatly exercised at the loss of certain trinkets which have to me a peculiar value, and which, to be frank, I staked in a moment of desperation. I had hoped, sir, to retrieve my losses o'er a friendly main this evening, for I have still to stake a coach and four horses—as noble a set of beasts as you'll find in England, aye, rat me. Your wound, sir, makes it impossible for me to ask you to give yourself the fatigue of obliging me. I come then, to propose that you return me those trinkets against my note of hand for the amount that was staked on them. I am well known in town, sir," he added hurriedly, " and you need have no anxiety——"

Crispin stopped him with a wave of the hand.

" I have none, sir. I am happy to oblige you." He thrust his hand into his pocket, and drew forth the rings, the brooch, and the ear-ring he had won. " Here, sir, are your trinkets."

" Sir," cried Mr. Foster, thrown into some con-fusion by Galliard's unquestioning generosity. " This is handsome. I am indebted to you. Rat me, sir,

I am indeed. You shall have my note of hand on the instant. How much shall we say ? "

" One moment, Mr. Foster," said Crispin, an idea suddenly occurring to him. " You mentioned horses. Are they fresh ? "

" As June roses."

" And you are returning to London, are you not ? "

" I am."

" When do you wish to proceed ? "

" To-morrow."

" Why, then, sir, I have a proposal to make which will remove the need of your note of hand. Lend me your horses, sir, to reach Harwich. I wish to set out at once——"

" But your wound ? " cried Cynthia. " You are still faint."

" Faint ! Not I. I am awake and strong. My wound is no wound, no more than a scratch. So there, sweetheart." He laughed, and drawing down her head, he whispered the words : " Your father." Then turning again to Foster. " Now, sir," he continued, " there are four tolerable post-horses of mine below, on which you can follow to-morrow to Harwich, there exchanging them again for your own, which you shall find awaiting you, stabled at ' The Garter Inn.' For this service, to me of immeasurable value, I will willingly cede those gewgaws to you."

" But rat me, sir," cried Foster in bewilderment, " 'tis too generous—'pon honour it is. I can't consent to it. No, rat me, I can't."

" I have told you how great a boon you will confer.

Believe me, sir, to me it is worth twice, a hundred times the value of those trinkets."

"You shall have my horses, sir, and my note of hand as well," said Foster firmly.

"Your note of hand is of no value to me, sir. I look to leave England to-morrow, and I know not when I may return."

Thus in the end it came about that the bargain was concluded. Cynthia's maid was awakened and bidden to rise. The horses were harnessed to Crispin's coach, and Crispin, leaning upon Harry Foster's arm, descended and took his place within the carriage.

Leaving the London blood at the door of "The Suffolk Arms," crushing, burning, damning, and ratting himself at Crispin's magnificence, they rolled away through the night in the direction of Ipswich.

Ten o'clock in the morning beheld them at the door of "The Garter Inn" at Harwich. But the jolting of the coach had so hardly used Crispin that he had to be carried into the hostelry. He was much exercised touching the *Lady Jane* and his inability to go down to the quay in quest of her, when he was accosted by a burly, red-faced individual who bluntly asked him was he called Sir Crispin Galliard. Before he could frame an answer the man had added that he was Thomas Jackson, master of the *Lady Jane*—at which piece of good news Crispin was certainly uplifted.

But his reflection upon his present position, when at last he lay in the schooner's cabin, brought him the bitter reverse of pleasure. He had set out to bring Cynthia to his son; he had pledged his honour to accomplish it. How was he fulfilling his trust? In his despondency, during a moment when alone, he cursed the knave that had wounded him for his clumsiness in not having taken a lower aim when he fired, and thus solved him this ugly riddle of life for all time.

Vainly did he strive to console himself and endeavour to palliate the wrong he had done with the consideration that he was the man Cynthia loved, and not his son ; that his son was nothing to her, and that she would never have accompanied him had she dreamt that he wooed her for another.

No. The deed was foul, and rendered fouler still by virtue of those other wrongs in whose extenuation it had been undertaken. For a moment he grew almost a coward. It even crossed his mind to bid Master Jackson avoid Calais and make some other port along the coast. But in a moment he had put from him that craven notion of flight, and determined that come what might he would face his son, and lay the truth before him, leaving him to judge how strong fate had been. As he lay feverish and fretful in the vessel's cabin, he came wellnigh to hating Kenneth ; he remembered him only as a poor, mean creature, now a bigot, now a fop, now a psalm-monger, now a roysterer, but ever a hypocrite, ever a weakling, and never such a man as he could have taken pride in presenting as his offspring.

They had a fair wind, and towards evening Cynthia, who had been absent from his side a little while, came to tell him that the coast of France grew nigh.

His answer was a sigh, and when she chid him for it, he essayed a smile that was yet more melancholy. For a second he was tempted to confide in her; to tell her of the position in which he found himself and to lighten his load by sharing it with her. But this he dared not do. Cynthia must never know.

CHAPTER XXVII

THE " AUBERGE DU SOLEIL "

In a room of the first floor of the " Auberge du Soleil,"
at Calais, the host inquired of Crispin if he were Milord
Galliard. Crispin caught his breath in apprehension.
What that question portended he guessed; and it
stifled the hope that had been rising in him since his
arrival, and since he had not found his son awaiting
him either on the jetty or at the inn. He dared ask
no questions, fearing that the reply would quench
that hope, which rose despite himself.

He sighed before replying. He passed his brown,
sinewy hand across his brow, to find it moist.

" My name, M. l'hôte, is Crispin Galliard. You
have news for me ? "

" A gentleman—a countryman of milord's—has
been here these three days awaiting him."

For a little while Crispin sat quite still, robbed of
the last shred of hope. Then, suddenly bracing himself, he sprang up, despite his weakness.

" Bring him to me. I will see him at once."

" *Tout à l'heure, monsieur*," replied the landlord.
" At the moment he is absent. He went out to take
the air a couple of hours ago, and is not yet returned."

" Heaven send he has walked into the sea," Crispin
broke out passionately. Then as passionately he
checked himself. " No, no, my God—not that ! I
meant not that."

" Monsieur will sup ? "

" At once, and let me have lights." The host withdrew, to fetch a couple of lighted tapers, which he set upon the table.

As he was retiring a heavy step sounded on the stair, accompanied by the clank of a scabbard against the baluster.

" Here comes milord's countryman," the landlord announced.

And Crispin, looking up in apprehension, saw framed in the doorway the burly form of Harry Hogan.

He sat bolt upright in his amazement. With a sad smile Hogan came to set a hand affectionately upon Galliard's shoulder.

" Welcome to France, Crispin. If not he whom you looked to find, at least it's a true friend you have to greet you."

" Hogan ! Why are you here ? How come you here ? What does it mean ? Where is Jocelyn ? "

The Irishman looked at him gravely for a moment, then sighed and sank down upon a chair.

" You'll have brought the lady ? " said he.

" She is here. She will be with us presently."

Hogan tightened his lips and shook his grey head sorrowfully.

" But where is Jocelyn ? " Galliard asked again, and his haggard face looked very wan and white as he turned it upon his companion. " Why is he not here? "

" Bad cess to it. It's the bearer of bad news I am."

" Bad news ? " muttered Crispin, as if the words were meaningless. " Bad news ? " Then he braced himself, " What is this news ? "

"And you have brought the lady too!" Hogan lamented. "Faith, I was hoping you had failed in that at least."

"'Sdeath, Harry," Crispin exclaimed. "Will you tell me the news?"

Hogan pondered yet a moment. Then—

"I will be after telling you the tale from the beginning," said he. "It was this way. Some three or four hours after you left Waltham, my men brought in the malignant we were hunting. I dispatched my sergeant and the troop at once to London with the prisoner, keeping just two troopers by me. An hour or so after that a coach comes clattering into the yard, and out of it steps a short, lean man in black, with as evil a face as ever I saw, and a crooked eye, who bawled out that he was Joseph Ashburn, of Castle Marleigh, a friend of the Lord-General's, and that he must have horses on the instant to proceed to London. I was in the yard at the time, and hearing the full announcement, faith, I guessed what his business in London would be. He entered the inn to refresh himself, and I followed him. In the common-room the first man his eyes lighted on was your son. He gasped at sight of him, and when he had recovered breath let fly as round a volley of blasphemy as ever I heard from the lips of a Puritan. When that was over, 'Fool,' he yells, 'why are you here?' The lad stammered and grew confused. At last—'I was detained here,' says he. 'Detained!' thunders the other, 'and by whom?' 'By my father, you murdering villain!' was the reckless answer.

"At that Master Ashburn grows very white and

very wicked. 'So,' he says, in a playful voice,
' you have found that out, have you ? Well, by God !
the knowledge shall profit neither you nor him. But
I'll begin with you.' And with that he seizes a jug
of ale that stood on the table, and empties it into the
boy's face. Soul of my body ! The lad showed such
spirit then as I had never looked to find in him.
' Outside,' yells he, tugging at his sword with one
hand, and pointing to the door with the other. ' Outside, you beast, where I can kill you ! ' Ashburn
laughed and cursed, and together they flung past me
into the yard. The place was empty at the moment,
and there, before the clash of their blades had drawn
interference, the thing was over—and Ashburn had
sent his sword through Jocelyn's heart."

Hogan paused, and Crispin sat very still and white,
his soul in torment.

"And Ashburn ? " he asked presently, in a voice
that was singularly hoarse and low. " What became
of him ? Was he not arrested ? "

"No," said Hogan grimly, " he was not arrested.
He was buried. Before he had wiped his blade I had
stepped up to him and said a word or two. I remembered the reckoning he owed you, I remembered that
he had sought to send you to your death ; I saw the
boy's body bleeding upon the ground, and I struck
him with my knuckles across his leering mouth. Like
the treacherous ruffian he was, he made a pass at me
with his sword before I had got mine out. I avoided
it, and we set to work.

" Men rushed out and would have stopped us, but
I cursed them so whilst I fenced, swearing to spit

any man that came between us, that they held off and waited. I didn't keep them overlong. I was no raw youngster fresh from the hills of Scotland. I put the point of my sword through Joseph Ashburn's throat within a minute of our engaging.

"It was then as I stood in that shambles and looked down upon my handiwork that I recalled in what favour Master Ashburn was held by the Parliament, and I grew just a trifle sick to think of what the consequences might be. So as to be avoiding them I got me there and then to horse, and rode in a straight line for Greenwich, hoping to find the *Lady Jane* still there. But my messenger had already sent her to Harwich for you. I was well ahead of possible pursuit, and so I pushed on to Dover, and thence I crossed, arriving here three days ago."

Sir Crispin sat very still, his elbows on his knees, his head in his hands, and for a while there was silence.

"That it should end thus!" he groaned at last. "God knows I had not dared look into the future. Here was a tangle from which I could see no issue, from which there could be no issue that was not fraught with pain." He looked up at last, and Hogan beheld a face distorted by suffering. It moved the Irishman to come and set a hand upon his shoulder.

"Aye, aye! Don't I know how you'll be feeling? It was your own son after all. And yet, could he ever have been a son to you? Maybe it's Fate's solution of a problem, after all."

"Don't I know it?" Crispin surprised him by answering; and he added—"That is what hurts."

Hogan's hand rested on the bowed shoulder.
" Courage, Crispin ! A man must be meeting what
Fate sends."

Crispin laughed without mirth. " That is the irony
of it." Then he looked up. " There's your part in
this garboil. Forgive me if I am slow to think of it.
I——"

" Och ! Do I need to be thanked, now ? "

" That and something more. You are in exile now
on my account. But I still have friends in France,
and through them I can provide. You shall not suffer
for having stood my friend."

" Is this a time to be thinking of me ? Haven't
you enough on your hands ? " Gravely he added—
" There's the lady, now ; and that's a grim problem."

Crispin stood up. " The least grim of all my prob-
lems. A priest will solve it."

" A priest ? Glory be ! " Hogan gaped. " A priest,
d'ye say ? "

" That's what I said. I hear her step upon the
stair, Harry. Leave me now."

The door was opened by Cynthia. Hogan stood
aside as she entered, then silently departed in deepest
perplexity.

Gravely considering her across the room, Crispin
asked himself in torment whether he dared give thanks
for this solution of the monstrous riddle that had
confronted him.

Smiling she came forward, to check at sight of his
countenance.

" What is it ? " she asked. " You have had bad
news ? "

A wistful smile broke across his pallor. " Bad news ? Do we ever know what is bad or good ? But it is news that hurts."

She came to him swiftly now, her eyes tender as her voice. " I am to help you bear it, my dear," she told him, and went to his arms.

THE END

PRINTED IN GREAT BRITAIN AT
THE PRESS OF THE PUBLISHERS

THE NELSON CLASSICS

AND THE

MODERN READER

" I want a good book." Who hasn't harassed a polite book-seller, or made a determined but unsatisfactory choice at a library, in an endeavour to find the " right " book ?

The Nelson Classics offer you a choice of the best books by the best authors, ancient and modern. Books for entertainment and information—books for pleasure and profit—books which the modern reader buys to build up his library.

These beautifully produced volumes—masterpieces in crafts-manship as well as content—are purchased in all parts of the world. Volumes marked * are issued also in the Winchester Classics, superbly bound in dark blue rexine, with gilt top and title.

R. M. BALLANTYNE : Martin Rattler, *Illustrated* ; The Coral Island, *Illustrated* ; *Ungava.

CHARLOTTE BRONTË : *Jane Eyre, Introduction by Rebecca West ; *The Professor ; *Shirley ; *Villette.

EMILY BRONTË : *Wuthering Heights. *Illustrated.*

SIR THOMAS BROWNE : Religio Medici and Christian Morals. Edited by Geoffrey Keynes.

ROBERT BROWNING : *Poems. Introduction by John Buchan.

JOHN BUCHAN : Greenmantle ; Prester John.

JOHN BUNYAN : *The Pilgrim's Progress. *Illustrated.*

EDMUND BURKE : Selections. Introduction by John Buchan.

ROBERT BURNS : *Complete Poems (Double vol.). Introduction by Lord Rosebery.

SAMUEL BUTLER : Erewhon.

THOMAS CARLYLE : Sartor Resartus ; Selected Essays.

LEWIS CARROLL : *Alice in Wonderland. Introduction by Langford Reed, *Illustrated* ; Through the Looking-Glass, *Illustrated*.

LORD DAVID CECIL : Modern Biography.

S. T. COLERIDGE : Poems. Introduction by Sir Henry Newbolt.

CARLO COLLODI : Pinocchio. *Illustrated*.

A. COMPTON-RICKETT : A Primer of English Literature, 56 *illustrations*.

JOSEPH CONRAD : Romance.

FENIMORE COOPER : The Deerslayer ; *The Last of the Mohicans ; *The Pathfinder.

WILLIAM COWPER : Poems. Introduction by John Bailey.

MRS. CRAIK : *John Halifax, Gentleman.

DANIEL DEFOE : A Journal of the Plague Year ; *Robinson Crusoe.

WALTER DE LA MARE : The Nap, and other Stories.

CHARLES DICKENS : *American Notes *and* Master Humphrey's Clock ; *Barnaby Rudge ; *Bleak House (Double vol.) ; *A Child's History of England ; *Christmas Books ; *Christmas Stories ; *David Copperfield (Double vol.) ; *Dombey and Son (Double vol.) ; *Great Expectations ; *Hard Times ; *Little Dorrit (Double vol.) ; *Martin Chuzzlewit (Double vol.) ; *The Mystery of Edwin Drood *and* Pictures from Italy; *Nicholas Nickleby (Double vol.) ; *The Old Curiosity Shop, *Illustrated* ; *Oliver Twist, *Illustrated* ; *Our Mutual Friend (Double vol.) ; *Pickwick Papers (Double vol.) ; *A Tale of Two Cities, *Illustrated*.

MARY M. DODGE : Hans Brinker or The Silver Skates, *Illustrated*. Introduction by Naomi Jacob.

JOHN DONNE : Poetry and Prose. Introduction by Desmond Hawkins.

GEORGE DOUGLAS : The House with the Green Shutters, *Illustrated*.

JOHN DRYDEN : Poems. Introduction by John St. Loe Strachey.

ALEXANDRE DUMAS : The Black Tulip, *Illustrated* ; The Count of Monte-Cristo (2 vols.), *Illustrated* ; Marguerite de Valois ; The Queen's Necklace ; *The Three Musketeers, *Illustrated* ; *Twenty Years After.

GEORGE ELIOT : *Adam Bede, *Illustrated* ; The Mill on the Floss, *Illustrated* ; Romola ; Scenes of Clerical Life ; *Silas Marner, *Illustrated*.

R. W. EMERSON : Selected Essays. Introduction by John Buchan.

JEAN FROISSART : A Shorter Froissart. The Chronicles, edited with an Introduction by F. J. Tickner.

MRS. GASKELL : The Cage at Cranford, and Other Stories. Introduction by Paul Beard ; *Cranford, *Illustrated* ; Mary Barton.

MRS. GATTY ; Parables from Nature.

OLIVER GOLDSMITH : Essays and Tales (selected by Rosalind Vallance, with Thackeray's Essay on Goldsmith) ; *The Vicar of Wakefield, *Illustrated*, with Sir Walter Scott's Life of Goldsmith ; Poems and Plays.

KENNETH GRAHAME : *The Golden Age ; *Dream Days.

J. L. and W. K. GRIMM : Fairy Tales.

JOHN HAMPDEN (Editor) : Sea Stories (by John Buchan, H. G. Wells, John Masefield, W. W. Jacobs, etc.) ; Nine Modern Plays ; Ten Modern Plays.

J. C. HARRIS : Uncle Remus, *Illustrated*.

BRET HARTE : Tales of the West, Poems, and Parodies. (New enlarged edition.) Introduction by John Hampden.

WILLIAM HAZLITT : Essays and Characters.

NATHANIEL HAWTHORNE : The Scarlet Letter ; Tanglewood Tales.

F. J. C. HEARNSHAW : The Development of Political Ideas.

ROBERT HERRICK : *Poems. Introduction by Sir John Squire.

MAURICE HEWLETT : The Queen's Quair ; The Forest Lovers.

THOMAS HUGHES : *Tom Brown's Schooldays, *Illustrated* ; *Tom Brown at Oxford.

HENRIK IBSEN : Four Plays—Ghosts, The Master Builder, The Wild Duck, and A Doll's House. Introduction by Desmond MacCarthy.

W. R. INGE : Protestantism.

RICHARD JEFFERIES : Amaryllis at the Fair. Introduction by Edward Garnett.

C. E. M. JOAD : Great Philosophies of the World.

JOHN KEATS : *Poems. Introduction by Sir Henry Newbolt ; Letters. Introduction by Hugh l'Anson Fausset.

THOMAS À KEMPIS : *Of the Imitation of Christ.

CHARLES KINGSLEY : Alton Locke ; Hereward the Wake, *Illustrated* ; *The Heroes, *Illustrated* ; Hypatia, *Illustrated* ; The Water Babies, *Illustrated* ; *Westward Ho ! *Illustrated* ; Yeast.

CHARLES LAMB : *Essays of Elia ; *Tales from Shakespeare, *Illustrated.*

LORD MACAULAY : Historical Essays ; Literary Essays ; Lays of Ancient Rome.

DR. R. R. MARETT : Man in the Making.

CAPTAIN MARRYAT : *The Children of the New Forest, *Illustrated* ; Masterman Ready, *Illustrated* ; Mr. Midshipman Easy, *Illustrated.*

KARL MARX : Capital. Abridged, with an Introduction and Commentary by John Strachey.

JOHN MASEFIELD : Lost Endeavour.

JOHN MILTON : *Poems. Introduction by Sir Henry Newbolt.

MONTAIGNE : Essays. Selected by Stanley Williams.

WILLIAM MORRIS : Poems *and* Two Prose Romances. Introduction by John Buchan ; News from Nowhere.

BARON MUNCHAUSEN, Travels and Adventures of.

SIR HENRY NEWBOLT : The New June. Selected Poems.

SIR HENRY NEWBOLT (Editor) : Devotional Poets of the Seventeenth Century (Donne, Herbert, Crashaw, Herrick, Vaughan, Traherne ; with an Introduction) ; New Paths on Helicon.

F. T. PALGRAVE (Editor) : *The Golden Treasury.

T. L. PEACOCK : Three Novels. Introduction by John Mair.

SAMUEL PEPYS : A Shorter Pepys. The famous Diary, abridged by F. W. Tickner.

EDGAR ALLAN POE : *Tales of Mystery and Imagination, *Illustrated.* Introduction by John Buchan.

J. B. PRIESTLEY : The English Novel (18 *portraits*).

SIR ROBERT S. RAIT, C.B.E. : A General Survey of British History. From Earliest Times to 1924. 8 Maps. Indexed.

ARTHUR RANSOME : *Old Peter's Russian Tales, *Illustrated.*

CHARLES READE : *The Cloister and the Hearth.

LORD ROSEBERY : Napoleon—The Last Phase.

JOHN RUSKIN : Modern Painters (Selections) ; *Sesame and Lilies.

SIR WALTER SCOTT : The Abbot ; The Antiquary ; The Betrothed ; The Bride of Lammermoor ; Chronicles of the Canongate *and* The Highland Widow ; *The Fair Maid of Perth ; The Fortunes of Nigel ; Guy Mannering ; *The Heart of Midlothian ; *Ivanhoe, *Illustrated* ; Journal (2 vols.) ; *Kenilworth, *Illustrated* ; A Legend of Montrose ; The Monastery ; Old Mortality ; Peveril of the Peak ; The Pirate ; Quentin Durward ; Redgauntlet ; *Rob Roy ; St. Ronan's Well ; *The Talisman, *Illustrated* ; Waverley ; Woodstock.

WILLIAM SHAKESPEARE : Complete Works (sold separately)— *Comedies (2 vols.) ; *Histories, Poems (2 vols.) ; *Tragedies (2 vols.).

P. B. SHELLEY : *Poems. Introduction by Sir Henry Newbolt.

R. B. SHERIDAN : Plays. Edited by John Hampden.

TOBIAS SMOLLETT : Humphry Clinker.

SOMERVILLE and ROSS : Some Experiences of an Irish R.M. ; Further Experiences of an Irish R.M.

ROBERT SOUTHEY : The Life of Nelson. With an Introduction.

JOHANNA SPYRI : Heidi. A Story for Children.

LAURENCE STERNE : A Sentimental Journey, *Illustrated*. Introduction by Dr. G. B. Harrison.

R. L. STEVENSON : *The Black Arrow, *Illustrated* ; *Catriona ; *Poems—A Child's Garden of Verses, Underwoods, Songs of Travel (1 vol.) ; *Dr. Jekyll and Mr. Hyde *and* The Story of a Lie ; Familiar Studies of Men and Books ; *An Inland Voyage ; In the South Seas ; *Island Nights' Entertainments ; *Kidnapped, *Illustrated* ; *The Master of Ballantrae ; Memories and Portraits ; *The Merry Men and other tales ; *New Arabian Nights ; Prince Otto ; The Silverado Squatters *and* The Amateur Emigrant ; *Travels with a Donkey in the Cevennes ; *Treasure Island, *Illustrated* ; Vailima Letters ; *Virginibus Puerisque ; Weir of Hermiston.

JONATHAN SWIFT : *Gulliver's Travels. *Illustrated*.

LORD TENNYSON : Complete Poems (3 vols., sold separately) ; *Poems, Introduction by T. S. Eliot ; *Idylls of the King ; *Later Poems, Introduction by B. Ifor Evans.

W. M. THACKERAY : The Book of Snobs *and* Barry Lyndon ; *Henry Esmond ; The Rose and the Ring, *Illustrated* ; Pendennis (Double vol.) ; The Newcomes (Double vol.) ; *Vanity Fair (Double vol.).

FRANCIS THOMPSON : *Poems.

LEO TOLSTOY : Anna Karénina (2 vols.).

G. M. TREVELYAN : Garibaldi and the Thousand (*Maps*).